Peggy Woodford

Peggy Woodford was born and spent her childhood in
Assam. She read English at St Anne's College, Oxford,
spent a postgraduate year in Rome and published her
first novel in her early twenties. She has since published
18 books in a variety of genres. She is married to a QC,
has three daughters, and lives in South London.

SCEPTRE

Also by Peggy Woodford

Cupid's Tears
On the Night

Jane's Story

~~PEGGY WOODFORD~~

Peggy Woodford

*for Carol & Thomas
with lots of
love – and
memories..
Peggy*

SCEPTRE

Copyright © 1998 Peggy Woodford

First published in 1998 by Hodder and Stoughton
First published in paperback in 1998 by Hodder and Stoughton
A division of Hodder Headline PLC
A Sceptre Paperback

A CIP catalogue record for this title
is available from the British Library.

ISBN 0 340 68569 7

Typeset by Hewer Text Composition Services, Edinburgh
Printed and bound in Great Britain by
Clays Ltd, St Ives plc

Hodder and Stoughton
A division of Hodder Headline PLC
338 Euston Road
London NW1 3BH

To my daughters Alison,
Frances and Imogen
with love and gratitude

PROLOGUE

My story? I didn't have a story until I was twenty-seven. Life was life. I fought against some of it and accepted some of it; I avoided things and people I disliked and took up with those I did. And used them and broke them and dropped them, both people and things. My life was not a story worth the telling. What happened to me day by day had all the importance of a television screen flickering in a suburban shop window. Happiness. Bitterness. Who cared? Then everything changed.

I told Nat it felt like judgement, a judgement for the way I was trying to wreck her life for my own ends. Wham. One day I was running round London making trouble, the next I was lying in hospital with a vampire tube in my neck sucking my blood out into a machine. I watched my own blood running in thin clear tubes in and out of this machine. I was shackled to it for hours on end; I dreaded the pain of connection and disconnection. An agonising spigot which felt as if it had been hammered into my neck ached and throbbed and never let me forget for a moment it was there, a malign presence trapped inside my skin. It was the last thing I knew each night and it woke me each morning.

I'd always been a control freak – manipulating people was a positive pleasure. And I was not used to uninvited invasions of my body – I never let anything or anyone come near it without my permission or active encouragement if I could help it. I hated dentists prodding about, drilling into my teeth, pushing stuff into cavities. I couldn't see what they were doing and I didn't trust them; with my eyes wide open, my hands clamped to the armrests, every muscle clenched, I was a tense and dreadful patient.

I remember the trauma of my appendectomy when I was ten. I didn't want to have parts of me cut away while I was unconscious and told my mother so while I was lying in the pre-med ward, a ramrod of fury and panic, waiting to be put to sleep by an unreliable-looking man. My mother tried to hold my hand but I snatched it away.

'I want to go home.'

'There's no need to be frightened, Jane.'

'I-am-not-frightened.'

'Relax, sweetheart.'

'I won't be able to see what they do to me.'

'Of course not. That's the whole point of the anaesthetic.'

The anaesthetist had thick glasses and hissed through his teeth (invisible behind his mask) as he prepared his instruments of torture. The last thing I heard as I slid in terror into blankness was this hissing.

Yes, I liked to be in control. To feel myself totally human, I had to be in control. Meekness, humility, acceptance: these were not attributes that held any attraction. They were meaningless to me, to be honest. They achieved nothing, they were vacuous, they did neither good nor ill to others as far as I could see. Life needed more, life needed harder qualities.

A little card with a prayer in the centre and a rope of assorted imaginary flowers trailing round the words once came into my possession via a book I'd borrowed; it had been used as a bookmark by someone, and I continued to use it as a marker myself until it moved on, forgotten between pages. The words hung about in my mind. *Lord, make me an instrument of Thy peace. Let me sow love – grant that I may not seek to be consoled as to console – to be understood as to understand . . . etc.* Proactive stuff. Doing, not being done to. Being an instrument. Sowing love, or its opposite in my case, when necessary. Keeping control, I ignored the last two lines: that in pardoning, we are pardoned, and in dying, born to everlasting life. I had nothing to pardon: people didn't mess with me. And death was a lifetime away.

I'm not jealous of Nat any more, though I don't think her feelings about me have changed much. She's still wary. But she's got a good life, a good husband and a good career, and it no longer bothers me in the way it did. All that aggro, all that shit, that pushing and destroying, I now feel someone else did that, not me.

The person I was did it, the person I was until my kidneys died on me. Any other century and I'd be dead too.

Jacob comes in with two Mars bars, a packet of crisps, a banana and his usual wide grin. 'All the wicked foods. Next time I'm going to bring in a tub of chocolate ice-cream with nuts and extra chocolate chips. Give us a kiss, then, Miriam.'

'Keep your hands to yourself, bad boy.' Miriam glares at him, but her mouth is soft and her eyes gentle. 'You're late. Come and get weighed.'

'The underground was stopped. Body on the line at Kennington. What a way to choose to die.'

The dialysis machines continue to hum as we all go silent. Chatter starts up again with the arrival of the tea trolley; Jacob finishes being weighed and comes over to me on his way to his machine.

'Not avocado again, Jane. And all this fruit. Boring. Have a Mars bar instead – this is for you.' He drops the chocolate on my table.

'Jacob—'

'Jacob! I'm waiting!' Miriam is over by his machine. 'Too much flirting this afternoon.'

'Thanks for the chocolate. I love Mars bars.'

'You eat it all up like a good girl.' He tap-dances across the ward, his hips ridiculously narrow in their well-worn jeans. He's West Indian, in his mid-thirties, and used to be a professional dancer. These days all he can manage is a couple of half-days teaching at a South London drama school. When his feet patter rhythmically across the hard ward floor I want to cry, but he's so funny I end up laughing. He's nearly always cheerful, even on a Tuesday after a long weekend off the machine, when his skin is a sort of matt grey and his bounce has gone.

Sixteen of us haemodialyse together for four hours in Renfrew Unit every Tuesday and Thursday afternoon and on Saturday morning. Fifteen of us today; Miriam has just told me that Angela is in Clarkson, the renal ward. She collapsed yesterday in front of her five kids as they were all watching *Neighbours* and things don't look too good. So there's an empty machine today. There's something about the layout of the dials and bits and bobs that give these machines two expressions: smug when our blood is whirling through them and morose when they're not busy.

Today I've got Eric on my left, who spent his working life driving buses in and out of Stockwell Bus Depot. Buses are what he likes to talk about, and football. When Nat told him Stockwell Bus Depot was one of London's really beautiful buildings, Eric looked at her as if she was out of her mind. (Nat often visits me here in the ward if she happens to be doing a case at nearby Southwark Crown Court. She whisks in wearing smart black and white clothes and carrying her large briefcase, and though everyone pretends they're asleep or reading, they watch her avidly from the corners of their eyes.)

On my right is poor Deirdre, the only other white woman on in the unit today. Everyone calls her poor Deirdre because of her woes which she constantly shares. She's got no money, only the memory of the comfortable life she used to live before her self-employed husband died suddenly of a heart attack revealing that he hadn't provided for any pension. Her only daughter has become a nun in an enclosed order (a good way of making sure she doesn't have to cope with Deirdre) and the shop she used to work in has closed. And now her kidneys have packed up. They do at least produce urine, but of such a poor quality (no toxins, only water) she's as ill as me. But at least she can drink more freely, drink as much as her bladder produces each day. A litre. Two litres. I am allowed, like most others, half a litre every twenty-four hours. I'm used to it now, but I hate having my mouth always dry and my tongue always furry. I see poor Deirdre swallowing carelessly and I have to shut my eyes in frustration.

Today poor Deirdre's got a cold. She had to wait too long in the road for her lift and caught a chill.

'It wasn't my regular driver, you see, and he couldn't find the flat. Nobody ever can. So I stood outside to wait and got frozen to the bone.'

'Poor Deirdre. You should've gone back inside.'

'I don't know how you manage to eat a whole avocado like that.'

'Easily.'

'This week I settled for Dundee cake.' She looks dispiritedly at her large slice of fruit cake wrapped in foil. Eating prohibited foods in the first hour of dialysis is pure delight to all of us. 'I bought a whole one – it's cheaper that way. But there aren't enough glacé cherries in it. I'm beginning to wish I'd got the Battenberg.'

'Cheer up, Deirdre. It's only food.'

Poor Deirdre sighs and ignores me. Fred, a large bearded man who is chronically depressed, is on her other side. She looks at him but he's got his eyes shut and his blanket pulled up to his neck. Opposite us, next to Jacob, is Mina, an Indian woman whose kidneys gave up after mine. She's always shy and confused, and cries quietly after the nurse has needled her fistula. Her husband often sits equally quietly with her, but he's not there today. Then there's Sonia further down the ward; she's Nigerian, and when her man comes in the din is deafening as their normal speaking voice is a shout. Jacob tells me she's being two-timed by her man and knows it. Losing your kidneys is not a great help to a relationship. Men on dialysis often become impotent; women stop menstruating. And it's odd, but if you're not peeing either, you begin to forget your sexual organs exist.

Nat gives me a lift home today; she's been working at home so she's in a jersey and jeans. She says, the moment we're shut in the car, 'That place is awful. You must let Freddie pay for a private room.'

'Don't be ridiculous. I'm fine and I like the unit. I'd hate to be on my own for all those hours. Freddie would be throwing his money away.'

There's a silence as she manoeuvres the car out into the traffic. I see her eye slide over the lump above my wrist, my fistula, which shows through the jersey I'm wearing. I always cover it; it's not a pretty sight.

'Why don't you accept our help, Jane?'

'Because I'm pigheaded. Anyway, I am accepting your help. You're paying my rent, you're keeping me afloat. Until I get a job, how could I begin to cope without you?'

'A job? How could you get a job?'

'Lots of people work part-time when they're on dialysis.'

Nat has a pinched look on her face, a look that often signals a moral dilemma. I know she's thinking that she's got two good kidneys and I have none. I've told her not to feel guilty, and not to consider giving me one because I wouldn't accept it. I haven't changed my position on that issue despite months of dialysis. It's asking too much of both of us.

'Would you like to come up for a bit?'

'I was planning to. I've had a letter from Dad which I want to talk about.'

'What's he say?'

'I can never park outside any more. What has happened to this street?' She tucks the car into a small space round the corner from the flat and we run through the drizzle.

'So where's the letter?' I ask when we're sitting in the kitchen. Nat is sipping weak gin and tonic but I've had most of my fluid allowance so I just suck an ice cube.

'I didn't bring it. But he said he thinks it's my duty to have my tissue-type done and to give you a kidney if the match is good enough. He reminds me, as if I needed reminding, that no one needs two kidneys – you can lead a normal life on one.'

'As if we don't know that. It's none of his business.' I'm angry with my father.

'He's worried about you. Everyone's worried about you. Freddie is coming round to the idea that I could save you from all this – the hospital, the constant dialysing, all your problems . . .'

'No, Nat. It's not as easy as that. I'm the one going through all this, and I *know* I couldn't accept your kidney. I couldn't put you through that awful op, much more invasive than mine will be. And say I lose it after all, reject it, you'll have made the sacrifice in vain. You and Freddie would never forgive me.'

'Of course we would.' Now we're both getting angry. 'But the real reason isn't that, Jane, is it? You don't want my kidney because it's part of my body and having it inside you is a prospect you can't bear. You haven't changed. I am beginning to think you'll never change.'

'Don't say things like that.'

'You just don't accept that people have good motives. Even Dad – you say it's none of his business but you ignore the fact you're his daughter, he loves you, he cares.'

'You shouldn't wear green, Nat. It does nothing for you. You never used to wear it.'

'Oh, for heaven's sake.' Nat gets up and pours herself a glass of water which she drinks off in four big gulps. 'I think green rather suits me, as a matter of fact.'

'Dad is only making suggestions because he's feeling guilty. He hasn't been over, he doesn't ring me much, he's bad at writing. So he's made the one suggestion that seems obvious to him, nice and far away as he is. But please, Nat, don't take what I've said about your kidney so personally. The Transplant Sister agrees with me. She's very aware of the effect of mind on body, and actually said that my state of mind when I have a transplant is crucial. She believes that sometimes the mind can trigger the body into the rejection process.'

No one has actually said this to me, but it seems so possible I believe it myself at once. Nat sits down again and fiddles with the pepper mill, which luckily is empty. The green cashmere jersey really doesn't suit her; it makes her skin look sallow and her brown eyes dull.

'I can understand that, Jane,' she says at last. 'So what's the news on a transplant?'

'Accident victims don't give advance notice.'

'Silly question.'

'Feel like a little outing?'

'Why not, Jacob? This is Thursday, always a good day.'

'My friend is having an opening, he said bring people. So come along, kid, let's have some fun.'

'Opening of what?'

'An exhibition of his paintings at the Court Gallery in Victoria. Devon Diamond is a good mate, we were at the same school.'

So we leave Guy's together, arms linked, both with that

post-dialysis buzz you can get sometimes when everything's gone well. Purified blood and renewed energy. Would that it lasted.

Devon Diamond is a huge man and his pictures are quite small, strongly coloured, full of oddly disturbing and distorted images. The immediate overall effect is attractive, very hangable in a home, and many have already sold. All I can see are the menacing and destabilising shapes behind the lovely colours. Nightmare stuff disguised as decoration.

'Some wine?' The woman speaking is beside a table covered with bottles and glasses. She seems to be in charge.

'No thanks.'

'Soft drink? Fizzy water? Have what you like.'

'I can't drink any more today. My kidneys don't work, and I've had my ration.' I don't usually say this at any point in a conversation, but certainly never point blank to strangers like this. We both stare at each other in surprise. The woman looks a bit shocked, too.

'Oh.' Her eyes are very warm, direct and frank, and I suppose they made me frank in return. 'I'm very sorry. What a calamity for you.'

'Yes. I'm rather aptly called Jane.'

The woman gives a quick bark of laughter. 'I'm Henrietta Court. I run this gallery with my brother. How do you like the show, Jane?'

'The pictures are quite scary.'

'My brother would agree. But they are also very beautiful and they're selling well, which is gratifying.' She smiles, a lop-sided smile showing uneven teeth. Her hair is thick and short, dark but full of grey. 'Are you a friend of Devon's?'

'A friend of a friend.'

'Thank you for coming, and I wish you – good luck.' She says it as if she means it. Then she moves away, and soon after I decide to leave with Jacob.

'Share my taxi, Jacob. I don't think I can cope with the underground. At least I'll get you over halfway home.'

'No thanks, Jane. I got other things planned.' He disappears into Victoria Station and I sit in the taxi on my way home to an empty flat. Mark's abroad for months, Sara's got a new boyfriend and spends most nights with him at the moment. I go home to watch the box or read, alone.

As the taxi crosses the river, I shut my eyes. I'm twenty-eight, I used to live a totally social life, always with people, always out and rushing about, always with more things to do than I had time for, more invitations than I could fit in. They don't come any more, because everyone knows I can't drink, I can't eat freely, I can't cope with crowds or go on late, can't get my blood racing with dancing or sex because I'm afraid it could make my fistula throb so much I would scream. And anyway that fistula is the ultimate turn-off for men, in my opinion.

Yes, I feel sorry for myself. Yes, I could cry and I often bloody do. I'm crying now. The taxi driver knows I am, and has turned up his radio.

Sara has left a note for once. *Come along to Joe's place if you feel like it – we're having a little dinner party tonight and it would be great if you came. Give us a ring when you get in. PS Joe sent you this book – he thought you might enjoy it.*

Under the note is a small hardback called *Last Count*, by Georgia Hill. I've never heard of it, and open it to see Joe's neat writing inside. *Joseph Macdougall.* I'm touched he's thought of me: he usually avoids meeting my eye, as if paying attention to anyone other than Sara was risky.

'Joe? Thanks for asking me over tonight, but I've been to a gallery opening and I'm knackered.'

'Sara said it was your dialysis day today, so I thought it was worth a try to get you over here. Promise you'll come some time soon.'

'I'd love to. Ask me again, Joe.'

'I will.'

'And thanks for the book.'

Joe is good news – Sara is lucky. And he's got a brother with cystic fibrosis so he knows about illnesses and is not fazed by mine. He gives me hope, to be honest, that I might meet someone one day who'll love me, fistula and all. One day. One day. Right now, my hormones have gone to sleep, along with the fact I haven't had a period since my kidneys gave up. No sex; no interest in it. What a change from the old Jane – I could never get enough of it in Sydney, particularly when I started living with Jake. At first we couldn't leave each other alone – we made love until we were raw – but as time passed and I was available every day Jake began to lose the urge. Not completely, but enough to make me feel annoyed and frustrated with him. I used to try masturbating in bed beside him to turn him on, or at least make him feel guilty, but he'd just grunt or laugh and turn over with his back towards me.

I look back at that Jane and, truly, she seems like someone else. My illness has utterly changed my physical life, and as for Jane the person – I know I'm too close to see how deep the change has gone. At the moment, I'm in limbo.

Let me admit it. I'm also frightened that if I have a new kidney, the old Jane will return to my body, and I'm not sure I want her back.

When I see Angela sitting there attached to the machine and tucking into chicken and chips, my heart leaps. I run across the ward to greet her and kiss her.

'Hallo, Jane. Yes, I'm back. Just a little crisis. I'm fine now.'

She looks terrible, grey-faced, deep bruised bags under her eyes, but she's alive and all of us rejoice. Even Fred is smiling. I sit beside Angela until a nurse is free to weigh me and do my monthly blood test.

'How long have you been on dialysis, Angela?'

'Four years.' She whispers this as if she doesn't want the rest of the ward to hear. 'My youngest is now six, and he was two when I realised I was in trouble. I'd blown up like a balloon, hadn't peed for days, but I put it down to post-natal problems. I should have guessed. But you don't want to face up to things like this, do you?'

'No.'

'How have you been, Jane? I remember your first day here. I felt really sorry for you.'

'Why?'

There's a pause. 'Because you were so angry.' There's another pause. 'And how do you feel now?'

'I'm not quite so angry.'

'It's a waste of time, love, being angry.' We smile at each other. This is the first time we have spoken like this, face to face, but somehow we've become intimate in one leap. I'm sorry I've never talked to her before, but in the past her family has been such a support and so often there it's put me off going over. Miriam calls me over to be weighed at this moment, and I pass a stranger moving from bed to bed. She stops me briefly and introduces herself as the new Renal Counsellor.

'I'm hoping you'll be free for a little chat sometime.'

'Sure.'

'Shall I come in at the end of an afternoon session?'

'Fine. I didn't catch your name?'

'Roberta Mason. I think the nurse wants you so I won't delay you.'

I can tell from Miriam's expression she doesn't approve of the Counsellor. I dread Miriam on duty; she has a heavy touch which of course makes me tense up. Even my regular blood test is not as neatly done as usual and I feel it. Chantal, a new staff nurse in the renal unit, is so deft I long for her but she's busy at the other end of the unit. When Miriam goes out for a moment, Jacob, on the next-door machine to me today, says:

'That Miriam couldn't hurt more if she used a hammer. She'd be better off filling cars with petrol than putting the needles in.' Chantal hurries past. 'Hey, Chantal, you're the best, you know that? I can hardly feel it when you're needling me – I wish I could do it so well myself.' Chantal barely stops. 'Why don't you teach the others to needle like you? It makes all the difference, I'm telling you, man.'

But cool, efficient Chantal is not going to allow herself to be charmed by Jacob. 'Everyone does their best, Jacob.' Off she goes without even a smile. Yet her detachment is probably what helps to make her such a good nurse: she's methodical, doesn't over-empathise, and really knows her job. Miriam is all friendliness, warmth and sympathy, but she hurts you and leaves you throbbing.

Needling our fistulas is something we all learn to do for ourselves if we can. But it's not always easy; to manage well, you need a good fistula, into which you gently insert the arterial needle and attach it to the red line which carries your blood out of your body into the machine, and then you attach the venous needle to the blue line, which brings the purified blood back. (Only about a cupful of your blood is ever out of your body at any one time.) The needles are more like fine hollow nibs with blue and red plastic wings on the ends, and the fistula – well, at first I felt too squeamish to want to understand what exactly has to be done to create an access point for your blood but I made myself learn all about it after the operation, when I began to feel an odd buzzing under the plaster on my wrist.

Actually, the idea is very clever. It was developed in the mid-1960s, and now it's standard for all haemodialysis. Because normal blood vessels would collapse under the strain of 300 millilitres a minute being pumped through them, two blood vessels are joined so that the arterial blood is made to flow through the vein, and within eight weeks the vein is greatly strengthened by this extra pressure and can be used for access. Mine is now quite large and it's this disfiguring lump that I hate so, even though three times a week it's the means by which I get clean blood. My fistula, my horrid buzzing bumblebee of a fistula.

I have become fairly adept at needling myself, and very matter of fact about the whole procedure as we all are on the ward; but I wish I could be as neat at it as Chantal. She is a revelation: I've put up with clumsy, sometimes painful needling without knowing it can be so well done. How we dread the student nurses on the renal course – they have to learn, poor things, but we all wish it wasn't on us.

Chantal has come up beside my machine, checking all is well. I smile at her, making her meet my eyes. 'Jacob's right,' I say quietly, my voice covered by the noise of dialysis. 'You're wonderful at needling, and you really ought to teach everyone.'

'We've all had the same training.'

'I have a better day if you start me.'

But Chantal is looking very uneasy, and clearly feels nursing solidarity comes before pride in her own skill. 'Everyone does their best.'

'Nurse!'

'What is it, Deirdre?'

'Can't I have my cake now?'

'Not yet. Nothing to eat at the moment.' Chantal goes over to Deirdre's machine and checks it.

'But I'm hungry, nurse.' Deirdre never calls the nurses by their names.

'I'm just obeying the Registrar's orders. There's nothing I can do.'

Poor Deirdre sighs and gazes at Jacob's chocolate biscuits. 'Everyone's had their breakfast except me.'

'You'll get it, don't fuss.'

Saturday morning's session has a different feel to the two afternoon shifts: we start at eight a.m.; we get given a full cooked breakfast. The sun, if there is any, pours into the unit first thing; by midday it's gone. When we leave Saturday afternoon stretches ahead of us and we go shopping, wandering, walking with energy to spend. By Sunday we're starting to save it, by Monday evening our energy's gone. Getting attached to the machines on Tuesday afternoon is so welcome we don't care if it hurts.

I have eaten my egg, my bacon, my toast. Poor Deirdre is muttering away on my right about the unfairness of doctors, and I keep my eyes shut, pretending to sleep. She moans at Fred instead. Her blood must be really screwed up if they're being so tough with her.

And then it happens, that moment we all dream about. The Registrar, Jamie Fearn, comes in, followed by the Transplant Sister; the staff nurses gather round and the atmosphere's suddenly electric. I hear Chantal say Deirdre's had nil by mouth. The Registrar turns to Deirdre:

'Congratulations, Deirdre, you're going to have a transplant. We're taking you away now to theatre.' He turns to us all. 'Rejoice for Deirdre, everyone. A kidney has come in that's a good match for her.' He's smiling as if he can't stop – so are all the nurses.

'Oh my God.' Deirdre is blank-eyed with shock, even when the whole unit erupts into a ragged cheer. 'Oh my good God.' She is wheeled away looking bewildered, her needles still attached, quite unable to reply to our shouts of good luck, good on you, Deirdre, go for it. When she has gone, so quickly that the whole scene seems like a mirage, I am crying and so is nearly everyone else.

I am crying with joy for someone else's good fortune for the first time in my life.

Anger came later.

*   *   *

'It should have been Angela, Jacob. Or you. Anyone but miserable old Deirdre.'

'It matched her tissues the best. End of story.'

Articulated lorries rumble past us even though it's Saturday. We wait in the dusty wind at a traffic light.

'The brutal fact is this, Jane: good road safety is bad news for renal units. Not enough accidents these days.'

'Is Deirdre's kidney from a road accident then?'

'Miriam said it was a bicyclist killed last night on Vauxhall Bridge.' We walk in silence as the traffic, restricted now by dusty roadworks, grinds past us. I suggest we walk down along the Embankment to Tower Bridge for a breath of fresher air, but Jacob hasn't got the time.

'I nearly forgot, Jane. Devon asked me if I was interested in a part-time job at the Court Gallery – I said no, I do my teaching, but I'd pass it on to you. The money's bad, it's probably boring, but it's only two days a week so you might want to consider it.'

A particularly heavy lorry has moved up beside us, every part of it emitting so much noise I can hardly hear him; I wait until the lights change and it stops before I reply. I remember Henrietta Court's nice eyes.

'What do I do if I'm interested? Have you got the telephone number?'

'Not on me. Did you keep the catalogue of Devon's show?'

'Yes, I believe I did. OK, I'll think about it. Thanks a lot, Jacob.' We peck cheeks and I watch his narrow body whizz away. I catch a bus and mull over this new opportunity. It's a sliver of light compared with Deirdre's wide-open door, but it's light. I'm smiling.

I don't want to go home. Harrods. I'm going to spend my Saturday afternoon wandering round Harrods. I haven't set foot in the place since I was in my teens, before I left for Sydney, and I collapsed so soon after my arrival in the UK I hardly saw any of London. I could go now to the British Museum or the National Gallery, but I know my limitations. I'm not ready for that sort of mental engagement. Meandering round Harrods would suit me better.

But it doesn't. The crowds jostle, someone bumps into my fistula and sets it buzzing with pain; everywhere I go there are too many people, too many goods, too much choice. I stare at the ranks of cosmetics and perfumes and feel suffocated by the ersatz conglomeration of scents; I push my way to the Food Hall and escape again immediately, tortured by the ranks of forbidden foods and drinks, and take the lift upstairs to Pets. Pets is closed, so I give up. I take the Fire Exit stairs, freshly decorated with thick carpet underfoot (who'd notice if they were fleeing a fire?) and debouch into a side street. The great square red-brick building squats behind me, its green awnings like rows of heavy lids. I think of the anthill of consumerism inside and rush off down a residential street.

I keep discovering I can't cope with things I have always taken in my stride. I know I'm tired most of the time, and anaemic, but it's not just that. As I walk away from Harrods, it occurs to me that it's not so much my illness but the loss of choice in my life that makes all my reactions new and strange.

The old Jane would have tried perfumes, found free samples of this and that, bought a new lipstick, tried shoes, tried clothes, bought something to cheer myself up with: a top, a skirt that she couldn't afford and didn't need but what did it matter. The new Jane is so daunted by the fact her condition is permanent, that she can't choose to shrug it off and try something new, that minor acts of choice have become meaningless.

The old Jane felt betrayed by her body when, aged fourteen, she had to wear braces on her teeth for two years. Rail tracks round the teeth making the lips bulge and look ugly, ruining every smile. Horrors. And all those visits to the creepy orthodontist, Mr Sedgmoor, who had big feet and regular teeth like a row of blank dominoes. Each time he tightened the brace I had a headache for days. Like everyone else, I threw a party when my brace came off and I could run my tongue round my pretty, naked teeth. Nat didn't have a problem with her teeth – straight and without fillings. Mine were a rotten lot, facing any old way. At least Mr Sedgmoor made them line up ready to salute; and my smile changed too. I had good teeth to show off at last.

I bare my teeth now, as I walk past a window. Lovely teeth, little straight nose. Oh, how that nose was envied by Nat.

'I'd rather have a nice nose and crooked teeth than the other way round. It's easier to do something about your teeth.'

'You could have a nose job.'

'Heaven forbid.' Nat echoed Mum, who often said heaven forbid. I used to visualise a booming voice saying no out of blue empty sky. It's a blue sky today, a pale cold March sky, and the fine afternoon has made the hawthorn in gardens start to break into flower, tiny little white flowers against dark bare branches.

I walk in the vague direction of South Kensington Underground Station, thinking of that moment when the braces came off my teeth (both jaws at once) and I was free of that betrayal of the body at last. Will I feel the same uncomplicated sense of lightness, of release, when I am given a new kidney? Will this sense of being permanently anchored, almost by an umbilical cord, to the dialysis unit, all pass with the same ease? Will I dance down the street and immediately plan a party? Of course not. My freedom will only be partial; I'll have to take drugs for the rest of my life, or the life of the kidney, to suppress rejection. I'll be tied to a renal unit somewhere, even if the best happens and I do so well I need only be checked once a year . . . Once a year. It's unthinkable.

By now Deirdre will have had her new kidney neatly tucked into her groin and she'll be round from the anaesthetic. Lucky Deirdre. A bitterness fills me, irrational but strong, with anger in its wake. Bloody Deirdre, as uninteresting as her wretched Dundee cake. Always moaning about how lonely she is, how mean everyone is to her. All she'll do is moan about her new kidney, about taking all those drugs. She'll probably even moan about—

I stop myself. Deirdre could change – she could even cheer up. She's been feeling ill for years and all that will end. She may never moan again. I tell myself to remember that Deirdre hasn't been given the kidney because she's the most deserving or needy. As Jacob said, she's the one whose tissues matched the best. End of story.

I take the tube to Victoria, and then walk again, this time to the Court Gallery. Devon's pictures are still on show; the three in the window all have red stickers on the little white title cards. Good for Devon. But the gallery's closed; a sign in the window says opening hours are Tuesday to Friday, visits at other times by appointment. I look at the two-storey house above the gallery –

it appears to be residential so perhaps the Courts live above the shop. I ring a bell that says Court, but with no result. I'm relieved – I pressed the bell without thinking through what I would say if Henrietta Court appeared. Do I want the job? Could I cope?

My fistula throbs as I walk back to the station; that knock has done it no good. Real exhaustion suddenly washes over me, and I take a taxi instead of the tube home. Nat's voice on the answerphone reminds me I'm invited for Sunday lunch the following day – Freddie will come and collect me at twelve-thirty.

'And Thomas is in London unexpectedly, so he's coming to lunch too. Nice surprise for us all.' Thomas? I don't know anyone called Thomas. I make a list of the messages for Sara and wipe the tape.

Thomas. Nat must mean that old brother of Freddie's who was lurking around at Elsworthy Avenue when I stayed there last year, before the wedding. He smelled of pee and whisky as far as I remember, and made me feel about twelve. Not a particularly nice surprise – I wonder if I can get out of going to lunch. Meals with Nat can be a problem anyway, not because she doesn't provide food I can eat – she knows my restrictions better than me – but because she can't resist drawing attention to it. 'Red cabbage is low in potassium, I checked. You can relax, Jane.'

Can anyone relax when people tell them to? And I don't want to sense that my condition has been fully discussed before I arrive, so that everyone except Nat is self-consciously keeping off the subject. And it hurts sometimes to sit at table with people who can eat and drink with the freedom I used to. Oh to be hung over, oh to drink freely of a good red wine, sip an ice-cold beer—

I stop myself. I remember the misery and anger I induced in myself in the early days, wallowing in longings. Jacob has helped with this problem; he says you've got to suppress the thought so early it simply dies before it has any flesh on it. He uses yoga techniques, but even if I don't know them – I've never been attracted to yoga – he suggests all I need to do is shut my eyes and concentrate on my breathing until all I'm aware of is the breath going in and out. 'As soon as your mind wanders to food and drink again, grab it and keep saying breathe, breathe to yourself as you breathe.'

It sounds futile but it works. I sit now and start to do it in the kitchen for a while, then fill the flat with music and have a bath. It's Mozart or something. I just want to kill the silence. I start to get my supper ready – pasta with boiled courgettes and a little olive oil followed by an apple – and pick up the book Joe left for me and flick through it while the food cooks so that when I give it back to him at least I've looked at it. I read the blurb at the front of *Last Count*. Georgia Hill is an academic, a philosopher, who has a killer cancer and has come to terms with it by writing this short book. A note falls out. *Dear Jane, Georgia Hill is a former tutor of mine. Enjoy the book – you remind me a bit of her. Love, Joe.* Joe's writing is small, condensed, as if paper is a problem. I stare at his nice signature – the 'J' trails unexpectedly, signalling that his control is partial.

I read the book straight through, while I'm eating and after. I'm aware as I rip almost breathlessly through it that I'm only taking in the top layer. And the best of the book won't be there, it's in the sediment which my brain occasionally disturbs so that a cloud of meaning rises through the seeming clarity above and makes me pause.

Georgia Hill has developed a cancer that eats its way unstoppably through her abdominal organs. There is a section of the book which deals with her two operations, invasive and of no ultimate success, which leave her with a permanent colostomy. (Colostomy. Fistula. How threatening these words are.) I read her description of her colostomy in tense fascination: the rose-like coil of red flesh protruding centre left of her abdomen, from which extrudes her shit, which for her is *the hourly transfiguration of our lovely eating of the sun*, a sweet-smelling fruit of the body that she celebrates, and not a negative substance that drops out unseen from an invisible anus and is flushed away rapidly. I tighten my sphincter muscles and feel the whole of my pelvic floor respond, including the neglected bud of my clitoris, and continue to read avidly.

Georgia Hill writes of her response to what she calls the *rancorous sentiment 'why me'*? She does not feel it, she says, because her life with a colostomy is so routine she can't imagine people aren't made with this new bodily function, an anus on the body wall. I find this difficult to take: I look at my fistula, and know there is a difference. Georgia Hill's routine care of her shit is a private thing done alone in the bathroom, with no pain involved. She doesn't have a machine, needles, the possibility of pain with each procedure.

Then she begins to write about control. She insisted she was told the whole truth about her condition after the second operation, given the facts undiluted by ambiguities. *I wanted control over the broadcasting of any ambiguities.* She defines control as the full taking-into oneself of the dreadful, unwelcome event that has arrived in one's life, so that it becomes one's own inner occupation. She uses the image of adopting a loveless, aggressive child as your own, a child that needs constant care and attention whom you don't leave to develop into an even more vengeful monster who constantly wishes you ill. You take into yourself the whole of your disease, unfiltered by other people. You take it right into yourself and care for it until it becomes part of you. You can then, paradoxically, release control without fear of unpleasant retaliations. (From what I can understand, she's not talking about death here.)

I sit back when I've finished the book and shut my eyes. The last sentences ring in my mind. *I hope that I am not deprived of old age . . . I will stay in the fray, in the revel of ideas and risk; learning, failing, wooing, grieving, trusting, working, reposing – in this sin of language and lips.* I have no idea what she means by the very last phrase, but the driving hope behind her words brings an itch of tears to my eyes. I long to meet this woman. The book has been recently published, and Joe might still be in touch with her. If not, I could simply write her via her publishers and say: I need you, Georgia Hill. I need you to help me see where I am, where I'm stuck. All I can still feel is the *rancorous 'why me'?*, though it's not as overwhelming as it was. Why me? Why Jacob? Why Fred, Eric, Mina, Sonia, Angela? And why oh why poor Deirdre, least suited to be a cupbearer of hope?

Freddie is looking tired. His hair is longer than usual, it's dragging a bit on his collar. I've always found Freddie attractive, but the urge to steal him really has gone. I'm currently married to my fistula. I laugh at the thought as I follow him downstairs.

'Nice to find you cheerful, Jane.'

'Black humour. How's life with you?'

'Exhausting. I've been doing a case in Birmingham all week, and chambers are about to move into different premises. All very tiring.'

'You're not leaving that lovely room?'

'I'm afraid I am. I was about the only person with a lovely room; in the new building there are many more rooms, all fairly small. Everyone will be more comfortable.'

'Except you.'

'Nat's very happy. She's got a tiny room to herself.'

'She'll miss sharing a room with Colin What's-his-name. She likes him.'

'He's leaving the Bar to become legal adviser to a group of charities – it'll suit him better. Philanthropists like Colin don't usually thrive in our cut-throat world.' Freddie's tone is dry. Conversation languishes. The bright weather of yesterday is gone, and it's drizzling again. I wrap my loose black clothes round me; I meant to add a red scarf but Freddie arrived early so my black outfit remains unembellished. I've let my blonde hair grow out, so I'm natural mouse at the moment. I look very plain with my short mousy hair – who'd have thought it possible that dashing Jane Harper should let herself look so boring. But I want to be invisible, I can't cope with the sort of attention I used to relish.

I needed everybody to notice me. I needed the men's eyes to glow and the women's eyes to go dead when I entered a room. It was a fix – if I didn't get that reaction, I'd feel cheated. And now I like to stand near the wall and watch; I know people find me hard to deal with at the moment because I am still saying, rancorously, *why me?* And I want to say as well to those who know me best: I am not the Jane I was, I don't even like her, but I haven't found the Jane I am. But it's not easy – I'm too tied to my hospital life, too dependent on my illness, I can't rise above it—

'You've been very quick, Freddie. Come in and get warm, Jane – join Thomas by the fire.' Nat is in hostess mode. 'I must pop down and take something out of the oven and I'll be with you.'

Thomas jumps to his feet as I go in; he's not quite as old as I remember him, and though he still smells, it's only faintly of aftershave and stale towel. He stares at me blankly; he clearly doesn't recognise me.

'Hallo. Nice to see you again, Thomas.'

'Er, hallo. I've got a shocking memory for faces . . .'

'It's Jane.' We shake hands.

'Goodness, Jane. Yes. Terrible business. Sorry to hear . . .' he tails off, looking for Freddie. I settle myself on the arm of the sofa and Thomas shifts about in front of the fire, breathing heavily, useless at small talk. I break the silence.

'Freddie said you were unexpectedly in England. Where have you come from?'

'Chile. Chile.' He says the word briskly, with the bite of chilly and chilli. 'I'm there on a UN mission. Yes.'

We stare at the fire, neither of us able to keep the conversation going. Thomas is so ill at ease it's infectious. A thaw sets in when Freddie returns with a glass of whisky for Thomas. I join Freddie in a glass of white wine (it will be the only drink I have, so I'll save most of it to go with lunch) and Nat comes in, flushed from cooking. She looks at my black clothes with irritation.

'Honestly, Jane, you look like a Sicilian widow. You never used to wear black.'

'How do you know – you didn't see me for eight years. I might have worn black all the time in Australia.'

'Did you?' I laugh as I shake my head and she goes on. 'I love you in blue, to match your eyes.'

'I'll remember.'

Freddie and Thomas are talking about some cousin called Ralph who's in trouble, and Nat goes to the door with her wine.

'Come down to the kitchen and chat while I finish getting the food ready. Sunday lunch is such a sweat.' Freddie often does the cooking and is very good at it, but obviously today is giving his attention to Thomas and carefully ignoring the fact Nat is making heavy weather of it all.

So I follow Nat down to the basement kitchen with its windows on the garden. Some changes have taken place down here since she moved in but the overwhelming good taste of Freddie's first wife, Anthea, killed in an accident, is still evident throughout the house. Nat's moved a round table into what used to be a sort of ironing area slightly apart from the main kitchen, and this is already laid up for our lunch. There's a dining room upstairs which Nat finds too formal to use. She starts crashing about the kitchen, looking harassed.

'God, I hate cooking. So don't expect anything elaborate.'

'You know I can't eat anything elaborate so it would be wasted on me.'

'Thomas doesn't notice what he eats. I could give him curried socks and he'd get through them.'

'Are you all right, Nat?'

'I was going to ask if you were.'

We stare at each other, a lifetime of poor communication between us. If you speak, I will . . .

'Not very, actually.'

'Nor me, Nat.'

A saucepan boils over with a hiss and Nat swings round to deal with it.

'I'm going to ruin the lunch if I don't watch out.'

'Do you remember how Mum hated Sundays? She saved all her housework for Sundays because she said it would make the day pass quicker.'

'I don't remember her saying that. I thought she hated Sunday because of the housework, actually.' Nat had drained the potatoes and a cloud of steam surrounds her. 'I've been thinking a lot about Mum recently.'

'Any particular reason?'

She turns, holding the bowl of hot potatoes against her body. 'I had a miscarriage last week, and I didn't even know I was pregnant when it happened. My periods aren't very regular, so it never occurred to me.'

'Oh Nat. I'm so sorry.'

'Freddie doesn't know, no one knows except you and my doctor.' She rocks the bowl. 'I needed to tell you. Not that I wanted a child yet, but it's upset me. Really upset me.'

I put my arms round my sister, and think of my own pregnancy, of my abortion, of my post-natal pain and confusion and Jake's insensitivity. 'It'll pass. Hang on to that.' She's stiff and unyielding but I think it's because we can hear Freddie's voice clearly upstairs. 'Why didn't you tell him too?'

'I can't. He's never had a child. I can't.' Now a timer on the oven bursts into an insistent tang, tang, tang. Nat doesn't seem to hear it. 'I'm not ready to face having a family. It's hard enough working full time and being married. I'm happy, Jane, don't misunderstand me. I'm really happy with Freddie, but the whole business of being married is much harder work than I expected. And his mother seems to think I married her as well.'

'You did, in a way.'

Nat switches the timer off, but doesn't open the oven. 'If she knew I'd been pregnant and lost the baby playing squash, she'd never forgive me.'

'Squash?'

'My opponent's racket hit me a real whack in the stomach. It was my fault, I ran up behind him just as he made his stroke. Next day I had this violent period, and my doctor confirmed it was a miscarriage. I think I actually saw the tiny little foetus without realising what it was before I flushed it down the lavatory. Oh God.'

We both stand in silence; I don't know what to say. Then we hear Freddie and his brother on the move to come down and join us, and Nat mutters, 'Never tell him. I'll give you a ring soon.' She opens the oven and gets out the blackened joint.

Family meals. Often people with nature and nurture in common but often little else rubbing along together, sometimes richly, sometimes in numb boredom. As a child I often found family meals an ordeal because I ate less and ate it quickly. I was always full before I'd finished what I'd been given, and would stare hopelessly at the unappealing remains on my plate while I longed to leave the table and do more amusing things than listen to the rest of my family chewing. Christmas dinner was a particular torture which suddenly ended when my father left us and we no longer had to try so hard to be a family. The first Christmas without him was a test for my mother, who by then had the cancer which would soon kill her, though none of us including her knew yet.

'We'll just have our very favourite foods. Make a list of what you like eating the best, and let me know in good time. It doesn't matter if everyone has something different.'

We stared at our mother: Nat looked worried; I looked happy. She chose fried chicken and roast potatoes and green beans. I chose salade niçoise – Mum had once made it on a hot summer's day and I'd never forgotten it. It wasn't a good choice for a particularly cold Christmas, but never mind. Mum had salade niçoise for a starter and chicken for a main course. We then all had different sorts of ice cream with hot fudge sauce. It was quite the most successful Christmas dinner ever.

The food restrictions (unlike the drink) I live under don't worry me unduly, because I know I can eat what I miss on dialysis days, and I never want much anyway. I suppose I'm quite a puritan about food – I often find myself disgusted by the stress laid on cooking and eating by the media. Jake and I never saw eye to eye about food: he'd plan and fantasise and fuss and spend money he hadn't got on food and eating out. A barbecue involved hours of marinading after hours of chopping up. Tedious.

I can tell Nat is right about Thomas by the way he eats. He shovels his food in, his mind elsewhere. He eats to refuel. He pushes his plate away as soon as it's empty and lectures us about the way changes in deep-sea currents can affect the economy of the Pacific seaboard countries like Chile. He forgets to eat his dessert until Freddie reminds him, disposes of it speedily, and goes back to the topic that engrosses him.

'Currents are strange things. I hadn't appreciated until I was at a conference in Istanbul recently that the Bosphorus has two layers of currents – the top layer sweeps you out of the Black Sea, but the very powerful one underneath it runs in the opposite direction, back up the Bosphorus. Extraordinary.'

'Why?'

'No idea, Freddie. I'm an economist, not an oceanographer. If I find out, I'll tell you. No cheese, thank you.'

'Are the currents of Chile changing because of the greenhouse effect?' asks Nat.

'No idea either. What an irritating tag that is. Do you remember our greenhouse when we were children – full of broken panes, broken pots and shrivelled vines?'

'Wasn't it dismal. Everything died of cold in it. Mind you, our cricket balls didn't help. Have you been in touch with Alice yet?'

'I can't call her Alice, to me she's still Mother. No, I haven't. Last time I spoke to her she seemed to be stuck on one topic of conversation, her Hopes for the Future. In other words, grandchildren.'

I spill some water and cause a useful diversion. Since the table is now wet, Freddie sends Thomas and me upstairs while they clear away and get coffee. Accepting our inability to make small talk, we both pick up newspapers. Thomas suddenly says:

'Of course, the lower current in the Bosphorus is denser and more saline than the water above it going in the opposite direction, so perhaps a chemist could explain the phenomenon better than an oceanographer.'

Silence descends again, the typical post-Sunday-lunch stupor.

By the end of Monday I am desperate for the unit. I can feel the weight of that extra day in my veins – I see the toxins that have built up as dyes staining and muddying my blood. Sometimes this illusion is so strong I dream that when the lines are attached blood comes out green or brown, or even several streams of colour bound together like the multiple-leaded pencils of my childhood.

I used to faint at the sight of blood. I remember Nat once cutting her finger very badly in the kitchen, right in front of me: as the blood spurted, I passed out at her feet. Nat had to stand with her finger under the cold tap while Mum fussed over me and made me put my head between my legs.

I was horrified by the redness of my own blood when I had my first period. I had somehow expected menstruation to be a tidier, more civilised affair, not this remorseless and crude seepage. (Now it has stopped completely, I don't miss it. It is the only aspect of my condition I don't mind.)

Blood. I had to have a blood test before my abortion, and I sat with my eyes tightly closed and head turned away while the nurse did what she had to. When I saw her label a little phial of my own blood, a wave of nausea filled me.

'How can anyone give pints of blood? I feel faint at the thought.'

The nurse was dismissive. 'You get used to it.' And you do indeed get used to it, though I would never have believed her.

Blood. Where does the word blood come from? Not the Latin word *sanguis*, or the Greek word *aima*. From Germanic roots, my dictionary says, but the original is unknown. It's a strong intimidating word, is blood. Red hearts, red anger. Seeing red. Blood. *Blood will have blood . . . I am in blood Stepped in so far . . .* The horror in *Macbeth* lies so much in this word, blood: Macbeth repeats the word again and again, and after the murder of the king, Lady Macbeth cannot get the blood off her hands. But it's when she says she never expected the old king to have so much blood in him that I shiver most. I never want to see that play again. I am in blood stepped in so far . . .

I think of my blood as a foe as well as a friend I can't do without. I watch it as it moves through the lines and I bless it, but I curse it for the useless sluggish muck it becomes by bedtime on Mondays.

'Jane?'

'Hiya, Dad! Brilliant timing – I was going to ring you.'

'How's my Jane?'

'Not bad, considering the bloody weather. Cold and wet and dark as night.'

'It must be midday with you. Dear old London, nothing changes.' I can hear my father yawning widely. 'It's still about forty degrees here, and I've had a hard day so I'm really bushed. But you sound good, Jane – haven't heard that note in your voice for a long time.'

'What note?'

'Perky.'

'I don't feel perky. I'm just about to go off for my haemo.'

'When you said "Not bad, considering" you sounded perky and the voice doesn't lie. Since your collapse you've mainly sounded angry and low, so it's a change.'

'I still feel anger a lot of the time.'

'OK, OK. Don't get angry with me now. Sorry I mentioned it. How's Nat?'

'Busy as usual.' It's on the tip of my tongue to tell him about her miscarriage, but I stop myself. It's up to Nat to tell him and she won't. 'Doing well, earning lots.'

'Good for Nat. I never expected either of you to become a barrister, but Nat especially. She used to be so tongue-tied as a child. She'd seize up completely when she had to justify something. Now she tells me she loves advocacy. It's strange. Do you see a lot of her?'

'In patches, Dad. We speak every week. I go round there for Sunday lunch occasionally. That's about it.'

'She's not a particular support, then?'

'I didn't say that. I don't expect people to support me, anyway. What can they do? They can't take my place and dialyse for me, they can't give me a break from my drink restrictions or diet.'

'So you *are* still angry.'

'Dad, I will get angry with you if you say that again. The point I am making is that no one can help me really, treatment can't cure me, only a new kidney will do that and until I get one I'm on my own.'

'You don't let people get close to you, Jane. That's always been your problem.'

'The hospital staff are close. They're really supportive. I sometimes feel my body's not my own, I admit, but I'd be lost without the renal unit. I spend upwards of twelve hours a week there, so it's a good thing I like most of them.'

'How's your social life these days?'

'I don't have a social life. I've forgotten what it's like to go wild.'

'No nice boyfriend?'

'No. Not at the moment.' I can't be bothered to explain my total lack of interest at the moment in men or sex.

'By the way, Jake rang me the other day. Just to find out how you were doing. He'd heard about – he'd heard about it all. He sends his love.'

'Just as well he's not around – he's so squeamish he'd pass out at the sight of my fistula.'

'Men are more squeamish than women.'

'You're right there.'

'Jake said to tell you he's getting married. Remember Sandy Jones? To her.'

'To *Sandy*? Randy Sandy! Well, well. You really surprise me. She's going to find Jake's libido a sad disappointment.'

'You are definitely better, Jane. You haven't been catty for months.'

Jacob is just going into a lift as I drag myself into the lobby, and he bangs the button to keep the door open. We're alone in the big metal lift, which starts an unsteady journey upwards. We lean against the silver walls and Jacob tries to laugh.

'We look a couple of wrecks.'

'We are a couple of wrecks. I did too much this weekend – you look as if you did too.'

'My cousins came down from Birmingham. Full house, up late, talk talk talk. I tell you, Jane, I don't care who helps me with needling today – even Miriam. I can't wait to get on that machine.'

The lift stops suddenly, jerks, stops again. Jacob pushes the fourth-floor button, but nothing happens. We stare at each other in panic. Jacob goes on stabbing the button to no avail. His hand is shaking.

'Jacob – what's happened?'

'Come on, come on.' He tries other buttons, and then presses the alarm button. 'Could be a sudden electrical fault. Don't worry, they'll fix it quickly. They know we're here now.'

'Help! Help!' My voice sounds feeble, and I stop. 'Oh God, I hate lifts.'

'Are you claustrophobic?'

'Not usually, but it won't take long before I am. I feel faint.'

Jacob presses the alarm button again, and then comes and stands in front of me. He takes my hand. 'Let's do the breathing technique, Jane. You mustn't panic. Shut your eyes, shut them, you'll make me panic too.' He leans against the wall beside me, still holding my hand. 'Slide down and let's sit. Come on, keep your breathing normal and your eyes shut.'

'I feel so ill. I'm going to pass out.'

'Breathe, Jane, don't go tense. Breathe. Breathe. Breathe. Breathe.'

His quiet steady voice, his regular breathing, help me calm down. But I find myself saying blood, blood, instead of breathe. Blood, blood, blood, blood. The minutes pass. A voice comes on the intercom and says don't worry, the lift is being fixed. Jacob prevents me from moving, and we keep up our regular breathing even when the lift judders briefly before stopping again. In the end nearly half an hour passes before the problem's sorted and the lift begins to move again, and all this time Jacob keeps me sitting still, his hand dry and firm in mine. He only pulls me to my feet when the lift door finally opens at the fourth floor and we stagger out.

'Thank you, Jacob, you were wonderful. I would have freaked out on my own.'

'You're a panicker, you are. Going ballistic never changes anything, Jane, remember that.' He is annoyed and tired and I'm not surprised. It must have cost him energy he didn't have to keep me calm. Poor Jacob. I am glad for him it's Chantal who needles him today. I get Miriam. I'm heavier than usual on the scales.

'Too heavy, Jane. You been abusing fluid?'

'Not particularly. I had more salad than usual, maybe. And it's cold outside.'

'You'll need extra time to take off that fluid.' She doesn't need to tell me that. She follows me and starts preparing the needles.

'I'll needle myself, Miriam.' But I've had a bad start to the day, and I need help to get hooked up. At last my lines are working properly, and as I settle back a new health-care assistant comes up and introduces himself. Ben Barton – he looks about twenty-five, red hair, freckles, twitchy.

'Do you mind if we chat for a bit?'

I smile to cover the fact I'd much rather he went and talked to someone else – Eric or Fred are looking bored and blank.

'Is that your first fistula?'

'If you don't count the emergency line in my neck when I first came in, yes.'

'Which is how long ago?'

'Five months. Seems like an eternity.'

'It must be difficult for you.'

'You can say that again.'

There's a brief silence and I shut my eyes, hoping he'll go away. But he's clearly got a list of questions in his head and he's not through them yet.

'Have they tried you on peritoneal dialysis? CAPD?''

'Of course. My peritoneum's scarred.'

'What a shame for you. You'd be so much freer.'

'But I'd also have an abdomen full of fluid and look bloated. I'm too vain – I like to keep my figure.' I watch his expression as he pigeon-holes me. 'So tell me, Ben, what's brought you into nursing?'

'Vac jobs in my local hospital while I was doing my degree.'

'In?'

'Business management.'

'So business management didn't fulfil you?'

'You could put it that way. But let's get back to you – why aren't you on home haemo?'

'It's not possible. Look, I'm sorry, but I can't talk any more. Another day.'

As I reach the end of this dialysis session, Roberta Mason hurries into the ward. I'd forgotten she'd arranged to have a chat with me today. More questions.

'You're still there – I thought you'd be gone. I'm sorry I'm late, but I had an emergency – someone came into my office and did their nut for a bit.' She pulls a chair up.

'I had a lot to take off today.' I see that Jacob's gone – he must have finished while I was dozing. Only Angela is left besides me.

'How did you come to have renal failure, Jane?'

I tell Roberta my story as briefly as I can and without any emotion. I'm not sure I like her: though her small brown eyes are bright with interest I can't believe it's any more than a professional veneer.

'How are you coping with haemo?'

'Loving it. Just what I've always wanted to do.' I shut my eyes before I add: 'What do you think?'

'If you want me to piss off, I will.'

My eyes flick open. She smiles and I smile back.

'Sorry, Roberta. I've had the new health-care assistant asking me questions too today. Everyone seems to be at it.'

'We forget you're sitting targets, so to speak. Really sorry to pile in on the same day. Let's leave it, and you can pop into my office and see me sometime if you'd prefer. Shall we fix a time?'

'I don't mind talking a bit now.'

'Good. But do you find it difficult as a rule to talk about your kidney failure?'

'Yes and no.' She waits, her eyes still warm from her earlier smile. I decide I do like her after all. 'I don't mind talking about it when I'm on top of it all, but when I'm not coping too well . . . it's harder. And I can go from coping to not coping in a matter of seconds, it seems.' Roberta waits neutrally for me to go on. 'I had a panic attack in the lift – it stopped for ages. Luckily Jacob was with me.'

'I heard about the stoppage – didn't know you were in it. Poor you. Tell me about the panic.'

'I kept thinking about my blood, I kept feeling it was getting more and more poisoned with every minute's delay. I felt pretty ill anyway – Tuesday blues. And there I was, stuck in the lift with nothing I could do about it.'

'Were you afraid you were going to die?'

I look at her. No one else on the hospital staff uses what Jacob refers to as the 'D' word. 'Yes. Yes, I suppose irrationally, deep down, I was.'

'Jane, hold on to the fact that you're unlikely to die of renal failure, you know. Related things maybe, but not renal failure itself.'

'But renal failure has removed my future. That feels like death sometimes.'

'It is a desperate loss, I'm sure.'

'I used to plan, think: I'll do that next year. I can change that in the future. Now I live from day to day, and the horizon's so low. When something goes wrong, I panic at once.'

'It's a natural reaction – don't let it stress you too much. Tell me what you feel when you do try to think about the future?'

'I can't think about it.'

'And you don't want to talk about it?'

'Not now. There's Miriam – I'll be coming off the machine.'

'I'll catch you some other time, if I may. And feel free to come and see me any time I'm on duty. I'm here three days a week, and Tuesday is one of them.'

'Fine.'

Miriam watches Roberta leave the ward. 'Can't think why they waste their money on that chatterbox. Renal Counsellor. Renal troublemaker more like.'

'I heard that, Miriam. I happen to disagree.' It's Vera Akram, the Ward Sister who first admitted me and whom I love. 'Surely you should be going off duty?'

'Any minute.'

'I'll finish Jane, off you go.' Vera stares down at me. She's one of the most beautiful human beings I've ever met – smooth brown skin, huge almond eyes, lovely body, and a personality to go with it all.

'Oh Vera.' I can't help it, but tears collect.

'What's the matter with my Jane?'

'Everything.'

'Let's get you disconnected.' She is gentle and deft, and I tell her about my day as she works. I know what she's thinking – that there's nothing particularly wrong beyond what's wrong anyway, and she's right. She insists on coming down in the lift with me, and gives me a hug as I leave. She's the best.

When I get home Sara and Joe are both there. My heart lifts when I hear them laughing in the kitchen – I dread the silence that greets me most evenings in the dusty empty flat.

'Hi, strangers!'

'Jane!' Both Sara and Joe give me a kiss. 'We felt bad about skipping off last weekend without warning you.'

'Why should you warn me? I had a busy time. Lunch on Sunday with Nat and Freddie.'

'Good.' Sara's cooking a chicken – that's good too. I accept a thimble of whisky from Joe, then remember the book.

'I loved *Last Count*, by the way. Tell me more about Georgia Hill.'

'She was a most extraordinary teacher, as you can imagine. Original, rigorous, exhausting, exhilarating – just extraordinary. Unforgettable.'

'Are you still in touch with her?'

'No. She went to America for a while, and I don't know where she's teaching now.'

'I'd love to meet her.'

'I'll try and find out where she is.'

'I can write to her publisher.'

'Who is this Georgia Hill woman?' Sara is chopping vegetables roughly. Pieces of carrot skitter across the kitchen table. 'You never talked about her before.'

Joe explains, adding that he'd only recently seen the book had come out. 'I had to pass it on to Jane the moment I read it.'

'I'd like to read it too.'

'I'll fetch it.' I leave the kitchen, aware that something has shifted; Sara is looking at me with that old wary look she hasn't given me for a while. It says don't mess with my man. Before I return to the kitchen I look at myself in the mirror: brown bags under my eyes, no make-up, wispy self-cut mousy hair, eyebrows that need attention, fingernails and skin ditto. I spend so much time tending my body's needs that the frills are beyond me at the moment. Sara need not worry. I can't believe that Joe will ever see me whole, see beyond my illness. The only reason he has taken the trouble to lend me this book is because he thinks it might help me. I flick through it before I leave the bedroom. He's right. I must buy my own copy, in case Sara removes it permanently from my possession.

I carry it back to the kitchen but they aren't there. I hear murmurs and laughter from Sara's room. I leave the book on the kitchen table and take my whisky into the sitting room where I turn the television on high. It's strange to find my role is playing gooseberry these days. I can hear the bed banging against the wall as they make love. I just find myself hoping that Sara won't over-cook the chicken, but I know better than to interfere in the kitchen – when she's in charge of cooking, she doesn't like help.

Luckily Jacob rings at that moment, and I turn the TV down.

'I'm sorry if I was rude to you, Jane.'

'When?'

'In the lift. I got angry with you.'

'It doesn't matter – I was being silly. You kept me going, and that's all that matters.'

'You should ring Henrietta Court now. Devon just rang to say she's there, and she's expecting your call.'

'I haven't quite made up my mind.'

'Yes, you have, Jane. You'll do it. Don't be crazy.'

'You're right. I'll do it. It's just taking the first step—'

'Dial that number, Jane Harper. Devon'll lose face if you don't do it now.' He's laughing. 'I want to hear the good news on Thursday.'

So I dial Henrietta Court's number as the banging in the next room ends with cries and groans, and her unmistakable voice answers, very brisk and matter of fact.

'Of course I remember exactly who you are. Come along soon for a talk about the job – what about next Wednesday? Any time except the lunch hour. I'm there all day. Excellent.'

I sip my whisky, amazed it should be so easy. Sara and Joe are now in the shower, and I long to tell them about this new development in my life. But somehow when they do appear and we sit down to eat together, the urge to talk about it has faded. Why should they care, with their high-powered jobs? They won't be impressed with my two days a week in a small gallery in Victoria, but they'll patronise me with their enthusiasm. I'll invite them to an opening when I'm good and ready.

'How's poor Deirdre doing, Chantal?'

'Mrs Elmcott?'

'I didn't know her surname.'

'Very well. You ought to go and see her in Clarkson before they send her home.'

But I don't have to. We're all well into our second hour of haemodialysis when through the ward door comes a woman with bright eyes, quick feet, and a glow on her face. She's laughing at something with Vera, who's holding her hand as she leads her in.

'Look who's here, folks.'

There's a silence before Angela cries out, 'Deirdre! It's Deirdre.'

We all stare in complete silence at Deirdre. I have never seen such a transformation; it's much more dramatic than those Weight Watcher ads with photos of Before and After. Deirdre hasn't changed in shape. She's changed in essence.

'Hallo, everyone.'

I hold out my free hand and she comes and takes it.

'Hallo, Jane.' Even her hand is different – not the floppy, flaky thing that used to fiddle with her blanket. Her eyes are clear – shy, but fully alert.

'I can hardly recognise you, Deirdre.'

She waves her hands in delight. 'I feel like I'm a new woman. I realise I must have been ill for years and years before I even went on haemo. I'm floating.'

'You look wonderful. Doesn't she, Jacob?'

Jacob nods at Deirdre, his face sombre, his skin lifeless. 'Yes, you look wonderful.'

'I feel wonderful.'

'You feel well, Deirdre. That's what.' He smiles at her, though it's clearly an effort. 'You look well.'

Deirdre goes round and speaks to each of us in turn: Eric, Fred, Sonia, even Mina who looks overcome. Then the doctors all sweep in for a ward round, and the old unsure subservient Deirdre takes over and she scuttles off, risking a small wave from the doorway before she disappears.

'The hard part for that lady is going to start when she gets home.' Jacob leans back, shuts his eyes, and switches off.

Eric is in trouble today. He lives with his brother Andy who refuses to accept that Eric is ill. He expects him to live as he always did – life revolving round the pub every evening and most of the weekend, gently but steadily drinking beer. As a result Eric regularly abuses fluid, is always too heavy even though he swears he's only had a half-pint an evening. The scales prove the opposite and he often comes in so ill he can hardly stand upright. But because he doesn't ever feel drunk, he can't seem to take on board that he's drinking too much. Today he was worse than ever, and the SHO – today it's Louisa McNally – has begun a serious conversation with him.

'Tell Andy to come and see us, Eric. We need to talk to him.'

'He can't abide hospitals. They make him come over all wobbly.'

'He's got to stop making you go to the pub with him. But you've also got to stand firm, you know. Resist the temptation. Say no.'

'He'll never take no for an answer. He means no harm.'

'He may not mean it, but he's doing it. He's harming you.'

'You tell him, doc. He won't listen to me.'

'That's why I said bring him in. I've tried to ring him, but there's never an answer from your phone.'

'He's at the pub when he's not working. He holds a man should drink three pints every night, and double at weekends.'

'You must stop going with him.'

'There's just the two of us at home now. I have to go. He'd be hurt if I didn't.'

'You do realise that beer is the worst thing you can drink? Shorts would be better, have a short and spin it out.'

'Goes in a flash, then Andy's getting me another.'

The SHO is obviously finding her temper hard to control. 'So what are we going to do with you, Eric? You come in here with a serious fluid overload three times a week, we clean your blood for you and off you go to do it again. Not good enough.' She's raised her voice to involve us all. 'Is it?'

'You got to live your life as you find it, doc. And nothing's going to change my Andy.'

When the SHO's gone, Fred says, 'You ought to listen to her, Eric. You're killing yourself, that's what you're doing.'

'Perhaps I don't care.' Eric leans back in his reclining chair, pulling his blanket right up. His face is grey and unshaven, his free hand is shaking badly. 'Perhaps I don't fucking care.' He shuts his eyes and turns away to face the wall.

'I get angry with his attitude,' mutters Jacob. 'Totally irresponsible. Wasting hospital time.'

'Maybe his problem is that he only feels responsible for his brother. He wants to keep him happy, and going to the pub's the only way. Maybe he's the stronger, older character.'

'Whatever, he'll surely die.'

'It's his choice.'

And indeed, at the end of the week we hear that Eric has collapsed and he dies over the weekend. This upsets me more than I expected – there was always something indomitable about Eric I couldn't help respecting. Despite everyone's best efforts he did what he wanted to do. He kept his brother company and lived life as normally as he could. And I can't judge him for wasting hospital time; I remember only too clearly how I pulled out my needles in that first nightmare period of confusion and despair. I was so mad with rage, I wanted the horror to end, I wanted to be free of it all, I could not believe that there was nothing I could do to help myself 'get better'.

3

The exhibition in the Court Gallery has changed. Hung on the walls now are big, stark, scribbly pictures. The tangle of lines makes me think of knotted hair, entwined creepers, barbed wire in untidy rolls. I don't like them. Perhaps I'm never going to like what they hang.

'Hallo, Jane. Welcome. I can tell you don't like these – this time they're Lawrence's choice.' Henrietta gets up from behind the reception desk and shakes my hand firmly. 'They're not going to sell like Devon's. He sold nearly everything – I was so pleased about it. Very good for a first exhibition. Let me get you a chair. How are you?'

'I'm sorry I'm a bit late.'

'It doesn't matter. But you haven't answered my question. I realise it's a silly question, to which you'll usually answer I'm fine. Do feel free to moan if you want to. Sometimes the stiff upper lip approach can be very cramping.'

'At the moment things are quite good.'

'You look well.'

That's because I've taken unaccustomed care this time: I'm wearing some make-up for once, I've got a smart suit on, and shoes with high heels. It's the first time I've worn this suit since my collapse, and the skirt's loose because I've lost a stone on dialysis. But the jacket is excellent at concealing my fistula.

'Are you from Australia? I catch a faint sound of it in your voice sometimes.'

'I lived in Sydney for years and went to university there, but I'm English.'

'I adore Sydney. I had a very happy time three years ago.' The phone rings and Henrietta picks it up, which gives me a chance to inspect her. She has heavy brows above dark eyes, her hair is a cushion of wiry black curls, she's tall, skinny, and doesn't wear a wedding ring. On her little finger she's got a beautiful carved stone signet ring. As she speaks, Lawrence Court comes in from the street; he too is tall, thin, dark, but weaker-faced. He takes no notice of me and is heading for the stairs when Henrietta ends her call and stops him.

'Lol, meet Jane Harper, who's come to see whether she'd like the job.'

'Goodness, I didn't realise you were coming today. What do you think of the paintings?'

'That's very unfair of you – take no notice, Jane.'

'It's not unfair. Jane's going to be asked questions like that all the time if she works here.'

I notice the if and take my time as I examine one or two pictures fairly closely, while the Courts discuss an invoice which is puzzling Henrietta. When I turn round they're watching me.

'I've never seen this artist's work before, but he might be influenced by an American whose name I can't quite remember – it was something like Tomby. Scribbly work like this – I saw some reproductions in a colour supplement not long ago. I find the pictures puzzling. I feel sucked into them by the tangle of lines, I can see shapes and the echoes of shapes but I don't think the artist wants you to see them particularly or they'd be clearer. I find the pictures a bit claustrophobic, haunting. I don't particularly like them, but I think they are strong. And as I said, they'll haunt me.' I deliberately used the word strong rather than good, hoping it would do to cover my lack of enthusiasm.

'What do you know about art?' He asks this most charmingly.

'Nothing.'

'Capital. The job is yours if you want it.' He laughs. Henrietta laughs, and then I do. 'Mind you, we haven't advertised so you're not exactly competing. Henrietta said she'd met you and that you might be ideal. We're both against anyone with any art training.'

'Can I ask why?'

'You go through these invoices again, Lol, and I'll take Jane upstairs for some tea and explain in comfort.' I follow Henrietta and we settle into a small crowded living area with a kitchen off it. 'I always find the intelligent amateur learns quickest, and it's obvious you're going to learn very quickly. The American you were trying to remember was Cy Twombly, by the way – you weren't far off. People who've had training are often full of preconceived ideas, and spend their time trying to think of something clever to say. We took on a dreadful mistake to help us last year when Lol had a bout of sciatica and it was such a trial for me I've learned my lesson.'

'What is your assistant expected to do?'

'To communicate, enthuse, help people form their reactions by sensible comments if they're asked. You did fine downstairs. When clients want to know more they can talk to us.'

'I honestly do know nothing.'

'But you've got a good visual memory?'

'I think so.'

'So have I – and it's the most useful of all abilities in this business. Would you like some lunch? It's sandwich time.'

'Thank you.'

'There's bread and ham and cheese – not that I'd recommend the cheese. With lettuce and tomato.'

'I'll just have the bread and ham, thanks.'

Henrietta puts the food together with a lackadaisical absence of care. Another non-foodee. I'll have to think of a generic term for them. Food phobics . . . No, too strong. Henrietta puts the tray between us. It's not inviting.

'Lawrence and I started the gallery when we inherited this house from an aunt, who'd run a most ladylike dress-making business here. The gallery was her workroom and showroom, with sweated labour in the basement and her home above. Lawrence had been made redundant, my husband died long ago, my twin daughters were out of the home, so it seemed an ideal opportunity to go into business together. The overheads aren't too big so we can occasionally take risks with artists, though obviously a success like Devon Diamond's is useful; too many exhibitions like the current one and we'd never pay the bills. The Court Gallery is regarded as eclectic and eccentric, but beginning to be recognised on the art circuit.' She stretches, her sandwich untouched. 'The only thing we find does begin to pall is that we're tied to the opening hours, and that we're endlessly housekeeping – banging nails into walls, polyfilling the holes, banging more nails in, generally keeping the walls clean and painted – it's endless. Then there's the packaging up of pictures for clients, the assembling and hanging of exhibitions, the dismantling. So what we need from you is a little assistance with jobs that are tedious but not heavy, and for you to look after the gallery on Friday afternoons and Monday mornings. We like to go to our cottage at lunchtime on Fridays, and up to now we haven't opened on Mondays because we like to return to London on Monday morning, but I know it's a mistake. People get into gear on Mondays, do things, get frustrated if you're not open.'

'Fridays and Mondays are fine for me. I'm quite handy with hammers and screwdrivers.'

'Excellent. Tell me about yourself, Jane. I've been talking too much.'

I tell her selected bits while she finally gets down to eating her sandwich. When I stop, she gives me a sly look.

'You haven't asked me how much you are to be paid.'

'I know I haven't. I rather hope it won't be much.'

She throws back her head and roars with laughter, revealing crumbs and dentistry. 'Your reactions are certainly different! Why not?'

'I might not be much use to you if I have bad days.'

'Even people without your serious condition have bad days. Coffee?'

'No thanks. A drink of water would be nice.' I bring out the little stainless-steel cup I found in a junk shop, which holds exactly 100 millilitres. It's extremely useful if I'm out during the day and want to measure my consumption. It makes it easier for me if Henrietta knows my system for controlling intake from the start.

'Or juice? I've got some nice apple juice.'

'Yes, please.' Considering her lack of interest in food, the juice is of very high quality. She pours it carefully into my cup.

'So how many of those are you allowed in the course of one day?'

'Five.'

'My poor girl. How old are you?'

'Twenty-eight.'

Henrietta goes over to the window and stares out towards a

distant redbrick very Italian-looking campanile. I sip my apple juice with intense pleasure and attention. When Henrietta turns round she has a tear like a drop of glycerine on one cheek which she wipes away unselfconsciously. 'My two girls are twenty-nine. I don't think they'd cope very well with your life.'

'I wasn't given any choice.'

'It must be hard for you, very hard. Now, to get back to your pay. I'll just go and check with Lol that the sum I have in mind is what we'd agreed when we discussed it some while ago. Won't be long.'

I wander round the room looking at all the books. The big bookcase holds archaeology, art, history. There's a desk, several boxes of card indexes, no computer (though I saw one downstairs). There's a photo of a much younger Henrietta with a blond man and two small girls.

I can hear a loud furious argument in progress downstairs and hope it's not over my pay. Henrietta bangs up the stairs and reappears breathing heavily.

'Impossible man. If there are two ways of doing something, the simple and obvious or the complex and obscure, Lol will choose the latter. He surrounds himself with a web of confusion and complication – rather like the mess in those pictures downstairs he so likes.' She drops into a chair. 'Sorry. He's just undone weeks of patient diplomacy.' She shuts her eyes and a few minutes pass. I'm beginning to wonder if she's dropped off to sleep when she says, eyes still shut: 'If we pay you eighty pounds a day, cash, to start with, will that do?'

''Sounds fine to me.' I hadn't really thought about what I'd earn; Freddie gives me a small allowance at the moment to cover rent and basic needs, Dad has sent me some money, I've got a bit saved; I get by. My life has been so circumscribed by my illness that taxis are my only extravagance. 'Since today's Friday, shall I stay for a bit and learn the ropes?'

'Wonderful. Let me just get rid of Lawrence – he's got to go to our framers to collect stuff so I'll send him off early. He'll just confuse you if he's around. He is very good at the money side of the business – don't misunderstand me. I couldn't run this without him.'

As I follow her down I hear her say, 'Off you go to Maurice.'

'I told him about four—'

'If you go now you'll miss the rush hour later.'

'Good plan.'

'Ring him and warn him you're coming early. Shall I do it?'

'I'm not a complete idiot, you know.'

'Only partial.' They smile at each other, and Henrietta leads me to the stockroom in the basement while Lawrence makes his call. It seems to take a long time; his voice goes on and on while Henrietta takes out stock to show me.

'Lol makes three phone calls where I make one. I sometimes think he's got three mouths, all weaving a new and complicated saga which counteracts the other. Sam Meredith.' She pulls a big abstract from the racks. 'One of our stars.'

'I like that one a lot.'

'So do I. Our other star is Alvin Seaton. If you like Meredith, you'll like Seaton – you probably know his work already.'

'I meant it when I said I knew nothing about art. You'll have to teach me.'

'A very good way of learning quickly is to look through our archive of exhibition catalogues. Seaton. There you are. Big exhibition three years ago.'

The catalogue has smart black covers; it contains abstracts of whorls and shapes which even in reproduction seem to move, and parallel lines doing funny things.

'A bit dizzy-making at first glance.'

'They fascinate and hypnotise. When you're in the gallery on your own with them, you begin to find each picture has such a powerful individual presence you feel quite insignificant. Whereas when you're surrounded by Mary Bredin's work' – she pulls out another painting – 'it's like a roomful of retiring aunts.'

'It's delicious at first sight.'

'Lovely colourist, I agree – yes, I was excited when I first saw her work. But she's one of our disappointments, though she sells well. She's stuck in a groove, alas. Now what?' She looks upwards.

'Hen, I can't find my umbrella.'

'The new one?'

'I know it's new, but I still can't find it. Can I borrow this red one of yours?'

'I haven't got a red umbrella. It must be Jane's.'

'You're welcome to it.'

'Don't let him take it, Jane. You'll never see it again. Take my black one, which I carefully hid behind my boots. If you lose it I'll be exceedingly cross.'

'The other thing I can't find is that catalogue for Maurice.'

Henrietta goes upstairs to sort her brother out, and I am left in the basement with Mary Bredin's picture. Henrietta knocked my fistula getting it out, but I don't mind. I like the Courts, I like the gallery, and I like this picture. Perhaps I'll save my pay and buy it.

I'm swimming in the sea, the Australian sea with big rollers, and I push into the blue-green curl under the frothing crest and the wave breaks above me, leaving me rolling in warm calmer water, a trail of weed touching my hand—

'Jane. Sorry to wake you, but I can't stay long.'

'Nat. Goodness, I was far away.'

She sits beside me, her eyes as usual avoiding the lines going to my needles. I straighten myself stiffly; after a couple of hours, the reclining chairs we have to use while we dialyse get very uncomfortable.

'Have you come from court?'

'Yes. I must hurry back to chambers. I've just rung my clerk, and had quite a row. I've got to sort him out.' She's clearly upset, and come for a moan.

'But I thought you had that wonderful clerk, Douglas Dean.'

'Douglas Dean has gone off with George Warne when he went on the High Court Bench. The man we appointed is not a patch on him, and he's not good at promoting the women in chambers. None of us are doing as well as we were.'

Nat's wearing a neat, very dark blue suit and an oyster-coloured shirt with smart gold cufflinks. She's got a simple gold chain round her neck. She looks good – I notice every eye in the renal unit is on my smart sister. I haven't seen her since that Sunday lunch, though we've spoken several times.

'Is your miscarriage still affecting you, Nat?'

'No. I'm now feeling more relieved than anything.'

'Have you told Freddie?'

'No. He knows I want to wait a bit. The thought hasn't crossed his mind I could have been pregnant.'

Don't bet on it. In my opinion Freddie is a lot more perceptive than he pretends. The tailored public-school image is misleading. And of course Nat knows that. Perhaps she's right, and Freddie never guessed. He, like her, is deeply involved with chambers life, and they probably talk mainly about work. She's banging on about the clerks now.

'That sort of thing makes me very angry. I mean, the case was mine, I did the pleadings, then I find quite unaccountably Francis bloody Bates is doing it. At the request of the client I'm told. Balls. The client was very pleased with what I'd done and said so to my face.' Nat takes off her jacket in the heat of the unit and reveals a bad under-arm tear in her shirt. 'One shouldn't get too upset about these things, I know, but it's difficult not to, particularly if you don't trust your clerk.'

'What's the new clerk called?'

'Terry Greener. He's wily, very good at spinning tales about "his barristers" to keep the solicitors happy, good at bringing new solicitors into chambers, but unfortunately, as Freddie says, some of them we'd rather not have around. Shysters, in other words. Not that they give me any work anyway.'

'What an unstable world you live in, Nat. A few months ago it was roses all the way for you.'

Nat looks quickly at me to make sure I'm not being sarcastic. I'm not.

'Sorry to moan about me, Jane. All you've got is thorns.'

'Not true, you know.'

There is one of those little silences between us in which large things shift, but do it with such a small movement nothing shows at first. I can hear Jacob singing to himself; Angela on my other side is asleep. No one is paying us any attention.

'Not true. I've just got myself a job.'

'A job!' Nat is completely taken aback. 'Surely you can't hold down a job, coming here as often as you do.'

'We're all encouraged to lead as normal a life as possible. I can do two days a week easily, and that's what I've found for myself.'

'Jane, is this wise? Think how tired you get.'

'Sometimes I wonder whether I get more tired because all I have in my life is this unit. You go out to work. I go out to the hospital. I need something else.'

'Tell me about the job.'

As I tell her, I can see she's really dubious about it all.

'Well, congratulations.'

'Don't sound so unenthusiastic.'

'I'm full of admiration actually, but I admit I'm also very surprised. You never told us you were looking for a job – perhaps we could have helped.'

'Jacob put me on to this one.'

'Jacob? Who's Jacob?'

'Jacob is over there. He's become a good friend.' Jacob is now listening to his Walkman, eyes shut, one hand tapping.

'How surprising – not that he's become a friend, but that he should come up with the ideal job for you.'

'It is ideal.' I don't explain about Devon; she probably doesn't realise what a snob she sounds.

'Make sure you invite us to the next opening so we can see the set-up.'

'Freddie probably knows about the Court Gallery already. They specialise in modern British painters, which is what he buys.'

'I'll ask him. I must go, Jane.' Nat stands up and puts on her jacket. 'Easter's looming. What are you planning to do?'

'Do? Go on as before.'

'We're going to Scotland, spending a week with a cousin of Freddie's. I'd rather be going somewhere warm, but the family want to meet me.'

'You'll enjoy it.'

'Will you be on your own completely?' She frowns.

'No idea. Sara and Joe don't tell me their plans much in advance – probably they'll be away somewhere.'

'I'll ring Sara. She's been very elusive recently.'

'Don't ring her on my behalf. I'm perfectly OK on my own. Don't fuss.'

'I wish we could whisk you away for a break. You've had such a hellish winter.'

I can feel my irritation building in spite of myself. Nat is being heavy-handedly kind, and sometimes I long for the old days of ice, suspicion and deep unease between us. There was a certain exhilaration in our enmity. Nat bends over to kiss my cheek (so many sisterly kisses now I'm ill, after a lifetime's dearth) and then walks off, showing a big ladder in the back of her black tights.

A hellish winter. She has a point.

'So when you've had a transplant, you'll come back to live in Sydney?'

'I can't think about the future, Dad.'

'Your voice has become all English again.'

'I am English. I've lived here three-quarters of my life.'

'When I was over, you told me you were going to return as soon as you could.'

'Yes, I know I did. That was before the full scale of my – of my condition had sunk in. When I still thought about the future because I had one.'

'Of course you have a future. I want you to share it with me – I'm thinking of buying a bigger place so that we can have half each.'

I stare at the phone. If he'd said this to me a year ago, I'd have been ecstatic. I'd have stayed in Sydney, never come over to London at all even for Nat's wedding, had a different life—

'Are you still there, Jane?'

'Yes. I'll think about it. But I can't leave Guy's, they know all about me . . .'

'Look, there are equally good hospitals here. You could transfer any time. But I know you're in a British queue for a kidney and you can't leave until you get one, but once you've had that transplant, what's to stop you coming back? One renal unit's as good as another, surely.'

'Dad, I really can't think about the future. There's a blank ahead of me, all I can do is get through a week at a time.'

'You mustn't be frightened of the future, Jane—'

'I'm *not* frightened of it. It's not fear I feel. You can be afraid of something that's not there. The future tense doesn't mean anything to me any more. *I will go back to Sydney* – I can't say it.'

'Your feelings will change when you have a transplant, you'll see.'

'How can you talk like that? First, there may be no kidney for me for ages – no good match might come up. And it's not a queue I'm in – people move up queues, they can see it's their turn next. We never know when it's going to be us. Sorry, I'll have to stop now. I'm feeling too upset to go on talking.'

'I only rang to tell you of my plan to buy a place big enough for you.'

'Thank you for the thought, Dad. I mean it.'

Do I want to go back to Australia and live with my father? I don't know. I can't at the moment imagine a life which offers such choices.

'What are you reading, Jane?'

Jacob makes me jump. He's finished dialysing and stands beside me.

'Rereading. It's called *Last Count*. It's a strange book by a woman who's got cancer. I keep dipping into it and finding something new.'

'Like?'

I hand him the book, my finger marking a sentence.

A crisis of illness, bereavement, separation, natural disaster, could be the opportunity to make contact with deeper levels of the terrors of the soul, to loose and to bind, to bind and to loose.

'What does she mean by to loose and to bind?'

'I'm not sure, but I'll tell you when I find out. If I find out.' We both laugh.

'Looks like a good book.'

'It is. It's not about grinning and bearing illnesses. It seems to be more about using them to fly, to float free.'

'Easier said than done, particularly when you're stuck in a lift feeling like death.' Again we both laugh. 'Anyway, if you're nearly through I'll wait for you.'

'I'm going to be at least half an hour.'

'I can't wait that long – I've got a busy evening. See you, Jane.'

'What are you off to do?'

'It's the end-of-term college show tonight. I've been coaching the students to do their tap routines in a rousing final chorus. I was going to ask you along.' He does a series of loose-ankled tap-steps.

'I'm really sorry. I'm bound and I can't be loosed yet. But good luck for the show.'

He smiles and raises a hand, poised to leave. 'I don't think she was writing about your haemo-lines.'

'Nor do I.'

'Come to the party at Ginny's tonight, Jane. She said to bring you if you were up to it. Do come.'

Sara and Joe are sitting drinking tea in the kitchen.

'I was going to celebrate with you anyway.' I pull a bottle of sparkling wine out of a carrier.

'Jane! Don't tell me they've got you a kidney!' Sara jumps up.

'I wouldn't be standing here planning to drink a glass of bubbly if they had. They don't hang about, Sara. If a kidney comes in for you, they have you there laid out for the op as soon as possible.'

'Silly of me. So what are you celebrating?'

'I've got a part-time job.'

'Fantastic!' Now Joe jumps up. We open the bottle and toast my good luck. They are so pleased for me – it's very different from Nat's pessimistic reaction. Though I know hers comes from a deeper knowledge of me and my illness, I love them for their enthusiasm.

'You must come with us tonight, Jane. Go on – you're looking well, you're feeling up-beat about the job, you must get out and celebrate. Everyone would love to see you.'

Ginny rings at that moment to ask them to bring cutlery, and Sara passes the phone over. 'Jane? Nat and Freddie are both coming – you must come too. Come and see my deeply scruffy but potentially lovely new flat.'

'I'd love to.'

A party. My first party since . . . I've been such a recluse. I go through my clothes and remind myself of them all. I pick a loose blue silk shirt and black silk trousers. I put a long vivid greeny-blue chiffon scarf over one shoulder, and wear an Indian lapis necklace and earrings given me by Jake. My eyes look extraordinarily blue against these colours. I stare into my eyes as I rim them with make-up. My face is thinner, which makes them look huge. Blazing blue eyes. I know from long experience what a hypnotic effect they can have on a man if I'm trying. I still don't feel like trying, but you never know. I can see by Joe's reaction as I walk in he's caught up by them. He's never seen me looking other than totally drab. He stares while Sara gets up briskly.

'Right. Off we go. The minicab's outside. You look wonderful, Jane. And that lovely loose shirt hides everything.'

Thanks a bunch, Sara. Joe opens the door for me, and I risk a quick blast of my eyes on his. He smiles and blushes.

'For goodness' sake, Joe, don't stare at poor Jane as if you've never seen her before!'

'I haven't.' Sara doesn't hear him say this as she bounces off down the stairs, but I do.

Ginny's flat is in an old mansion block that has seen better days, but in my view it's a perfect space: well-proportioned rooms with good windows, plenty of period detail still in place. The walls are covered with dreadful colours, the squeaking wooden floors are bare except for some bits of matting, but she's got some good lighting installed already and it's enough to give an impression of a warm and welcoming place.

'I love it too, but I'm never going to have enough money to get it the way I'd like it. Come and meet some of my friends, Jane.'

I panic. 'Is Nat here yet?'

'Somewhere. She arrived a few minutes ago.' Ginny takes my arm solicitously (like many people, she can't help treating me like an invalid) and leads me towards a room where jazz is playing. But I see Freddie in the kitchen and pull away to greet him.

'Hallo, sister-in-law. You look very well.' He gives me a hug and Ginny disappears as more people arrive.

'Thank you.'

'Your eyes look normal.'

'What do you mean exactly?'

'They've looked deadened for a long time.'

'I've been feeling deadened for a long time.'

'What can I get you to drink?'

'Nothing, Freddie.'

'This is rather good apple juice. I'm driving.'

'An inch then, to keep you company.'

Freddie is still in his working dark suit and stands out against Ginny's casually dressed friends. He needs a shave, but his stubble is not quite designer-stubble.

'How's life, Freddie?'

'Not so great at the moment. I'm doing a stressful case, and Douglas Dean's replacement is proving a disappointment.' He sounds quite depressed, so I wonder if Nat has told him about her miscarriage after all. 'Do you mind if we sit down? I've been on my feet all day in court.'

'Suits me.'

There are two chairs under the window, and we sit on them even though they are both unsteady. The kitchen fills up with noisy people, screening us from the door.

'Nat told me she wasn't very pleased with the new clerk.'

'With reason. He's got to change his attitude towards women, but it'll take time.'

'Couldn't you sack him for discrimination and get another?'

'Some people are very pleased with him. Their view would be if you don't like the clerk, then move chambers. And they have a point. Anyway, enough of our life. How's yours? And congratulations, by the way, on your job at the Court Gallery.'

'So you know the gallery?'

'I've been to see exhibitions there of Sam Meredith's work.'

'Have you ever bought any of his paintings?'

'Not yet, but mainly because he paints on such a large scale. If he did something smaller, I'd be very interested. It does sound a bit bourgeois but I do like to be able to hang works in my house. Let me know when he has his next show, won't you?'

'Of course. I'm excited about this new job, Freddie.' I know my eyes are shining, as they used to, by the way he's looking at them. And I am excited, by the job, by the fact that I seem to be getting a life back. 'I'm going to meet all the artists, go to their studios sometimes with Henrietta Court.'

He laughs. 'In my experience, meeting artists can be a disappointment. Best to keep one's illusions about them.'

'But I'd like to see their studios. Surely that's interesting?'

'There you are! I've been looking everywhere.' Nat's wearing a beautiful black velvet dress which I stroke.

'That's nice.'

'One of Anthea's – you remember, Freddie's first wife. Her designer clothes are gorgeous, and one or two suit me.' Nat perches on Freddie's knee because there isn't another chair and she won't let him get up and give her his. He looks uncomfortable.

'Your bottom's bony.'

'So's your knee.'

'I'll try and find another chair.' He pushes away through the crowd. The noise level all through the flat is rising as it fills up.

'My God, Ginny's invited Dave Rosenberg. She must be mad. Duck, Jane, I really don't want to talk to him.'

Nat and I bend towards each other as if we're exchanging the most intimate of private information, but it doesn't deter Dave.

'Well, the beautiful Harper sisters. What luck.' He squats before us, bouncing on his heels. He's cut his hair off at ear level very roughly and it sticks out all round his head in a wild bob. He's grown a beard, neatly trimmed, and looks in his strange clothes as if he's come from Paris in the 1890s. He takes Nat's hand and kisses it, then mine.

'Nat, the elegant North London wife. And Jane, you must be wearing blue contact lenses. Love it – I've never seen your eyes looking so blue.'

'I don't wear lenses.'

'Then your eyes have turned bluer.'

'Eyes don't change colour.'

'Why not? Hair changes colour, skin changes colour, why not eyes?'

'It's only that scarf she's wearing – it emphasises their colour.' Nat is brusque. She's looking round for Freddie, but he's disappeared. 'So what are you up to, Dave?'

'Up to. What a negative tone. The naughty boy must be up to mischief.'

'You usually are.'

He laughs and sits back on the floor. 'Your eyes are wonderful too, Nat. Almost black when they're cross. Such a temptation to make you cross so that I can see them at their best.'

'You still haven't said what you're doing.'

'Sitting at the feet of the Harper sisters, drinking their every word.'

'Have you finished your novel yet?'

'Everyone is so keen on achievement these days. What do you do, have you finished it, what do you earn, what are your goals. I have no goals, I live on benefit, I do very little. But I think. I think a lot, which makes other people think I'm doing nothing. There you are, Nat. That's what I do. I think. If I was an artist I would simply have DAVE IS THINKING in elegant black capitals on a white wall, and sit in front of them.'

I stare at Dave and remember how he tried to seduce me, waving some list at me which he said contained all the women he hoped to seduce or had seduced. Mad. At the time I was already feeling so ill he didn't get past trying to kiss me. He's looking at Nat with a speculative expression.

''So how's the successful barrister? Raking it in as usual?'

'No. Well, yes, compared to you. Life's tough at the Bar, so don't think it all comes easily because it doesn't.'

'Would I think that?'

'Yes.'

'When are you going to let me have your wedding dress?'

'Dave, you really can't be serious about that dress.'

'I am. I always was.'

'What about the wedding dress?' I'm puzzled, and Nat's clearly quite upset suddenly. She mutters that she'll explain some other time, and jumps up to escape when she sees Freddie. He's trying to work his way towards us with a chair, and Nat heads him off plus the chair. Dave sits in the empty one beside me.

'Why are you being so annoying to Nat?'

'Just getting a bit of my own back. She had me thrown out of her wedding party, if you remember.'

'I wasn't there.'

'Yes, you – Of course you weren't. You were in hospital.'

'You never came to visit me either, you coward.'

'I would have fainted at your feet.'

'Nat said you'd promised to come.'

'I promise Nat anything when she's determined. It gets her off my back.'

Dave is a vocal eel, entertaining but imprecise, unpinnable

down. When Joe drags me off to dance, I realise I still know nothing about him and what he's doing.

Joe is clarity by comparison. He apologises for the fact that he can't dance very well, which suits me because I'm nervous of someone hurting my fistula.

'I'm happy to shuffle in a corner, Joe.'

'You should go out more often, you know. It's brought you alive. You look a different person this evening.'

'I've been camouflaging myself for ages.'

'Why?'

'Protection.'

Joe is staring at my eyes as he dances stiffly. 'Protection from what?'

'Myself as much as anything?'

'Why would you need that?'

'I can't explain.'

'Or won't explain.'

'Maybe. My life's been too full of change.' I'm dancing stiffly too, but enjoying it more than he is.

'Change . . . some people never change at all except to turn into their parents! A friend of mine was thirty recently and there he was at his party with an expanding stomach, set ideas, looking just like his father, and no change looming ever except in his income. Depressing.' He takes my hand as we dance. 'But you're not depressing, Jane, despite everything you're open to change, you're a seeker.' He's a little drunk, and stumbles. We stop dancing and stand in the corner, still holding hands though I'm hardly aware we are and mean nothing by it.

'I don't feel like a seeker, Joe, whatever you mean by that. The last few months I've hardly had enough energy to cling to what I know.'

'You've got yourself a job. You're trying to meet Georgia Hill, presumably to talk to her because she interests you. I call that seeking.'

'I haven't heard from her.'

'I could try and get hold of her if you fail. But watch out, Jane – you may find her hard to take. She's fire and ice.'

'Fire and ice.' As I repeat this, Sara pushes up to us. She's pretty drunk, and grabs at Joe.

'Stop making passes at Jane and dance with me, you bastard.'

'He wasn't making passes.'

'Then you were. I don't trust you, Jane Harper.'

'Don't talk rubbish, Sara.' I push my way through the throng and find Freddie out in the corridor looking tired and bored. 'Freddie, I think I've had enough.'

'I certainly have. Midweek parties are hard when one's in the throes of a case. I'll take you home if you like. Nat could stay on – she's not in court tomorrow.' He waves at Nat. 'I'm going to take Jane home. What are you going to do?'

'I'm coming with you. Give me five minutes.' She looks in my direction, just a quick glance, but it's the old look, like Sara's, with no trust in it.

4

I take the train to Brighton one cold Thursday morning. Thin March snow is lying trapped by the wind in tight corners. The sky is heavy, grey, and merges with the sea's horizon. I'm wearing boots, heavy coat, woolly hat, scarf, and good thick gloves but I'm still cold.

Georgia Hill lives in a flat off the sea-front going towards Hove, and the wind bites less as I turn into her street. Her telephone voice was light and warm: she spoke quickly and energetically and wasted no words. There's no photo of her on the jacket of *Last Count*, but I know she's in her late thirties, and I imagine her young for her age, open-faced, full of life.

So nothing prepared me for the human frame of that voice. Gaunt, dark, witch-like, with burning greenish eyes in a wasted, prematurely old face. She is propped on an odd-looking walking frame, stuck all over with labels covered in writing.

'Jane Harper? Come in quickly out of the cold and shut the door. Do go ahead of me into the flat – I'm so slow these days. Go on, go and get warm.'

I can't answer and she doesn't seem to expect me to. Her flat is brightly lit and heated to a high temperature; it smells sweetly of lavender oil. I see she has a scented oil burner glowing gently on the mantelpiece and stand near it to soak in the warmth from the open fire while she struggles into the room and lowers herself awkwardly into a chair, pulling her frame in front of her feet. She holds out a slim hand.

'Sorry about the way I have to welcome you.' We shake hands – hers feels soft and firm. Mine's frozen. She smiles at me, a vivid quick smile that fills her eyes. 'I liked your letter. Sit here, would you. It's near me, near the fire – it's where my students sit.'

'You still teach?' My voice is unsteady.

'A bit of post-graduate supervision. That's my forte, and I like to keep my hand in.' She looks sharply at me. 'I may look a wreck but there's still plenty of energy there – I'm just finishing a new book, actually. But I had to cut down my teaching because I get so tired.' The phone beside her rings and she deals with an academic query with speed and lucidity. I can feel my tongue going flaccid, my thoughts faltering. I can't think why I have come. I have nothing at all to say to this woman which would remotely interest her.

'Do take your coat off, Jane. You'll get very hot in here, the central heating's always on so high. Would you like a drink of some sort? Help yourself – there's a tray over there in the corner with a kettle and a choice of teas.'

'No, thank you. I'm fine.'

'As I said, I liked your letter. I was particularly interested in your comment that while your renal collapse removed the power of choice from you, the very constriction was beginning to offer you certain new freedoms.'

I stare at Georgia Hill, unable to answer. I've never met anyone who unnerved me so. Fortunately the phone rings again, she rolls her green eyes in apology, and picks up the receiver.

'Mo, darling, this is not a good moment. My visitor's just arrived. I'll ring you back later on. Well, after your bridge session then. No, of course I haven't called the doctor in this time – there was no need.' She ends the call and puts her hands through her frizzy hair. 'My mother. She can't cope with the fact I ignore my condition as much as I can.'

'*Medicine and I have dismissed one another.*' My tongue and brains return to me suddenly as I remember this phrase from her book. She laughs.

'Precisely. Mo is always ringing up with news of some new cancer cure she's read about. She never notices those important qualifying words in the report. Possible. Hopeful. Promising. No, medicine and I have dismissed one another.'

'I found the descriptions of your operations unbelievable. How could two top surgeons disagree so radically?'

'How, indeed, one could say I am riddled with cancer and

another say the same patch was scar tissue and lesions? The former was right, clearly. Look at me – I am being eaten away!' She raises her singularly thin arms into the ancient orant position, her eyes merry. *'Keep your mind in hell, and despair not.'*

Keep your mind in hell and despair not – I remember how puzzled I was by that phrase when I read it, and am just about to ask her to explain it when I see the very phrase written on one of the labels on her walking frame. All the labels seem to bear quotations. As I look up at her she asks:

'Tell me why you have come to see me, Jane Harper.'

'Because I hoped to meet in you a more developed version of myself. I'm sorry if that sounds arrogant . . .'

'Go on.'

'I've read your book more than once, and sometimes I feel I understand less and less. I don't know where to begin . . .'

'Wherever we begin we won't get far. Just now, my mother said, angrily: "Why are you spending your energies seeing a complete stranger, when you've got so much work to do and so little time?" I told her I wanted to stay in the fray – I didn't want to pass up the chance of making a new friend.' She smiles. 'Tell me about yourself. Do you have a lover, Jane?'

'No. I've been so submerged in my condition I haven't wanted one. And I hate people to see my fistula. It's a turn-off.'

'I've had a colostomy for some years.'

'I read that.'

'It doesn't bother my lover. And though he's in America now and I'm here, my illness is not the reason we're apart. But this fistula . . . to start with, where does that word fistula come from?'

'I've no idea.'

'Please get my dictionary from the bookcase over there and we'll look it up. Read it out to me, would you. I do so love dictionary definitions.'

Fistula, from the Latin=a pipe, flute.
1. Pathological. A long, narrow, suppurating canal of morbid origin in some part of the body; a long, sinuous pipe-like ulcer with a narrow orifice.
2. A natural pipe or spout in cetaceous animals, insects etc.

3. Ecclesiastical. A tube through which in early times communicants received consecrated wine; now used by the Pope only.
4. Musical. A reed instrument or pipe of the ancient Romans.

Georgia listens intently as I read, and laughs at the papal definition. 'Do you think he still uses one? But I didn't know the Latin word either, I confess. And it's odd that its original medical usage should be so unpleasant, and now it is reused for something so different. Would you show me your fistula?'

'Of course.'

'What's going on inside there?'

'It's a joining of artery and vein where they both lie close together. The extra pressure makes the vein stronger so it toughens and knots up like this, and can be used for access. It took about six weeks for this fistula to get strong enough to take needles.'

Georgia is not in the least squeamish, and inspects my fistula with interest. 'Very clever. Until it was ready, how did they clean your blood?'

'They made a temporary access point in my neck, here.'

'That sounds an unpleasant process.'

'It was horrible. Anything after that was an improvement. When they operated to make my fistula, they also prepared me for Continuous Ambulatory Peritoneal Dialysis – CAPD – which meant they put a catheter in my abdomen.' Georgia nods. 'Unfortunately, my peritoneum was very inefficient, so I have to rely on haemodialysis.'

'So you've got a couple of scars to remind you of the other methods.'

'Little ones.'

'I think your fistula is incredibly neat. I somehow expected a great thing with a spigot. And the beauty of it is that it's an integral part of you. No bits of plastic sticking out, no pipes to stopper and keep clean. It's brilliant. I love it. You must love it too.'

'I can't. It's so ugly. Look at it. Ugh.' I hold up my other forearm as a comparison.

'It's all a matter of perception, Jane. Some tribes think that stretching of the earlobes or the lips or the tongue with weights and straps makes for beauty. I think your fistula is beautiful. I can imagine others feeling the same.'

'I can't. Some people have enormous ones that extend up the arm in a rope-like twist. I'm frightened mine will grow like that – I've always had such a good body.'

'What has changed? You still have a good body.'

'My whole view of myself has changed. My future has become my present.' We stare at each other; she waits for me to go on. 'A part of me still can't accept that this condition is permanent, and the rest of me knows that my whole future is taken away by the fact I have lost the use of essential organs. I'm on borrowed time.'

'You'll have a future again if you are given a transplant. Or do you have too many antibodies in your blood for that to be a viable option?'

'Luckily my antibody count is lowish. But a transplant isn't plain sailing either.'

'Jane, I know it would be foolish to think of it as a perfect escape route. But it would lift your horizon.'

'Most people don't understand what it's like to be without a horizon. I suppose you can't conceive of what it's like until you've been there.'

'Of course.'

'Yet despite the fact they don't understand, I need people more than I used to.' I meet her eyes. 'I find that very hard to admit, but it's true.'

'The same thing has happened to me. I was the super-achiever, alone but never lonely, always in control of my life. Or so I thought.' She smiles. 'I felt healthy, I looked healthy, I was healthy, yet my body was full of cancer. My brain was bruised for days when I learned this. You know, Jane, that as humans we have lost the sense of the irrevocable. We've tried to rewrite the myth of Orpheus: we want to break the rules and still get Eurydice back. But we haven't succeeded in changing anything. If we get too sick we die, and there's an end to it. No one has banished death. Nor will, praise be.' She eases herself into a more comfortable position, tossing back her hair. 'Embrace the irrevocable, love your fistula. If you're hugging it, it will do less damage to you!' She laughs and I try to join her, but I can see her mind is moving to some new topic when she turns those piercing eyes on me again.

'Are you agoraphobic at the moment?'

'Open spaces don't frighten me at all—'

'No, no. The word is specific: *agora* means the market place, the public space for talking, connecting with people, doing deals. To feel agoraphobia is to think yourself on the sharp rim of the world.' I wait for her to go on, wondering briefly if that phrase is to be found somewhere on her walking frame. 'A tribulation like yours can cause agoraphobia – you're so busy surviving the trauma you can't cope with people very well. Or at all.'

'In that sense I've been agoraphobic. But it's passing – here I am, after all.'

'Here you are indeed.' Her hands clutch the cross bar of her wordy walker. I can see she's tiring and I will have to leave soon. The phone rings and she promises to ring back.

'I must go. But just before I do, do you think you could explain what you mean by that quotation in the front of *Last Count*?'

'*Keep your mind in hell and despair not*? Well, I was angry with modern solutions to the pains of living – for instance, all the dictates of New Age Buddhism, which urged one to become edgeless, translucid, without inner or outer boundaries, so that the difficulties of life disappear. In my view, keeping the mind out of hell in this way is a counsel of despair. A soul which isn't bound is as mad as one with cemented boundaries. We need to accept our boundaries, however deep we plunge into the terrors of the soul. We need to remain vulnerable. We need to accept pain, accept hell, in other words, in order to grow. We need our boundaries in order to push against them. Keep your mind in hell and despair not!'

There's a knock at the door at this moment, and a friendly woman comes in with a carrier bag of groceries.

'Hallo, hallo.'

'Is it twelve already, Liz?'

'It is.' She looks firmly at me.

'This is Jane, Liz. She's come down from London just to have a talk—'

'And I'm going back now. Thank you for giving me so much of your time.' I stand up shakily in the hot room, aware I have been in a heightened state of concentration for some time and keen to hurry out before Liz, who's clearly the day nurse, destroys it. 'And thank you for all you've said, all you've written.'

Georgia Hill grins at me. 'Don't be too serious about life, Jane. See the funny side. Comedy is homoeopathic – it cures folly with folly.' We laugh, she raises a hand in farewell, then Liz shows me out.

I go into an unpleasant little café and sit with a cup of orange-coloured tea I hardly touch. I feel as if I've been close to an elemental force; I've never in my life met anyone like Georgia Hill. She may be physically weak, but the sharp power of her restless, driving mind has bruised me. I sit on, a strange anger building in me as my elation fades, fuelled by the feeling I have been given more than I bargained for, that I haven't the resources to cope with the onslaught I invited.

I would love to walk along the beach to clear my head, but I know I haven't the energy against the cold and the violent wind. I ask the café proprietor to get me a taxi and he rings while yawning and scratching his crotch. I leave a tip beside my cup and go out into the cold, aware I'm going to be late for my dialysis session if there isn't a convenient train. The minicab comes at last, and of course I find I've just missed a London train. I'm not feeling very good now; I'm shivering while I sit in the cold waiting room. I haven't told anyone I was going to Brighton to see Georgia Hill, not even Joe. No one knows where I am. I'm on the sharp rim of the world.

'We were getting worried about you.' Vera Akram is in the unit when I arrive.

'I missed a train. I'm sorry.'

'Are you all right, Jane?'

'I think I might have a temperature.'

'Let's check you.' Her bleeper goes at this moment and she has to rush off, leaving me in the care of Miriam of the hammer-hands, as Jacob has taken to calling her. As I follow her, her broad back and solid shoes make me quail. My temperature is a tiny fraction above normal, which Miriam decides isn't significant. As my needles are being put in I notice that though the unit is now full, there's a strange girl in the far bed and no sign of Jacob.

'No Jacob?'

'He's been transferred to the satellite unit at St Thomas's.'

I stare at Miriam, aghast. 'He never said anything about that on Tuesday.'

'He didn't know until yesterday.'

I lie back, ignoring the plate of food that is brought to my table. Angela is next door to me today; she's lying back too, but fully alert.

'You're going to miss your friend Jacob.'

'He might be moved back here just as suddenly, I suppose.'

'They never seem to do that.'

'What am I going to do without him, Angela? He's been such a help.'

'We're all going to miss him. Such a lovely sense of humour. And the dancing. What a laugh when he did that, eh. Tap tap tap across the floor. Dear Jacob.' She snuggles further down her chair and shuts her eyes. I lie there stiffly, near tears.

I feel bereft, utterly bereft.

Ben sits beside me as I enter the second hour.

'Why has Jacob been transferred? No one tells me anything.'

'Nor me – I'm just a health-care assistant, don't forget. The lowest of the low.'

A horrible thought grips me. 'He hasn't died, has he? They're not lying to me?'

'He's fine, Jane, stop panicking.' Ben is obviously a little uneasy at the extent of my distress.

'I'm just feeling paranoid. On the sharp rim. Plus I got frozen today and I can't get warm.'

'It's bloody cold for March.' Ben has a threadbare look about him – tattered jeans under his hospital coat, shoes that need new heels and a good polish.

'Where do you live, Ben?'

'End of the Northern Line. Grisly flat but cheap.'

'So you've got a long haul ahead of you to qualify?'

'My understanding of life is that all the good things demand a long haul.'

'And don't pay much at the end of it.'

Ben and I are at that stage of an acquaintance when the clichés dribble along while one's antennae are honing in on other things. I can see he picks the skin round his nails, that he holds his head very tensely even though his smile is easy and his red but nicely shaped hands rest loosely on his knees. Getting through the day is not easy for Ben.

'You do look pale today, Jane.'

'I'm feeling lousy, actually, but Miriam says all is well.' I shut my eyes and Ben drifts away. On the sharp rim, Georgia Hill comes back into my mind. Ben and my talk with him are like a pastel wash against the burst of primary colour that is her. She may rail and beat her head against the wall, but Georgia Hill would never have a problem getting through the day.

The whirring of the machines seems louder today. I think about Jacob; I know we are unlikely to meet again unless one of us makes a big effort. Like friends made on holiday or on a journey, the bond is part of the shared experience and when that ends, nothing is left. I'm afraid my friendship with Jacob could be like that. I could put it to the test, do what I half planned to do: ask him over for Easter Sunday lunch. I'll see how I feel when I get over this cold or whatever it is.

I doze, and when I wake my body seems to have become an aching, throbbing boil. I see Louisa McNally the SHO going past and call her over.

She touches my forehead. 'You've got a temperature.'

'Miriam said I didn't really have one.'

'Well, you've got one now.' She sticks a thermometer in my mouth, and I try to keep my eyes open while she deals with another problem. But my brain feels as if it is being crushed and whatever is trying to crush it is about to succeed and wipe me out. I can't kep my eyes open, I'm shaking, I feel sick, I seem to be going deaf. Voices are there but far away. I can feel my body sliding, plunging, into a featureless jelly-like darkness.

Gardenias, I smell gardenias. Dad grew them in Sydney, and the scent was so strong it was like a drug. I smell gardenias faintly, only faintly—

'Jane?'

I must open my eyes. I love the scent and sight of gardenias. I must open my eyes.

'Jane, it's Nat.'

At last I manage to lift my eyelids and there's Nat, sitting close beside me, all worried brown eyes. But the gardenias . . .

'It's me, Jane.'

'Where are they?'

'There's only me here—'

'Gardenias. I can smell gardenias.'

'Look.' Beside her on the ward floor is a well-grown pot plant with dark green glossy leaves and white camellia-like flowers. 'Freddie got it for you. Isn't it beautiful?'

'Dad's favourite flower.' Tears drip uselessly from my eyes as I touch the tough dark green leaves of the plant Nat is now holding in front of me. 'How I love that smell.'

'He sent you his love.'

'Thank Freddie.'

'No, Dad sent you his love. Freddie sent the gardenia, with love, of course, too.'

'Where's Dad?'

'Where he always is, in Sydney. He rang this morning for an update.'

My eyes can't stay open. Coming back to life is all too much. I drift again.

The garden flowers are floppy and brown-edged; even the dark leaves look tired. Water. The plant needs water. As usual there is none beside my bed.

'Water.'

'Hallo, Jane.' It's Roberta; she's sitting quietly at my side. 'I thought I saw you waking up.'

'My plant needs water.'

'So it does, poor thing. Hang on.' She returns with a beaker full of water and pours it carefully round my gardenia.

'I hope it doesn't die.'

Roberta looks at me. 'It'll be all right. You gave us such a fright, my dear. It's lovely to see you alert again.'

'What's been going on?' I'm hooked to an intravenous drip; my fistula is aching as if it's recently been used. 'How long have I been like this? I can't remember anything since feeling groggy on dialysis.'

'A couple of days. Apparently a particularly virulent little bout of septicaemia got you – our old friend Staphylococcus aureus.'

'How did I get infected?'

'Dirt got into your bloodstream somehow.'

'I know you said renal failure wouldn't kill me, but I really thought I was dying, Roberta.' I smile weakly, but she doesn't smile back.

'Septicaemia can kill anyone if it's allowed to take hold and go too far. You were lucky – you were here when you collapsed.'

'Lucky?'

'In a manner of speaking.' This time she does smile, and we chat comfortably until Nat comes in. Nat ignores her as Roberta slips away, and bends to kiss my forehead. It's funny, but people who normally kiss your cheek, kiss your forehead in hospital.

'You look better.'

'I feel almost normal, except for all this pipework.'

'Here's a present. I can't think why we didn't give you one of these long ago.'

I try to undo the present, but one-handed I'm so awkward Nat has to do it for me. It's a very small personal CD player.

'Isn't it sweet, Jane? And the sound is supposed to be excellent. Anyway, it'll help pass the time. I've brought a few of our CDs for you to borrow as well.'

A staff nurse comes and puts a thermometer in my mouth as Nat is talking, so all I can say is fantastic before I'm gagged.

'It's normal. Well done.' The nurse scribbles this down and hurries off again.

'Thank you for my lovely present. You and Freddie are so good to me.'

'Don't be silly.'

'Are you all right yourself, Nat? You look whacked.'

'I am. Our social life's gone crazy recently, I've been in court a lot – it all gets a bit much.'

'Are you still feeling low?'

'About the miscarriage? No. It was more a strong physiological reaction than a psychological one. I'm fine. Relieved, actually. I'm not sure I'd cope with a baby quite yet.' She's rolling and unrolling the strap of her bag; I can tell she's got something on her mind. I remember how she used to stand in the kitchen at home and do the same thing with an apron string, a tape measure, even strips of pastry if Mum was trimming a pie. Fiddle, fiddle, until she came out with what was on her mind.

She pushes the bag away and crosses her arms. 'Anyway, I haven't come to talk about me. You've given us another fright. You live on such a knife-edge, Jane. Please won't you accept the idea of my kidney? I'm consumed with guilt about you, and all I can do is give you silly CD players when what I should be giving you is a chance of health.'

'I can't think about it now.'

'I thought now would be a good time – surely you're desperate for a transplant, and any kidney would do, even mine.'

'Don't be so bitter about it, Nat. Give me time. A couple more bouts of septicaemia, another year of dialysis, and who knows what I'll say!' I laugh, but she remains grim-faced. Then we hear hesitant footsteps coming into the ward, and I look beyond Nat's shoulder and see it's Joe Macdougall. I can feel Nat's annoyance that we can no longer talk freely as I welcome him.

'Joe! How nice to see you. Did you have a problem finding the renal unit? Lots of people do.'

We chat uneasily – two visitors is one too many – and soon Nat says she has to go.

'Thanks for everything, Nat. I mean it.'

'Enjoy the CDs.'

'I will.' I watch her leave while Joe takes some letters out of his pocket.

'Sara says she's very sorry she hasn't been in to see you, but she's had an awful work crisis. I've brought your mail.' I leaf through the envelopes which Sara has put a rubber band around with a note to me, and notice one has a Brighton postmark. The handwriting is very small and clear. I bundle the letters up for later, but say to Joe:

'By the way, I managed to get down to Brighton to see Georgia Hill.'

He looks at me in complete surprise. 'When on earth did you do that?'

'On the morning of the day I collapsed in the unit. It was that very icy day.'

'How did you get on with her?'

'She's extraordinary. Absolutely extraordinary. I felt as if I'd been put through a mental mincer.'

'Sounds all too familiar. Her tutorials could be killers. But I found I'd be thinking about what she said for days, weeks afterwards. In the end it would come clear – more or less.'

'I've had to put the whole experience on hold.'

'How ill is Georgia now, Jane?'

'Pretty bad. She couldn't walk very easily. She used a frame.'

Joe stares at me, upset. 'How awful. When I last saw her she was bicycling like the wind through the campus, on the way to the pool to do her forty lengths.'

'I'm sure that's the way she'd like you to remember her.'

'Are you implying she won't live long?'

'You never know with cancer, but she said she was riddled with it.'

'It could go into remission, even reverse itself. It's happened to others.'

'Let's hope it happens to her. Enough of Georgia Hill – tell me about the new job. Sara said you were after one.'

'I got so fed up with the City. Yes, I've become the finance director of a wildlife charity, the Noah Trust, with a role to play in campaign strategy as well so it won't just be figures. I'll earn half the money but get twice the job satisfaction.'

'Do you know much about wildlife?'

'No. It didn't seem to matter. I offered them the broad view, and they liked it.'

'You're clearly thrilled.'

'I'm thrilled, Jane. Yes. Life as a City financier just wasn't me.'

'What does Sara think?'

'She thinks I'm crazy to take such a massive drop in salary before I've managed to save enough to buy myself a flat. She's probably right.'

I can feel my eyelids suddenly drooping. I can't reply – I feel as if my current's suddenly been switched off. Joe leaves and I sleep for a while, the packet of unopened letters under my right hand.

Brighton, Thursday

Dear Jane,
Thank you for coming to see me. I have been thinking over your

remark that your future has become your present. Your tone when you said it was recriminatory, implying that your disease, for which there is therapy but no treatment, has restricted your future, limited your options, taken away hope. A new kidney would give you some of your future back, but I know that you are not stupid enough to expect that it would all open out as before. So my advice is: don't conceive of your life as a linear progression through time. A little poem by e. e. cummings has ever pleased me.

seeker of truth

follow no path
all paths lead where

truth is here

Come and see me again if you can.
Yours,
Georgia.

I fold up the crisp sheet of white paper. She wrote and posted this the day after my visit. I decide then and there to ask Joe to drive me down to Brighton as soon as I'm out of here, which will be any day now. When Roberta returns for a chat, I feign sleep. I need to see Georgia Hill again, I need her to explain the poem.

5

'Come on, Jane. Lawrence can hold the fort for once – we're going to visit Sam Meredith.'

'Don't go yet, Hen – what are we going to do about Morgan's letter? It's getting ridiculous.'

'You caused the problem, Lol, and you can solve it.'

'But now he's saying he doesn't even owe us the final £250—'

'He certainly does, but I don't think we'll ever get it unless you take him to the small claims court.'

'I can't do that, he's an old school friend.'

'Then write the debt off, my dear. And tell him not to show his face in this gallery again or I personally will eject him.' Henrietta glares at her brother, who is shuffling paper about and ignoring the ringing phone. 'I mean that, too. Off we go, Jane.' She takes my arm and leads me out down the street. 'Lawrence let this rascal Morgan Yeats buy a picture on the never-never – £50 here and £50 there – and didn't keep a proper tally of the payments – old school friend, of course we can trust him – but apparently you can't.'

We set off in Henrietta's small car towards the South Bank. Sam Meredith has a studio in Bermondsey, with a flat attached. 'He's got a home somewhere else, but never seems to use it. He had a wife too, but the poor long-suffering woman walked out on him ages ago. His studio is freezing, by the way, like all studios, but you're well wrapped up.'

'I'm always well wrapped up. I feel the cold terribly – my sister says those years in Sydney have softened me.'

'I shouldn't think that's got anything to do with it. Much more likely to be your disease.' Henrietta has a forthright confidence which I find very comforting. As she blasts her way through a problem she can seem insensitive, but if one stands up to her she listens and often changes her views. 'My husband used to suffer from the cold. I'd be wandering round sleeveless in bare feet and he'd have a thick jersey and socks on. How I hate the drive to London Bridge – I wish they'd get on with these wretched roadworks, they've been like this for months. Yes, Jeremy would be shivering and turning up the heating and I'd be opening windows. I sometimes wondered whether his feeling the cold so was connected to the leukaemia he developed – that's what he died of, by the way – but his doctor pooh-poohed it.'

'When did he die?'

'A long time ago – fifteen years. It feels like another life lived by someone else, to be honest. The girls were saying the same the other day. I told you I had twin daughters, didn't I? Poppy and Grace – non-identical twins who live in Ireland where they run a weaving business together.'

'Has Lawrence ever married?'

'Goodness, no! Can you imagine him getting to the point of committing himself to anyone? The complications would swarm until they overwhelmed him. Unthinkable. And I'm glad, because we share the gallery and a little house in Devon very amicably and it all works well, much to the relief of my daughters. They keep telling me to marry again but I haven't got the energy.'

'Nat agrees being married is hard work.'

'Very hard work. Sometimes rewarding, sometimes not.' She is peering at street names; we've been circling streets in the shadow of Guy's Hospital, but to the south-east where I have never ventured before. 'Keep a look out for Pilgrim's Place – I always forget which turning it is.'

'We've just passed it.'

'Blast. And this street's one way. Let's park here and walk.'

It's strange to look up and see the modern blocks of Guy's so near me, where I spend so much of my life. Pilgrim's Place is full of old warehouses which are now being converted into flats and studios. Henrietta rings a bell and we climb a dusty concrete staircase to the top of a warehouse. Sam Meredith's studio fills the top floor; big north-facing windows scummed with grime look out on the railway tracks leading into London Bridge Station. Against the facing wall lean rows of large paintings. In the middle of the studio is a table crowded with paints, bottles, brushes, empty coffee mugs, empty milk cartons and cigarette packs. The floor is dense with dried splodges of paint. Meredith seems to be working on several pictures at once; there's a step ladder in front of one. He's wearing many layers of aged stained jerseys, mittens, and overalls which would probably stand up on their own, there's so much paint on them. He's short and fair, and in his way attractive. He greets us with a wave of his paint-encrusted hands, and kisses Henrietta.

'Sam, this is our new assistant, Jane Harper, who's started work at the gallery this week.'

'You're looking well, Henrietta. Hallo, Jane Harper of the amazing blue eyes. Let me look at them.' Then he is looking at them, not into them, and it's most disconcerting. I feel as if I'm not there.

'Deep cobalt aureole of the iris, shading inwards in striations to mid-cobalt, touch of ultramarine round the pupil. Very fine eyes.'

I close them briefly, and when I reopen them Meredith has moved away, his interest in me over, towards his new paintings. Henrietta's already staring at them. I stand nearby, listening. They are talking about Poppy and Grace while they gaze at the work.

'I'm glad their business is going well.'

'Mainly because Knock Airport is so close – three-quarters of an hour's drive. The Liberty's buyer was over recently – she flew over in the morning, saw their stuff, and was back at her desk in London by five. Makes it easier to get orders.'

'All tweed?'

'Some wool and silk mix. I like this new one, Sam. It reminds me of the paintings you showed with us in '89, and I don't mean it's looking backwards – it's just the use of that green there in that way – your special green.'

'Well, I'm returning to the same theme I worked on then – ancient field patterns.'

'W. G. Hoskins again.'

'W. G. Hoskins again.'

'*The Making of the English Landscape*. Do you know it, Jane?' Henrietta is kind.

'No.'

'You should read it. Seminal book.' Sam Meredith implies it's a serious lack on my part I haven't read it already. He goes to a rack and pulls another picture forward. It's almost identical to the first, but Henrietta gives an ooh of pleasure. 'Like that even more.' They talk on, looking at pictures, discussing when he's going to be ready to exhibit them. Then a phone rings in one of the rooms off the main studio, and when Meredith returns he's clearly keen for us to leave. As we go I notice his paint palette: a piece of board with inches of dried oil-paint built up into a sort of pitted landscape of colours. It is almost an exhibit in itself.

Henrietta gives me a simple lunch on the way back to the gallery, and then leaves me in charge for a few hours while she and Lawrence disappear upstairs to work on the accounts. It's very peaceful; I read former exhibition catalogues and the afternoon slips by. A couple come in to buy a small painting they have been thinking about, and Henrietta comes down to talk to them while I make out my first invoice.

'Court Gallery on the cheque?'

'Court Gallery Limited, please. Let me stamp it for you.'

'Too late.'

'I don't know why we bothered to have that stamp made. Nobody ever waits. Well done, Jane. Immaculate. I didn't expect that pair to come back – they were so indecisive when they left last week I was sure they'd get home and change their minds. So you never know, is the message. Make no assumptions about anyone. The most unlikely looking person will suddenly write out a cheque for £5000 without blinking, and another who's dripping with money will suffer over £500. I think there's a friend of yours outside.' She nods towards the window before going back upstairs as I see Jacob's smiling face peering in.

'Came to wish you luck. Devon told me you were starting this week.'

'Jacob!' We hug. 'I've missed you. I began to think I'd never see you again.'

'Didn't you get my note?'

'No.'

'I left a letter with Miriam when I heard I was being transferred.'

'She forgot to give it to me. Mind you, I collapsed the same day, so it could be forgiven.'

'What do you mean, you collapsed?' Jacob is upset when he

hears about my infection and my stay in hospital. 'Why didn't someone tell me? I'd have come to see you. The water closes over your head so quickly in hospital life – and it's as if you've never been there at all once you leave.'

'I was only in for a few days, and my blood's stabilised now.'

'No wicked new antibodies running around making trouble?'

'No, thank goodness.'

'You look well, Jane. Better than before.'

'I think it's the fun of having a job, getting a bit of a life. And you, Jacob – you look a bit under the weather, to be honest. Are things OK?'

'I'm low. When I think about it too much, I get low. You know how it is. It affects me at this time of year – birds in the trees getting on with it, birds on the pavements ditto. But I've got no sex drive any more and yet I can't believe I don't want it. This year I'm extra restless.'

Somebody comes in at that moment to look round, and Jacob looks round too. I watch him. He's just pretending to look; his shoulders are rounded, his head's bent forward. I hadn't really thought about it before, but the impotence that often goes with kidney failure must be worse for young men. When the visitor leaves Jacob's mood has changed.

'I gotta go, Jane. Anyway, you need to get on with the business.'

'I'm so glad you dropped in. I was going to ring you, but you know how it is.'

'Only too well.'

'Let's meet soon for a meal.'

'Cool. I'll ring you to fix something up.'

'See you, Jacob.' We kiss cheeks, and he hurries away. I don't think either of us expects the meeting to take place.

People who would never drop in to see me at the flat, come and visit me at the gallery. Friends of Nat and Freddie come, no doubt encouraged by them. Half an hour after Jacob leaves, Thomas Mentieth appears.

'I've been to a meeting nearby – Freddie said you were just round the corner.'

'Thomas, what a nice surprise. Henrietta, this is Dr Mentieth, my brother-in-law's brother. Is there a correct name for that? I've no idea. Anyway, meet Mrs Court.'

'Miss. Actually, my married name was Snodgrass. I went back to using my maiden name when my brother and I started this gallery.'

'I used to know a Snodgrass at Cambridge – Jeremy Snodgrass. He married a Henrietta, I clearly remember. Could it be you?'

'It is. Tell me your name again?'

'Thomas Mentieth. I was invited to your wedding, you know – couldn't make it, I was abroad. How's Jeremy these days? Still writing?'

'He died.'

'Oh no. Oh dear. I didn't know. So sorry.' Thomas is all wrists and elbows; his grey hair is its usual tufty mess. His trousers are too short, so his ankles add to his total air of awkwardness.

'It's years ago now – as I was saying to Jane, it almost feels like another life. Are you also a journalist?'

'Oh no, dear no. I'm a scientific economist, so to speak. I work for the UN. Jeremy was an economist too, wasn't he, but more interested in the theoretical side.' Thomas puts down his worn, bulging briefcase. 'I'm so often abroad on missions I must have missed the announcement of his death.'

'Come upstairs and have some tea and tell me about your time at Cambridge with Jeremy. How fascinating this is.'

'I'd love to.'

'Oh, Jane—'

'Don't mind me, Henrietta, really. Don't feel you're excluding me, because you're not. I must finish this filing.'

'We'll bring you down some tea. Dr Mentieth, come and meet my brother.'

'Thomas, call me Thomas.'

I've never seen Thomas looking so lively. He nips up the stairs behind Henrietta with positively gleaming eyes. He can't begin to relate to me or Nat because he's plainly terrified of us, but for Henrietta, widow of his Cambridge friend, a different Thomas is unfolding. I sit there smiling to myself. Nat and Freddie say he has no women in his life because he's always travelling and never permits himself a social life when he's working. And when he comes back to London, he's still working all hours of the day and night. I tip back my chair, my smile growing. Thomas is just the sort of man to surprise everyone and propose to Henrietta within the week. *Look, Henrietta old thing, I'm just off to Timbuktu for six months, but before I go, erm, er, ah, erm, will you marry me?*

I almost ring Nat to tell her my fantasy, and then decide that it's such a fantasy she would just groan. So I go back to the filing, aware that the voices above me are particularly animated, and when the time comes for closing the gallery, the tea party has become a drinks party.

'I've come to get you, Jane. You must join us for a drink before you go off. Thomas has been entertaining us with such amusing stories.' Henrietta puts an arm around my shoulders. 'Did you know he was coming here to see you?'

'No idea. I didn't even know Thomas was still in the UK.'

'He has such a lovely dry wit, hasn't he? Oh well done, you've finished the files. You deserve a drink, you really do.'

'Would you mind very much if I didn't? I feel quite tired, and I've had most of my fluid ration already.'

'Forgive me. I keep forgetting the constraints on your life. Let me call a minicab.'

'I've done that, actually. In fact, I think it's just arrived.' An unsavoury-looking character has tooted and tapped his watch. I wave and he nods and taps his watch again.

'Graceless lot, our local minicab firm. Never mind, they're just round the corner and that does have its advantages. See you on Friday, Jane. Look after yourself.'

I half expect Joe Macdougall to cancel our trip to Brighton because Sara has been so touchy about it. But he arrives as planned on Wednesday morning and we edge our way through the ugly southern suburbs listening to jazz and saying little until we reach the M23 and the straight run to the coast. Joe yawns and offers me a sweet.

'How's the job, Jane?'

'Perfect.'

'We were afraid you might find it a bit tedious, sitting about all day waiting for people to wander in.'

'There's plenty to do and the Courts are fascinating.'

'Really? I'll have to come and see the gallery.'

'You do that.' I'm annoyed; he's patronising me and I don't like it. I'm also beginning to realise that visiting Georgia Hill *à deux* is a mistake. Georgia Hill is going to talk to Joe about their subject and their shared friends and experiences. I'm going to be a silent witness. I shouldn't have asked Joe to do this for me during his week off between jobs; it's upset Sara and caused a temporary deep freeze between us because she mistrusts my motives.

'Sorry, I didn't hear what you said.'

'I was suggesting we went and visited Charleston after we've seen Georgia. It's not far from Brighton. Important house where some of the Bloomsbury group lived – I'm sure you'd love it.'

'Good idea.' I find the Bloomsbury group rather tiresome but one can change one's mind. 'Bloomsbury might not mix very well with the rigorous Georgia Hill.'

'Oh, I don't know. By the way, will you remember which turning it is off the sea-front?'

'I'll try.' I fail dismally and have to resort to directions from a policeman. We find a meter and feed in all our change.

'Only an hour.'

'It'll probably be more than enough, Joe.'

'Really?'

If Joe says really once more in that tone of voice I'll whack him with my bag. 'Well, she was very weak when I came recently. Shall I wait in the car and let you have her to yourself?'

'Jane, what's the matter with you? You're the one who was so desperate to see her again.'

'You wanted to see her too. You go – two of us could be too much for her.'

'Don't be an idiot. Of course we'll both go together. Come on.' There is anxiety at the back of his eyes; I realise then that he's very nervous of his old tutor, and would never have come without me as moral support. I smile, and Joe smiles, and the atmosphere between us lightens.

Life is full of the unexpected. We are let in by a good-looking man in his mid-thirties – tall, broad, dark-haired and tanned. He's wearing a navy tracksuit and trainers.

'Hi, I'm Tim Clancy. Jane and Joe, I take it. Come right in. Georgia's through there. Coffee? I've just made some.'

Joe asks for coffee and I for hot water, and we follow him into the room. It looks different, but that's because all signs of illness – walking frame, medicines etc. – have been cleared away, and Georgia is lying by the fire on a sofa, wearing a long dark red woollen dress with her hair in a knot on the top of her head. Shorter lengths hang round her face in wiry curls. Her eyes glitter as she holds out her hand to us. She looks magnificent; her extreme thinness is masked by all the folds of wool keeping her snug. As usual there's a strong smell of lavender.

'Joe Macdougall! How lovely to see you again. And Jane, my newest friend. Tell me what you're up to now, Joe, and Jane, come and sit here beside me on the sofa. There's plenty of room in the corner.' She gives me a wide smile and I hope my tears don't show as I smile back. 'Isn't it wonderful that Tim's back from Chicago for the Easter vacation. I was fading away without him, fading away.'

'Don't talk rubbish, my darling. You were fading away because you weren't looking after yourself well enough – my absence has nothing to do with it.' Tim puts a tray of mugs between us and gets us all settled with what we want. I hold my hot water between my hands and listen to Joe telling Georgia about his various jobs since leaving university, and about his contemporaries, while I watch. Her beauty today has surprised me. She's a woman whose body radiates sexual interest when her lover is near her, and lacks it completely when he's not. Her alertness and her driving sense of focus are as I remember them, but the crackle of sexual allure was missing then. Tim, like me, sits in silence and I turn to him after a while.

'How boring of us to take up your precious time here.'

'Not at all. Georgia has hosts of friends, and she loves seeing them. If it wasn't you, it would be someone else.'

'She's looking so much better.'

'She says she's feeling better, but don't be fooled. This is a good day. Tomorrow she could just as easily be lying grey-faced in bed all day. That's the way it goes.'

'I love her book, Tim.'

'Which one?'

'Oh. Has she written many?'

'Five or six. Mostly on her particular subject – German philosophy and Hegel in particular. Is that your field?'

'I'm just a humble admirer of *Last Count*. I've never read any German philosophy, Hegel or otherwise. I did an ordinary degree in history at Sydney university.'

'I nearly went to Sydney – there was a post going in the university that was very attractive – but in the end Chicago won.'

'What did Chicago win?' Georgia's voice cuts into our conversation. She's smiling at Tim as if she can't smile enough.

'Me. Instead of Sydney. But what's this new book, Georgia? What have you been keeping hidden from me?'

She waves a hand. 'Nothing, nothing. It's not important, just an extended essay really.'

'What about?' He's frowning; his index fingers are tapping his thighs.

'Something you know too much about. My illness. Me. I was going to surprise you with a copy on your birthday. Never mind, I'll give you *Last Count* later on today. You'll be bored by it.'

'You are a devil, Georgia. Writing and bringing out a book without saying a word about it. I'm quite hurt.'

'There's no need to be. I was a bit ashamed of it, to tell the truth.' She laughs. 'When you read it you'll see why.'

'Show me a copy.' He's imperious.

Georgia laughs again. 'Later, Tim, later. I don't want to talk about it now, and I'm sure Jane and Joe don't want to talk about it either.' She takes my hand and gives it a little squeeze. 'Jane and I exhausted the topic last time we met.' She pats my hand and releases it. No, I don't want to talk about her book now, and certainly not in front of her clever, cross lover. Luckily the phone rings at that moment, and it's an academic colleague of Tim's so he goes elsewhere to talk, looking huffy.

'Dear me.' Georgia's eyes are alight. 'Ruffled feathers. I adore Tim when he's mad at me.'

And I think of her loving him, of her making love, with her scars and her colostomy and her emaciated riddled body, and feel humbled as I think about something she wrote:

Matured by love, practised in the grief of its interminable exercise, I find myself back at the beginning.

Lightheartedly we drive away, full of the pleasure the visit has given us. We eat excellent plain beef sandwiches at a pub near Charleston, and then we join a group about to go around the house on a guided tour. Charleston is a pretty, medium-sized farmhouse, which surprises me – I'd expected more of an ancestral pile. We gaze at the cosy minutiae of Bloomsbury existence; I stare at a bath strangely placed, at painted surfaces busy with the loose designs favoured by Vanessa Bell and Duncan Grant, and feel sad to be examining these domestic things of no special importance except to those who had once lived here. I feel stifled by the weight they are all given by the guide, and in the library I turn to Joe and tell him I'll wait for him outside.

'Are you all right?'

'I'm fine. Take your time, Joe. I'll be in the garden.'

I've never much liked going round country houses peering at the way other people live, and Charleston is so individual, so much the special space of that strange group of people, that staring for example at their clutter of private ephemera on a mantelpiece seems wrong to me. Either destroy it, all that private mess, or store it away, and leave the mantelpiece bare.

Joe doesn't agree. He thinks the restoration of Charleston has been wholly successful, he likes the fact the intimate flavour of the house and its inmates has been frozen for lucky posterity. He doesn't feel it's an invasion of privacy. Anything's game, in his view.

'If they found a cupboard full of bondage gear, it should be opened and left for us to look at and speculate whether Clive Bell brought tarts in from Brighton when the others were away.'

'I'm beginning to feel the less we know about creative people the better.'

'How can you say that, Jane, when you admire Georgia's book so much? It's painfully revealing.'

'It's different. It's a summary, a sort of testament refined for public consumption. She'd be angry if all her mess and notes and all those stickers on her walking frame – sorry, you didn't see it – were ritualistically preserved after her death. There would be a sort of theme-park sentimentality about it which I am sure she wouldn't like, just as in my view there is about Charleston. It doesn't add anything to the reputations of those who lived and worked there, it just gives us a keyhole to peer through, it satisfies our curiosity but doesn't increase respect or understanding.'

'You're being very purist. I think people need all the help they can get to understand the artistic or creative mind.'

I shrug, but I imagine most people would agree with him. I'm really tired now and we drive back to London mostly in silence.

I spend the Easter holiday as I spend most weekends these days: doing very little. I walk, I go to a museum (more successful than my visit to Harrods), but the gap between Saturday's dialysis and Tuesday's seems longer than usual. London is full of foreign visitors, but none of my friends. I think of ringing Jacob, but somehow can't; I begin to wonder whether I will see him again. Probably not. Our friendship was based on a shared experience in a shared place; when he came to the gallery I think we both felt the thinning and weakening of that bond. Anyway, I can't ring him, and he doesn't ring me. It's lovely to return to work, to the gallery, to the warmth and kindness of Henrietta.

'Jane, do you get to see *The Times*?'

'The Courts read it. Plus the *Independent*. I haven't seen either yet. Why?'

'Terrible news. Georgia—' Joe stops. I stare at the receiver in my hand.

'She's dead.'

'You knew!'

'No.'

'There's an obituary in *The Times*. I just happened to see it – I don't usually read them. I had such a shock. It must have happened over the Easter weekend.'

'While Tim was still with her, then. Perfect for her.' I am surprised at my reaction. All I can feel is a strange delight. 'Lucky Georgia. She might have had to die in hospital without him.'

'You don't sound at all upset. I thought you'd be devastated.' Joe sounds quite accusing.

'I thought I would be too. I dreaded hearing it. But now it's happened I don't feel anything except' – I can't say the word joy – 'relief for her.'

'I'm feeling very shaken. She meant a lot to all of us.' His tone is sombre, hushed. It makes me want to giggle, make jokes, do anything to dispel it. I take a deep breath, still surprised at myself.

'It'll hit me later. I must go and find the newspaper. Thanks for letting me know, Joe. Did you and Sara have a good Easter break, by the way? I've hardly seen her to ask her.'

'Very relaxing.' He sounds guarded. 'And you?'

'Positively geriatric, it was so quiet.'

'I feel choked about Georgia. Aren't we lucky to have seen her when we did?'

'Very lucky, Joe. Very, very lucky.'

'I really feel choked.'

'I know.'

And I do know. Joe's reaction to this death is normal, mine isn't. He's probably never known someone well who has died. It's out there, far away, not a consideration in his existence except perhaps during those paralysing moments of terror when one's awake in the small hours. I know that my reaction has been conditioned by the last few months; I also used to ignore death, treat it with blithe and blind indifference; now I feel a grudging even affectionate respect for it. Death is one of the doctors; he'll bail me out when the others fail. He doesn't need a bleeper, he's caring enough to know exactly when he will be needed to play his part. In my worst moments, I've felt him near, as if he's been capped and gowned ready for the final operation. We've had a practice run together, and I know he's there.

I didn't really talk to Georgia about death itself. I've no idea if she viewed him at the end as friend or foe. I hope the former, but I know she loved life more than I do. I didn't realise this until I saw her with Tim. Her whole being sang with hope. And hope is not death's friend.

I sit quietly in the gallery for some time, thinking about Georgia. And then, without premeditation, I pick up the phone and ring her Brighton number. What I am half hoping for is her voice on the answerphone, but instead Tim Clancy replies and I nearly put the receiver down.

'Hallo? Hallo? Tim Clancy speaking.'

'This is Jane Harper. I came down before Easter . . .'

'Of course. Georgia was so glad you did. She was on great form that day.' He sounds so normal. I don't know what tone to take.

'Wonderful form.'

'You've heard what's happened to her?'

'Yes. I'm very . . .' But I can't say I'm sorry. I can't say anything. Luckily Tim says plenty, a torrent of words he clearly needs to use to help him come to terms with Georgia's death. He tells me how she grew suddenly weaker on Good Friday, and kept talking about the harrowing of hell and the nature of purgatory while she lay in bed and listened to the Bach *St Matthew Passion* on the radio.

'Georgia asked for a prayer book, the 1662 *Book of Common Prayer* to be precise, and of course there wasn't one in the flat, nor could I find anyone who had one. So on Easter Sunday her mother Mo went to church hoping she could borrow one, but they only had little booklets of the latest version of the liturgy, and that wasn't what Georgia wanted. When I told her this errand was out of character, that she'd been heard to say that faith was a crutch for the wounded in body and mind, she said: "So? What am I?" and laughed. She'd been very cheerful all weekend in fact.

'Well, after lunch Mo and I went for a good walk round Brighton, sure we could find another more fruitful church, but they were all shut, so we gave up and walked along the beach instead. When we got back, Georgia was dead.'

I wait, knowing he will go on again. I want to ask whether Georgia knew she was on the point of death, and he indirectly answers my unspoken question.

'She'd dressed herself up. She was wearing her red dress, she'd even varnished her nails; she smelt of lavender, she adored the scent of lavender. Of all colours, red suited her best. She was lying on the sofa, where she'd been busy taking the labels off her walking frame until she must have felt dizzy and leaned back, a clump of stickers rolled up in one hand. Then her heart gave out.

'Jane, she looked so calm and relaxed – death when it came was a gentle visitor. Mo and I sat beside her for ages, just sat there in silence holding her hands. What was the point of calling the doctor and ambulance yet, and filling the flat with bustle and strangers? Photograph her, said Mo. So I did, very carefully, only to find out next day there was no film in her camera.'

'So no death mask.'

'Sorry? I didn't catch what you said.'

'You must be exhausted, Tim.'

'Completely exhausted. Yes. Drained.'

'Thank you for talking to me. And forgive me for disturbing you.'

'I keep her alive by talking about her.'

He tells me to try and come to the funeral, but I know I won't. I can't. My part in Georgia Hill's life was so peripheral to her, so brief and recent, that it would be quite inappropriate to be there. And too painful.

I buy myself *The Times* during my lunch break, but I don't read it until I get home that evening. As usual the flat is empty, though I'm expecting Sara back at some point.

I open the obituary page, my hands beginning to shake. A photograph of Georgia stares out straight at me: messy hair, big focused eyes, a faint smile at the edge of her strong wide mouth. Her face is thin, but not as thin as it later became. Under the photo is written: *Georgia Hill, philosopher and sociologist, died of cancer in Brighton on Easter Day, April 19, 1992, aged 39.*

Georgia Hill's early death has silenced a great scholar in her prime: an authority on all continental and especially German thought; a world expert on Hegel; widely respected for her work on theology, sociology, political theory and post-modernism. But it has also extinguished a new star in the world of literature. Late in 1991, already gravely ill, Hill published her last book, an autobiographical meditation entitled Last Count. *It has resonated far beyond her usual academic sphere, and received rapturous reviews and wide acclaim. In this remarkable book her prose attained a concrete simplicity and existential intensity; her eloquent suffering was transfigured by a radiant spirituality. She dealt in her philosophical books (particularly the collection of essays on Buber, Simone Weil, Derrida and others entitled* The Problem of Modernity) *with what she called 'the crisis of self-comprehension', but nowhere more accessibly and movingly than in this short last book. Into it she concentrated the essence of her life and thought. The book dwells on sickness and mortality, on friendship and betrayal, on the most intimately personal and the most sublimely universal. To quote*

> *her: 'This is not love of suffering, but the work, the power of love, which may curse, but abides.'*

I collapse. All the emotion that Joe expected pours out of me like a river bursting its banks. I lie on my bed and sob until I have no tears left, then I just go on lying there. The flat is in darkness around me, but I cannot move. Sara comes in and switches lights on while she calls me. I pretend to be asleep, and having peeped round my door to check I'm there, she leaves me alone. I hear her beating eggs, smell the heated butter, know she will take her food to eat in front of the television as usual. But she doesn't – she must be in a hurry and have eaten it quickly in the kitchen, because very soon after the front door bangs and she's gone again. Later when I get up I find a note to say she's gone to the cinema with Ginny.

I thought I wanted to be alone but now the flat's empty I bitterly regret not going out with her. Yet I know if she'd asked me I'd have probably said no. I cut myself a piece of bread and spread it thickly with marmite. Full of salt, utterly off limits, but sod it. I pour myself a beer. It will put me over my day's allowance of liquid but sod that too.

Calm now, I read through the obituary again. It lists all Georgia Hill's publications, and goes through her life and career. Her family background seems very ordinary, not so her working life. I had not in the least appreciated her academic stature; she was introduced to me by Joe as his tutor, and he gave me no inkling of her many books and breadth of influence. I feel shrivelled by this long, weighty obituary; shrivelled with embarrassment that I approached her with such confidence, wasted her time with my boring ideas and thoughts. Professor Georgia Hill was an eminent academic figure, and I didn't even know she was a professor.

By the time I'd had a bath and reread the obituary several times, I realise how lucky I have been. If I'd known anything about her beyond the book I love so, I would never have dared told her I wanted to meet her. And she rang me so quickly, said come down to Brighton, I'd love to meet you too. I stare at her haunting face with its invitation of alert encounter, and smile through fresh tears.

6

The rest of April and the whole of May pass uneventfully, as if the sources of emotion in my life have been turned off. Freddie and Nat are both involved in long cases and also very tied up with Alice Mentieth who's beginning to show worrying signs of dementia. Thomas has been visiting the Courts with unusual enthusiasm before disappearing on another of his special missions. Sara has forgotten her suspicions of me, mainly because she and Joe are showing signs of pulling gently apart. Joe I have not seen at all since our visit to Brighton.

One late May night the phone rings at about 3 a.m. and Sara and I bump into each other as we go to answer it. My heart is racing, I push her aside roughly and grab the phone from her as she lifts it. But it's not that call from the renal ward that I hear subliminally in every ringing phone, it's a drunken voice on a wrong number. Sara watches me replace the receiver, my face and heart wiped blank.

'Sorry I shoved you.'

'It's OK, Jane. Poor you.'

'It doesn't matter.'

'It does matter. What a pig I am. I never think about your life. I'm very sorry to be such a useless, selfish flatmate.'

'It doesn't matter.' I only want to get back to bed, but Sara's now wide awake.

'Let's have a hot drink. Hot chocolate for me. Something for you?'

'No thanks.'

'Will they really ring you like that in the middle of the night?'

'Yes. The renal ward's staffed twenty-four hours a day, and if the right kidney comes in, they get hold of you at once.' I follow her into the kitchen.

'So it could come at any time.'

'Any time. I have to make sure I always let them know my whereabouts.'

'Somebody medical asked me the other day why you weren't on home haemodialysis. They said hospital dialysis was the worst option.'

I lean against the fridge as she warms milk. 'You can't dialyse at home unless you have someone there with you, trained to help you. In other words, either you have your family or your partner helping you, but if you're single, it's not an option.'

Sara stirs her drink fiercely. 'I should have helped you. I've been absolutely useless.'

'Sara, I couldn't have asked you. Nor Nat – which is one of the reasons I didn't want to live in their flat. The commitment is total, and can last for years. It was bad luck for me I couldn't get on with CAPD, because it's the most benign form of dialysis. But a lot of us can't use it for one reason or another, and unless we have someone at home who can help us to needle, we're stuck with the unit.'

'Needle?'

'Putting the two needles into your fistula when you connect up to the lines that go into the machine.'

Sara is staring at me as if she's never seen me before. 'I've deliberately closed my mind to everything you go through all the time. Do you actually have to stick needles into your own veins? Oh Jane.'

'It's a lot less painful doing it oneself than some heavy-handed nurse doing it! I'm quite good at it now. The needles are very sharp, and if you're careful they don't cut you.'

'Oh God, Jane. It makes me feel sick just to hear you talk about it.'

'I'm not surprised. It makes me sick to look at my fistula and think about what it's for. I hate the way my vein has thickened.'

'Show me. You always keep it covered.'

'You won't like it.' *Love your fistula, Jane. Love it.*

'Show me just the same.'

I put my arm out, pulling back my sleeve. 'Not very nice.'

Sara starts to smile as she looks. 'Oh come on, Jane. I was expecting a ghastly mess. That's very neat.'

'Compare it with the other arm.'

'Don't compare it. That's stupid.' I cover up my arm. 'Can I come in one day with you and watch you dialyse?'

'Of course you can. Anyone can visit as long as we warn the nurses. Come on a Tuesday – I'm always there until six on a Tuesday. Come just before I finish and then we can go home together.'

'I have departmental meetings on Tuesdays, but I'll make sure I leave early one day and come. I've been a complete squeamish coward about your illness. Joe's right. He told me to face it, it won't be nearly as bad as I think. I've been a bloody hopeless flatmate, let's be frank.'

'Why should you have done more, Sara? I was wished upon you; you're Nat's friend, this was her flat. It suited me to come here – no one really asked you or Mark what they thought. I know Mark was going away so he didn't care, but I never asked you. And you must have wondered why I didn't do the obvious and live with Nat.'

'I thought you didn't really get on, so that was the reason. But you seem to get on OK now.'

'There's nothing like a nasty crisis for improving relations.'

'And changing people. You've changed, Jane.'

'I think I have, but what I don't know is how much of it is part of the illness. You know, give Jane a new kidney and she reverts to type.' I meet her gaze. I know at the beginning she was Nat's spy – I overheard a conversation that made me very angry at the time. Nat was clearly asking: Are you surviving my dreadful sister? Has she done anything awful yet? Not said anything too bitchy? But things have shifted since then, and now Nat moans to me about Sara not being a good friend any more – too absorbed in her own life and Joe.

'But when you get a transplant, you'll also be cured in a sense. Good as new.' Sara sits at the kitchen table and I join her. I'm wide awake now.

'I can never be good as new.'

'A hell of a lot better than you are now, then.'

'I'm afraid of false hopes, Sara. I've accepted so many things – I've accepted that I'm unlikely to live a long life, make old bones. I've accepted that I am no longer in control, and the funny thing is, I no longer mind. I used to resent bitterly that I was only alive because of my dialysis, that I was completely in the hospital's hands. At the beginning they were the enemy, now they're my allies, my best helpers. I couldn't live without the idea they are there, at the end of a phone, twenty-four hours a day. I'm too dependent on them probably, but until I have a transplant what can I do about it? I've given up being angry that I'm not in control, and that's not something I could have remotely expected eight months ago. That's the biggest change in me.'

'Is it really eight months already?'

'Just about. Unbelievable, isn't it?'

'Jane, we all expected you'd have a transplant immediately. Freddie said it to me himself at the wedding; he said he'd pay anything to give you one, and that you'd have it by Christmas.'

I hesitate. It seems unfair to worry that what I say will get back to Nat. Perhaps it should get back to Nat. And Freddie. I don't think they've ever really understood my reasons.

'Sara, where do kidneys come from? Think about it. Either dead people, or family donors, or poor people in Turkey or India or wherever who sell them to unscrupulous middlemen. And if they come from dead people, those kidneys usually go into the NHS pool and get allotted immediately to the best recipient. It's not something you can order. The tissues have to match as well as possible – you can't buy a kidney unseen and hope it will do. I don't think Freddie has completely understood the way it all works – he and Nat seem to think money will buy you into the queue or something. It doesn't work like that. There are a limited number of cadaver kidneys, they always come unexpectedly, and I really feel strongly they should be matched through the NHS base.'

'So how's the pecking order determined?'

'There's no pecking order. The best match gets the kidney. You may have waited five weeks or five years, you may be an elderly single drone with low life achievement, you may be a young parent of five children. It doesn't matter. I don't know what they do if there are two patients whose tissues match a transplant kidney equally – perhaps they toss up, perhaps they give it to the youngest. I don't know and I don't want to know.'

'I had no idea tissue-matching was so crucial. I thought they had drugs to control the rejection.'

'They do, and if I have a transplant I'll have to take them permanently. But they still have to start with as good a match as possible. Somebody on the ward was whisked off suddenly to be given a kidney. I'm sure we all privately felt we were more worthy than poor Deirdre. I certainly did. But at least I also felt a bit of joy for her before I started grinding my teeth!' I laugh.

'But they must sometimes make judgements and say, look this chap's a criminal, he doesn't deserve a kidney, we ought to choose her, she's a mother of five.'

'They try not to.' I yawn hugely as Sara gets up to make more hot chocolate.

'Do you know, this is the first time you have *ever* sat gassing like this with me?' She has her back to me. 'I was beginning to think you'd never let your hair down and talk about yourself.'

'If you're born a control freak, you can't take risks like that.'

'I can't see it's much of a risk chatting round the kitchen table.' Sara sits down again.

'One's guard is down. Look at the things I've been telling you about myself. Dangerous stuff!'

'You sound as if you regret it already.'

'I probably will tomorrow. Assessing change, confessing change – not easy when you've never done it.'

'It's not easy for any of us to talk about the things that really matter. I'm – I'm at a crossroads myself. I find I enjoy work more than people – Joe made me realise it. Things are not as good as they were between us and I couldn't think why. He put it down to my attitude to work, told me I was a real career woman, and he didn't mean it as a compliment.'

'Don't take any chauvinist shit from him, Sara. If you want to be a career woman, why should he stop you?' I sound more vehement than I mean to, and she stares at me, her eyes full of thoughts.

'Joe isn't a chauvinist. I don't think he meant I should be a little home bird, I think he meant that my career was taking over to an unhealthy degree. He's probably right.'

'But work is wonderful. You're so lucky you enjoy it.'

'Yes.'

Intense exhaustion is spreading through me, my feet are becoming so heavy I can hardly lift them. I somehow manage to pull myself upright. This small hours chat will take its toll tomorrow; I'll have to stay in bed almost till the moment I leave for the hospital. 'Sorry, Sara, I've had it.'

'You've gone grey. Are you all right?'

'I feel a bit dizzy suddenly. It'll pass.' I lean on her arm as she helps me to my bedroom. It is a strange feeling, accepting help from Sara. She even tucks me in.

'Jane, what time do you leave tomorrow for Guy's?'

'About one.'

'I'm working on a report which I can easily do at home. I've got my lap-top with me – I'd half thought of finishing it here, one gets interrupted so much at the office. So I'll stay, and I'll go with you tomorrow, give you a hand.'

'You don't have to.'

'I know I don't have to – I want to. It's time I opened my eyes to your situation, instead of pretending you have a cosy disease that is easily treated.'

'Treatment implies cure.'

'I get your point. Contained might be a better word. Good-night, Jane.'

'Good morning would certainly be the better word!'

So Sara calls a taxi and comes with me to Guy's, and I am very grateful for her company. Even after spending the whole morning in bed, I'm feeling ill and leaden. Sara comes right up to the unit, and watches me weigh myself. I'm quite a bit overweight – I'm going to need extra time on the machine. Chantal is on duty, and helps me connect to the machine with her usual deftness. Sara is sitting staunchly beside me, watching the whole process even though I can see from her tense hands how difficult she's finding it.

Chantal goes over to Angela to check her levels and Sara smiles ruefully at me. 'I'd no idea it was all quite so physical. What happens now?'

'I lie here and go to sleep.'

'When do you finish?'

'In about four and a half hours' time. With luck I'll sleep for a good part of it.'

'I can't come and collect you this evening, I'm afraid . . .'

'Don't even think of it. You've done enough. Thanks for the support, Sara.'

'Here's a little prohibited treat for you. You said you could eat what you liked in the first hour.' She puts a plastic picnic box beside me, picks up her heavy briefcase and leaves with her characteristic over-the-head backwards wave.

She's made a beautiful salad of avocado, onion, tomato, and green beans.

'Do you drive, Jane?'

'I haven't driven much since I came to London, but my international driving licence is up to date.'

'Would you take my car and drive to Bermondsey to collect some stuff from Sam Meredith? He's done a new series of small works and wants me to sell them quickly if I can. I can't go – Mr Pimble's here to do the accounts.' She rolls her eyes. Mr Pimble is the cause of much groaning between brother and sister. He's got a square flat face, a square flat body, a high precise voice and soft white hands. Henrietta says he's the human equivalent of a column of figures.

'The car's fully insured for any driver, and old and battered so I don't mind what happens to it. Enjoy your trip.'

As I set off, I remember the last time I drove a car: it was Freddie's Saab, and we were on the way back from his cottage in the country. He'd hurt his hand and Nat was drunk on lunchtime champagne. Jane Harper, destroyer of relationships, smugly driving with her eye on the main chance – Freddie – while Nat lay on the back seat and slept. Perfect. But in fact Freddie fell asleep too, and Nat sobered up, and by the time we arrived back in London after a horribly slow and congested journey, I felt aggrieved rather than smug. I haven't been back to that cottage. Weekends in the country aren't possible if one has to dialyse every Saturday morning.

This time I park right outside Sam Meredith's warehouse; the meter still has half an hour on it, and I reckon that will be enough. I climb up the concrete stairs, and he takes a while to open the door.

'Oh, no Henrietta?'

'She couldn't come.'

'It's Joan, isn't it?'

'Jane.'

'The last painting isn't quite dry – tell Henrietta to be very careful until it is. Here they are.'

A series of small canvasses lean against the studio wall, scaled down versions of the last works I'd seen last time I was here. I squat in front of them.

'I decided to try and condense what I was doing. Like painting sonnets, I suppose. I even thought of calling these my Sonnet Sequence, but decided that was a bit twee. Do you agree?'

'I do, rather.'

He doesn't look very pleased with my answer. We both turn back to the little oil paintings. They are subtle and wonderful. Each one is very similar in design to the next, but with telling differences of colour and texture.

'What do you think they look like?'

'They look beautiful.'

'No, no, what do they make you think of?' He almost snarls at me for misunderstanding him; there is something feral and predatory about him, and he smells strongly of oil paint, turps, and sweat.

'They make me think of maps. Organic maps.'

'Ahh, do they?' Now he purrs, pleased. He prowls about. 'Go on.'

'I know nothing about modern art, Mr Meredith. I think you'd find my comments banal. I'm learning as I go, and I've not learned much yet.'

'Don't study "Modern Art". Fatal. Just keep your nerve ends sharp and look, look, look. Don't let Henrietta try teaching you!'

'She doesn't. She leaves me be.'

'I like Henrietta. Can't stand her brother Lawrence. What does she call him, Lolly?'

'Usually Lol.'

'Apt nickname for a stupid man who's only interested in money.

By the way, talking of money, tell Henrietta that if she sells the whole series to one buyer, she can give a discount but not of five per cent as she suggested. One per cent max. I don't particularly care if they all go to different buyers. Each stands on its own. So you think they are like organic maps, then, Joan?'

'Jane. Yes.'

'Not a bad description. Not bad. I have a little map of the village in Essex I was born in, now too near Stansted Airport for comfort. The map is seventeenth century. The configuration of fields inspired that.' He points to one of the series. 'I then looked the village up in the Domesday Book, took it back to before the Norman Conquest. Lots of oak forest then. The old greenwood of England, in which the merry men did "fleet the time carelessly, as they did in the golden world". Then along came the despotic Normans, and they promptly destroyed the system of common woodland rights. The old greenwood was a vigorous working society, you know, nothing as soppy as that quotation from *As You Like It*. The Normans took the forest as the King's property, policed it with his minions, and dedicated it to *la chasse*. Bang went the liberty of the greenwood for ever.' He points to another picture. 'By the seventeenth century and my little map, the oaks had all been felled to make ships for the King's fleet, and it was downhill all the way for the next two hundred years. The forest completely disappeared. Until 1918, when a rich landowner's widow planted an oak forest in his memory – he fell at Ypres – and *voilà*, today they are good big trees. Not quite the greenwood of old, but a creditable little forest.' He has been staring over my head as he speaks, as if watching a film over my head. It isn't clear at all which pictures go with which stage of the story, but it doesn't matter anyway. I'm certainly not going to ask.

At this moment a tall girl with long tangled hair staggers out of a side room. She's wearing an old shirt and nothing else. It's unbuttoned and she doesn't bother to do it up as she wanders groaning to a sink and pours herself a glass of water.

'What the hell did you put in my drink, Sam?'

'Lots of neat whisky. Nothing else. You drank too much, Ingrid. By the way, this is Joan.'

'Jane.'

Ingrid ignores me as she drinks a second glass. 'What's the time?'

'Midday.'

'God.' She goes back through the door, carrying a third glass of water. Sam Meredith watches her with goatish glee.

'She has no concept of self-control, does my Ingrid. In anything.'

I start to fill in the receipt book Henrietta gave me. 'What shall I call the series? *Ten Sonnets* – just as a working title?'

'No. Call them *Arboreal Memory One to Ten*.' With quick efficient movements he stacks the pictures in boxes divided internally so that each picture does not touch the next. 'And remind Henrietta that I want those crates back.'

'I'll add a note about that to the receipt. Perhaps you'd like to check it all before you sign it?'

'Goodness me, how businesslike. I don't remember Henrietta ever wanting me to sign anything.'

I stare at him. His patronising manner is getting to me. I'll be rude soon.

'Henrietta is a friend of yours. I am an employee of hers, collecting some valuable items, and she needs to have paper evidence that I've done that.' My tone's crisp but I wasted my breath because Ingrid has started calling him and his attention's elsewhere.

'Just coming, my sweet. Have to help Joan carrying this stuff down and then I'll be with you.'

I don't bother to correct him.

Henrietta is excited by Sam Meredith's new paintings and lines them up as he did along the wall. 'I've never known Sam to work on so small a scale, and so quickly. They're wonderful. So confident.'

'How are you going to sell them?'

'On the grapevine. I'll ring the serious collectors I know and tell them to come in. There's an American who'll buy his work sight unseen, but he's a bit like Saatchi – fills warehouses with the stuff and occasionally brings them out for exhibitions. I'd prefer to sell these to smaller-scale collectors who'll hang them now and live with them. As I don't need to tell you, Jane, I'm a bit of a romantic.'

'I know someone who might be interested. He said he'd love a Meredith but they were always too big for his house.'

'Who's that?'

'Freddie Mentieth, my brother-in-law.'

'Thomas's brother, the QC.' Her expression softens at the mention of Thomas. 'I don't think he's been to the gallery ever.'

'He's been to see a Meredith exhibition here, but perhaps you weren't around.'

'Well, go on, Jane, try and make a sale. Ring him and tell him to come and view them if he's interested. But he can't hang about – these will sell at once when the word gets out Meredith has painted small works. And I know Sam wanted them sold quickly, didn't want to wait for his exhibition. Said he needed money for a holiday.'

'I'll ring Freddie now.' He's in court so I leave a message in his voice mail-box. Freddie gets back to me at half past four.

'I'm very interested – how small are they? . . . I see, for Meredith real miniatures! I've got a consultation about to start which will last until five-thirty – I'll come over then.'

'I'll keep the gallery open until you arrive, don't worry.'

'How many in the series?'

'Ten.'

'To be sold only as a group?'

'Not necessarily.'

'Thanks for thinking of me, Jane. See you soon.'

Henrietta and Lawrence are upstairs when Freddie arrives. Henrietta has told me to call her at some point because she'd love to meet another Mentieth, but otherwise is leaving the transaction (if it was to be) to me. Freddie looks taller than usual as he steps into the gallery, perhaps because of his very dark suit. He's wearing a bright blue tie on a darker blue shirt, which greatly flatters him. He's a handsome man – I thought so when I first set eyes on him, and I haven't changed my mind.

'No Nat? I thought you might bring her along too.'

'She's on a case up in Manchester, returning tomorrow. I spoke to her just before coming, and she sends her love.' His eyes are raking the walls in vain.

'The new Merediths are kept downstairs, out of sight. Henrietta doesn't want people to see them yet, unless they are seriously interested in them.' Freddie follows me downstairs, where the pictures lean in their appointed order against the wall. He examines them in silence while I tell him what Meredith told me about their origin.

'So he called them *Arboreal Memory*.'

Freddie examines each picture with great care; I can sense his interest and enthusiasm even though he's silent for many minutes. I sit quietly waiting.

'It would be a crime to separate them.'

'Meredith didn't care if they were sold separately.'

'Painters can be barbarians.'

I'm laughing at this when Henrietta appears looking feisty.

'You must be Frederick Mentieth – I'd recognise you as Thomas's brother anywhere. I'm Henrietta Court.'

As they shake hands I can see Freddie looking puzzled.

'Thomas was a friend of my husband's at Cambridge – he dropped into the gallery and we all met again. Didn't he mention it?'

'So he did. I'm surprised you see a likeness – most people don't.'

'Oh, I do. What do you think of the Merediths, by the way?'

'They are wonderful. Quite wonderful. I would love to buy them, but only the whole series, because I feel strongly they shouldn't be split up. But it all depends on what you are asking for them.'

Henrietta names a figure and there is a small pungent silence.

'Well, that's much what I expected, multiplying what each picture would fetch by ten. No discount if one takes the lot?'

'One per cent only, I'm afraid.'

'Fair enough. I'd have to sell a couple of pictures to afford the Merediths, but they are too good to miss. How much time will you give me?'

'If you're in earnest, whatever it takes to sell your others.'

'I want to buy *Arboreal Memory*.'

'Please do come upstairs and have a drink while we discuss all this. Bring him up, would you, Jane, while I just go and open a bottle?'

I am filled with a strange excitement which began to build as I watched Freddie fall in love with the pictures. I suppose it's also from the making of my first sale.

'Where will you hang them?'

'It's a good question. But I think what I'll have to do is take the other pictures out of the drawing room and hang them there. I'll redecorate it first in cooler colours – it needs to be done again. It hasn't been painted since Anthea had it done ten years ago. If I have the walls painted off-white, the Merediths will sing against them.'

'Come on upstairs, Freddie.' He's unwilling to leave the pictures, and follows me with his eyes turned back to them. As we pass through the main gallery he says, 'I wonder what Nat will think of them.' I don't need to answer, because Henrietta is waiting on the staircase and the conversation becomes general for a while until she asks Freddie what pictures he's considering selling.

'One I'm sure about. It's a Peter Blake I bought right at the start of my collecting years ago but I've lost interest in it. Pop Art doesn't attract me any more.'

'One Peter Blake could fetch enough to pay for all the Merediths.'

'Not this one – it's not one of his best.'

'I'll put you in touch with a collector who specialises in Blake. And if you need any other help, please don't hesitate to ask. I wish we could do a swap with the Blake but we don't deal in Pop Art. But if there's anything else you're thinking of selling, let me know.'

'Why don't you come round some time and see what I've got?'

'I'd love to.'

Conversation continues, but I can see Freddie isn't listening to a word. Lawrence is boring on about one of his obsessions, mobile phones.

'They're supposed to oil the workings of social life, but in fact in my view they destroy it. Nobody will commit themselves – everyone is late because they know they can ring up and explain they're on their way—'

'On the subject of social life, I've got a suggestion to make.' Freddie leans forward. He hasn't touched his wine. 'Why don't you all come back with me now, and continue this drink? And perhaps I could take a couple of Merediths to see how they'll look in their new home, and you can give me some advice about what else to sell.'

The Courts look surprised, but Henrietta agrees it would be a good idea not to waste time and since she's free, she could come.

'I've got a dinner. In fact I ought to be changing. So thanks, Mr Mentieth, but no thanks.' Lawrence stands up as he empties his glass.

'And you, Jane?'

'Jane should come if she feels up to it.' Henrietta is firm.

So we all get into Freddie's car and drive up to the house near Primrose Hill. I sit in the back in silence while Freddie and Henrietta talk about Thomas and the UN mission he's on. Beside me on the seat are two fresh-smelling oil paintings. I was impressed with the sure way Freddie picked out the two he wanted to take. I carry them in when we arrive, and Freddie immediately takes down a picture over the mantelpiece and props the Merediths on it. They don't look good against the apricot-coloured walls, but they look wonderful with each other.

'I can see why Meredith says you could sell them separately.' Freddie has taken off his jacket and is standing looking ecstatic. 'Each is so interesting in itself, and yet two together start talking. All ten will have a conversation of unending interest. What do you think of the room, Henrietta? Can this space absorb all ten?'

Henrietta has taken in the room in a long sweeping stare. 'They'd fit. I'm not sure you'd want all ten in one room though. To use your image, the conversation might be deafening. People can be too rigid in their treatment of series. Have a couple in your hall, move that mirror so they are reflected in it when the door is open. Play around with them a bit. But don't also feel that you have to have them all, you know. Just two look powerful enough.' She gives Freddie her lopsided grin. 'Thomas will never forgive me if he thinks I've made a hard sell.'

'Thomas probably won't forgive me for filling the room with a whole set of new pictures. He's a complete philistine.'

'He knows nothing about modern art and cares less. So refreshing.' Henrietta laughs as she takes the wine Freddie hands her, after he's given me my usual apple juice.

'What do you think, Jane?' Freddie turns to me.

'I've never talked about art with him—'

'No, no, about how the Merediths will look in here.'

I walk to the window and look down the long room; the far window opens on to a wrought-iron balcony, from which a small staircase winds down to the garden. Wisteria, now in full flower, crowds the fragile-looking iron with its fresh light green foliage nd racemes of pale mauve flowers. The window framed with all this is a very attractive feature of the room, at its best just now.

'If you stand here looking at the greenery over there and imagine what they'd look like, all full of green too, and well, organic, there's no doubt the effect will be stunning. I'm sure Nat would agree. But can't you wait until she's back from Manchester and involve her in the decision?' Henrietta's reservations about Thomas's view of a hard sell are also mine as regards Nat.

'She won't be back until Wednesday. She tends to leave buying pictures to me.'

'That's a lovely Roger Hilton.' Henrietta has ben examining it closely.

'I know. I'll never part with that one.'

'Where's the Peter Blake?'

'Upstairs, in my study. Let's go and have a look at it.' But the telephone rings at that moment, and Freddie leaves me to show Henrietta the house. When we pass all the photographs of Anthea hung in a group I point them out.

'Freddie's first wife, Anthea. My sister Natalie insisted these were hung here. Anthea was much more interested in art than my sister is – Nat's a bit like Thomas in that respect. She doesn't care much either.'

'And also, if she's got any sense, she won't try and compete with a dead wife.'

'I hadn't thought of that.'

'I expect she has. If she's managed to land Freddie Mentieth, she can't be a fool.'

'She's not.'

Perhaps I sound glummer than I mean to, because Henrietta puts an arm round my shoulders and says, 'Nor, my dear Jane, are you.'

*   *   *

'My advice is to sell the Blake as you already decided, but also that drawing upstairs by Nicola Spurgeon. Since the BBC did a programme on her, her work has been fetching silly prices. I don't think she'll last or develop much, and you clearly don't rate the drawing very highly or you wouldn't have put it on an awkward bend in the staircase where one's attention is more on one's feet than the walls!'

Freddie laughs as he fills up Henrietta's glass. 'That's a very good idea, and I probably wouldn't have thought of it. I am tired of the drawing, but I had no idea Spurgeon was a celebrity. Right. Let's hope the two of them fetch enough.'

'I can get you almost as much for the Spurgeon as the Blake with a couple of phone calls. It's the best Spurgeon I've seen, as they go.'

'Done. Now, when we've finished our drinks let's continue this delightful evening over some dinner at the Italian restaurant round the corner which has fed me so well over the years.' And it continues to be delightful, and though I'm very tired when the taxi (paid for by Henrietta) finally drops me off after leaving her in Victoria, I still feel some of the buzz that's been with me all evening.

The answerphone is winking in the dark flat: five messages. I yawn hugely as I play them back; one from Sara to say she's at Joe's; one from some workmate of hers with a message about some meeting. I yawn again as the third message begins and nearly miss what it says. It's the hospital, telling me there is a kidney for me. Come at once. The next two are also from the same nurse, her voice growing increasingly fraught. Where are you, Jane? Hurry, hurry.

7

I replay the messages. I don't need to, but I can't either believe them or move. My heart is racing and my brain's gone blank. At first I can't even remember the hospital number which I know as well as my name. I'm just about to enter the number when the phone rings again.

'Jane! Thank God! We were really getting concerned. There was no reply all evening from any of your numbers – the gallery, your flat, your sister's place – we were beginning to think you'd gone away without telling us.'

'I'm so sorry, I was out to dinner, I'm full of food, how can I possibly have an operation? Oh, I wish I'd known, I'd never have gone out—'

'Don't panic, Jane. Just rejoice and don't worry about anything. Go and pack what you'll need for a week or two in, and we'll send a regular taxi for you at once. He should be with you in twenty minutes or so. Don't forget your record book and medication in your excitement.'

'I can't believe there's a kidney for me.'

'It's a seventy-five per cent match – very good. See you soon!' The nurse's voice (which one?) calms me a bit, but it's still the oddest sensation to be rushing round the flat collecting my things together. I put the heap on my bed – sponge bag, make-up bag, hairbrush, two nightshirts, extra underwear, tissues, clock, earplugs, books. My little CD player and a few CDs. Two towels, hand and bath size. My dressing gown. I'm now grinning like someone who's suddenly been offered a perfect holiday – quick, we're going to the Seychelles, get packed. I almost look out my bathing suit.

I put everything into a tote bag and I'm ready, but the cab still hasn't come.

I must tell people. My father – he'll just be starting his morning consultations – I'll ring him. My hands shaking, I key in the Sydney number and get the answerphone. His receptionist is obviously not in today, and I curse.

'Dad, this is Jane. Good news – what I've been waiting for. They've got a kidney for me, and I'm going in now to have the transplant. It's late, no one's around – Nat's out of London, Sara's not in, you're the first person I've told. I can hardly believe it, but I'm getting a new kidney.' Without warning, I start to cry, and can barely finish the message. I control my tears and ring Sara at Joe's place. Another answerphone, and I start to gabble a message when Joe picks up the receiver.

'It's Jane, can I speak to Sara?'

'Of course.'

I hear the rustle of bedding and then Sara's sleepy voice.

'Hiya, what's the problem?'

'Sara, they've got a kidney for me!' And I burst into tears again.

'What? I couldn't hear what you said – are you all right, Jane?'

'Guy's have rung and told me there's a kidney for me. I'm going in for my transplant now, and I'm crying because the waiting's over.'

'Fantastic!' I can sense her sitting up in her excitement. 'Fan-fan-tastic! Do you want me to come over and hold your hand? I'll leave now – Yes, she's going in for a transplant.' I can hear Joe shouting terrific in the background as I blow my nose and try to collect my wits.

'Don't worry, I'm OK. The hospital have sent a cab and it'll be here any minute. I'm all ready. But if you could come and see me tomorrow – Nat's away . . .'

'Of *course* I will! Give me the ward number. What else can I do? Ring your father?'

'I've done that and left him a message. And could you ring Freddie first thing. And the Courts. That's it, really.'

'Give me all the numbers now and I'll do it from here tomorrow morning early.' As she is writing them down, the doorbell rings.

'The cab's here. Oh God.'

'*Coraggio*, Jane, *coraggio*. Though why I'm saying that to you, I've no idea. You've got more courage than the lot of us put together. I think you're great. I mean it.'

'I must go – I'll leave the answerphone on—'

'Just go! Don't worry about anything except locking the front door. I'll see you tomorrow. Good luck.'

Good luck . . . I need a good kidney, a good surgeon, a good reaction to the foreign organ about to be inserted into my body which will do its utmost to unseat the unnatural intrusion, destroy it, render its efforts useless. Good luck isn't going to play much of a part. I sit in the taxi as it dashes through the almost empty streets of South London and hug my body as if to will it to accept the outrage it is about to undergo. Please, please, body, break the habits of a lifetime and tell your little armies of antibodies not to fight too hard. I hug myself and talk to myself as a comfort; I wish, I piercingly wish, that I had Nat or Sara with me. The taxi driver is whistling quietly through his teeth, and I shut my eyes to stem new tears, this time of panic.

When I reach Clarkson Ward, Sheena, a staff nurse I don't know, and Ben the health-care assistant, go through the routine admittance procedures. I'm weighed – too heavy – and given a blood test, and the Senior Houseman takes over and gives me a thorough examination before sending me down for an ECG and an X-ray. I'm so tired now I feel quite deadened, so the prospect of being put on haemodialysis for a few hours is a relief. I'm given the only vacant bed in Clarkson Ward, surrounded by sleeping or dozing patients, and the needles are inserted into my fistula and I'm connected to the machine. It flits through my mind this could be the very last time I dialyse, but I banish the thought before it becomes a hope.

'We need to leave a litre of fluid in your blood for the new kidney to work on.' Sheena hangs a Nil By Mouth notice above me, smiles encouragingly (a brisk professional smile) and departs. All my adrenalin has gone, and I long for sleep but it won't come. I feel confused, disoriented and lonely. At last Sheena returns and holds my hand as she tells me that my transplant is scheduled for 10 a.m.

'Now try to sleep, Jane. Rest is important. I'll be off duty by the time you have your pre-med, but the Transplant Sister Esther Fisher will be looking after you.'

'I'd love to see Vera Akram . . .'

'She's bound to pop in and see you when you come back to the ward.'

'I feel terrified.'

'Of course you do – it's the suddenness of it all.'

'Sheena, whose kidney am I getting?'

'I honestly don't know, beyond the fact it's a young woman's. She was killed in a traffic accident. The Tissue-Typing Unit say that for a cadaver kidney, it's a very good match. Now go to sleep, Jane, if you can. You've got a big day ahead.'

But I can't sleep, though I doze. Just before dawn someone wakes in the corner and starts calling for a nurse. The whining voice is very familiar, and as I listen a coldness fills me. It's poor Deirdre, back in hospital. A nurse comes in on squeaking crêpe soles.

'I feel sick, nurse.'

'Shsh. You'll wake everyone, Deirdre.'

'Give us a bowl. I don't feel good at all.'

'Please think of the others and keep your voice down.'

'Who's moved my pink towel?'

'I think one of the nurses must have.'

'No business touching it. Where's that nice Miriam? I haven't seen her this time.'

'Sh, Deirdre. You must be quiet.'

'Miriam would never move your things without your leave.'

'She's gone. She's not with the renal unit any more.'

'Shame. I feel sick again, nurse.'

The rest becomes inaudible, and at last I fall asleep.

Roberta comes in after I've had my pre-med but before it starts to take effect so I'm not yet woozy. Her face is full of delight. 'I've just heard! Oh Jane, how wonderful. I had to catch you before they took you down to theatre. How do you feel?'

'So nervous it reminds me of stage-fright.'

She laughs. 'How appropriate that is – you'll be on stage in the theatre in less than an hour.'

'Can you stay with me now?'

'Of course. And I'll come down as far as the anaesthetic room, but they won't let me come in with you.'

'I can't tell you how pleased I am to see you.'

'I saw them taking Deirdre off for an ultrasound, so I knew we'd have peace and quiet.' She winks at me. 'Enough said.'

'I haven't seen my Consultant yet.'

'Mr Stewart's away on leave, as it happens. Who's your surgeon?'

'Mr Fellows.'

'He's lovely. And very good. Lucky you.' At that moment a staff nurse comes in briefly to say Nat has rung to wish me luck, and five minutes later, when I'm beginning to feel the effects of the drugs, tells me that Dad has also rung with the same message.

'Luck.' My voice is going blurred. 'I'm going to need more than luck.'

'Luck's useful too. It's a funny word, luck. It doesn't sound right for its meaning.' But my eyes are shutting, and Roberta's voice comes and goes. She holds my hand as my bed is taken down in a lift to the first floor, and squeezes it goodbye as I'm wheeled into the anaesthetic room. Two women anaesthetists immediately start the final preparations.

'Hallo, Jane. I'm Helen and this is Fiona. We're going to start by putting you on a drip – your fistula's on your left arm, isn't it? So we'll use your right hand.' As they work, a gowned figure comes up beside me, very short with cat-like yellow eyes. He bounces as he talks.

'Hallo, Jane. I'm Henry Fellows. I expect you know what I'm going to do, but I'll just remind you.' They talk to me as if I'm a child, but I'm past caring. 'I will be making an incision in your left side above your groin, and the kidney will be inserted deep inside, behind the peritoneum and right in your pelvic girdle so that the little chap's well protected. I'll plumb it in and there it will stay even if your body rejects it – no point ever taking it out because it becomes inert and does no mischief. But it's such a good match I'm sure it's going to work an absolute treat. See you in a minute.' He disappears back into theatre, and I lie there hanging desperately on to my consciousness as it ebbs away. I feel as if I'm in a river heading for the edge of an unimaginable waterfall. The rushing water engulfs me.

Trees, trees, with sunlight slanting in beams like soft searchlights, and my mother saying: don't pick the flowers, Jane, don't touch those mushrooms, they might be poisonous, and don't hit those pretty ferns with a stick, and the trees thinning into fields stretching out green and neat, or brown and ridged, and my mother pinching my neck—

'Jane, Jane. Wake up, Jane.' The Transplant Sister's face is close to mine. I don't know Esther Fisher very well, because she's been off having a baby.

'Your baby. Did you have your baby?' It doesn't sound like my voice, it sounds like a blurred version of my mother's.

'You sweet girl, to think of that now. Yes, I had a little boy. How do you feel?'

'Where am I?'

'In the recovery room. Your op took four hours, and all is well.'

'Something's wrong with my neck.'

'You've got a neck-line in it. Just a small one, to give you the drugs you need.'

'Oh no!'

She obviously sees the horror in my eyes and understands my phobia of the neck-line. 'It's only there for a few days, Jane, and it really won't give you as much trouble as the first one you had. You've also got a temporary catheter in, a drainage tube in your abdomen, and a drip – the stand looks like a Christmas tree with all the bags and bottles!'

I'm not amused; I shut my eyes in despair that the vampire's back in my neck and slip into semi-consciousness. When I come round properly, I'm no longer in the recovery room but back in Clarkson and Vera Akram is with Deirdre across the ward. She hurries across when she sees I'm awake, and draws the curtains round my bed.

'Well done, Jane – everything's going beautifully. Let me sit you up and have a listen.' She puts her ear against my stomach; it's all very tender down there, in fact it's pretty sore all over. 'Good – I can hear encouraging sounds. You must start drinking a lot.

And look, I have something that will cheer you up – proof that the new kidney's working.' She shows me the catheter bag, and there it is – the first urine I've made myself for all these months. I can feel my smile spreading across my face as if it's got a life of its own. 'Now, drink this whole jug of water as quickly as you can, and drink another litre before you go to sleep. Two litres. You'd better start now.' She hands me a glass brimming with water, and all my conditioning comes into play. Half a day's ration. I sip it.

'Glug it down, Jane! Come on.'

It's an extraordinary feeling, opening my throat to drain that glass. And another. By the third I feel as if I'm so full of fluid I'll burst.

'I can't drink any more, Vera.'

'Yes, you can.'

'You're bullying me.'

'Absolutely – this glass has got to go before I stop.'

'Drink up, Jane!' Deirdre's voice comes from the end of the ward, interrupting our illusion that because we're hidden we're inaudible. 'You got to change all your habits now.'

Vera rolls her eyes as I finish the third glass. 'I'll remember your advice, Deirdre,' I call back and then mouth at Vera: 'Why is she in?'

'Rejection, alas. Poor Deirdre. We're still trying to save the kidney, but . . .' she shrugs. 'She's had an infection – it's very bad luck.'

'Poor Deirdre.'

'Are you whispering about me in there?'

'Of course not.'

'You are. It's not kind.' Deirdre's whine drops to a mutter.

'Vera! Look, my bag's filling up!'

'Wonderful. That's what we want – to change it all the time. Water in one end and out the other!'

'Nurse. Come quick. I feel sick.'

Sheena puts her face through my curtains, and then goes to see to Deirdre. Vera stays to check all my bags and bottles, and bends over me before she leaves. 'I know you feel invaded by all this, but none of it will be in you for long. If all goes well, you'll be home by the end of the week.' I look at her disbelievingly. She laughs as she pushes the curtains back. 'Tomorrow we'll get you on your feet, and if you keep drinking your drip will come out tomorrow as well. Another glass, come on.'

I sleep but wake often, and once, when something tickles my throat and I start to cough, I nearly scream from the pang of pain in my abdomen. I'm afraid of turning over on the new kidney side, in case I disturb things. So I lie on my back, dozing, waiting for morning. As dawn starts to break I hear racking sobs from Deirdre's bed. For once she's not shouting for nurses, but breaking her heart in despair all alone. Her breaths are sharp and panicky; she's obviously woken out of a nightmare. There's nothing I can do, tied as I am to my Christmas tree, and I'm nervous of speaking to her.

Then I hear her voice whispering, muttering. '*Hail Mary, full of grace, the Lord is with thee.*' The words come out between gulps of her panicky grief. '*Please let it not fail, Holy Mary, please save it. Holy Mary, Mother of God, pray for me. Please God, don't take my new kidney away, please let me have it for life. My kidney was fine, why is it failing now, why is it failing . . .*'

Every word is clear in the otherwise silent ward. I wonder if anyone else is awake and listening as I am. My whole being freezes as I wait for her to stop, for the day's routine to start, for the nurses to come in. I'm not strong enough to bear her grief, even though I've fully understood that life with a new kidney is an uncertain and fragile alliance, that out of every ten kidneys transplanted six fail. Not even half succeed.

Poor Deirdre is not particularly unlucky seen in this light. From what I knew of her, she always wanted her life to be simple, for solutions to be clear-cut, cosy and hopeful. She never wanted to face reality; she clearly thought that life with a new kidney would be like the romances she always read: happy ever after. How I hate those words. They are full of equivocation and untruth. Give me instead Georgia Hill's spare and bony maxim: *Keep your mind in hell and despair not.*

Sara and Joe come in, carrying a small hamper between them. In my state of post-operative sentimentality, I start to cry as soon as they kiss me. They put the hamper near me.

'Pzzaum! Fortnum and Mason's best fruit selection.' Sara whisks the lid up, revealing a mouth-watering selection of fresh tropical fruit, dried fruit, and other goodies, in the middle of which sits a small toy kangaroo. 'Very silly, I know, but I couldn't resist this little fellow and I thought he might make you laugh. Your father asked me to get you something, so the kangaroo is from him. I'm sure he didn't mean this sort of something, but who cares.' She's talking too much to cover up the fact she's moved by my tears, and gives me a hug while paying due care to all my tubes.

I hold the kangaroo above my head. He's got a contented, sly expression, as if he's just committed a clever act of mischief undetected. 'I love him. I'm going to call him Sydney, naturally. Thank you, Sara, thank you, Joe . . . Oh dear, I'm going to cry again. Take no notice – I think it's all the water I have to drink now. Three litres a day – my eyes aren't used to it.'

'So the kidney must be working?'

'A treat.' We're all smiling as if we can't stop.

'Your father said he's going to try and ring you on the ward phone tonight about eight o'clock our time. And Nat's back tonight as well, but too late to come in so she'll ring as well.'

They don't stay very long because they're aware how tired and generally dopey I am; when Sheena comes to take my temperature and check me over, they stand up to go. Sara takes my hand. 'I swear your eyes have got two degrees bluer, Jane. And your cheeks are pink again. It's a most remarkable change.'

'It's wonderful what a bit of new plumbing will do.'

They laugh and leave me; Sheena finishes and moves across to another bed. As I lie there and eat a fresh fig, a curious almost physical wash of realisation courses through me, through the haze of drugs, of post-operative emotional see-sawing. My life has changed. A woman's death has given me a degree of freedom. Not total freedom, not a future without walls, but freedom as I have never known before, because when I had it, I didn't know I had.

'Jane. At last. Getting through to your ward has taken quite a while.'

'Dad!'

'How are you feeling, girl?'

'Sore. Reborn. Happy. Apprehensive. And sore.'

'What's this apprehensive bit? You're not rejecting the kidney already?'

'No, no. I'm on too many drugs for that to happen. My antibodies are being zapped to extinction at the moment. But they're just waiting for their chance, Dad. That's what makes me nervous – they just sneak up on you without giving any warning and the next thing you know they show up in a blood test and you're rejecting. I hate the word antibody, I really do.'

'They are little bastards, too right. But they also do a good job, don't forget. Concentrate on the reborn feeling, Jane, it must be wonderful to eat and drink as you please again.'

'I find it so odd, Dad. It's ingrained in me now to weigh and balance everything, measure my fluid – not to think about almost every mouthful is extraordinary.'

'Enjoy it, darling girl. You've had a hard time, a terrible time, and now it's over and done with.'

'No it's not.' I can't let him talk so confidently.

'What do you mean?'

'Nothing's ever over and done with in my life now – you should know that. I can't count on this kidney.'

'The success rate is pretty good these days, and you're in a good hospital—'

'Agreed, but I can never forget that six out of ten new kidneys fail, so my joy is qualified.'

'You always were a wary little person when it came to the future. I remember you saying: "I don't want you to take me all the way to Disney World, Dad – what if I don't like it?" You must have been about six.'

'That sounds more like Nat.'

'No, it was you. Nat couldn't wait to go.'

'Whatever I was like then, I can't help being wary now – people all round me are being so bloody optimistic all the time.'

'Be optimistic yourself then! What a strange girl you are – I thought you'd be over the moon.' He sounds almost annoyed with me.

'You should have seen me when I got the phone call. You wait and wait for that call, and when it finally comes it's fantastic.'

'I wish I could come over, Jane, but life is frantic at the moment. And I'm still house-hunting. Very time consuming.'

'I thought you'd found a house.'

'It fell through. But I do intend to try and come to England soon and see my girls.'

I do wish he'd stop calling us his girls, but never mind. As he talks I have a new idea. 'If you came over later on, we could go travelling together – go to Paris, go to Rome. Why don't we, Dad?'

'Good idea. Let's work towards it.'

Roberta comes up as Dad's call ends and stands staring at me. 'You look very happy – it transforms you.'

'I've just realised I'll be able to go on holiday again. It's been impossible during dialysis.'

'Well, people on dialysis can have holidays away, but I agree with you they're not the same. You remain shackled.' She sits down beside me, smelling slightly of soap.

'I had another dream last night, Roberta. It was horrid – you'll enjoy analysing it! I was watching a play in a very confusing theatre with funny red curtains all over the place and lights doing odd things, and then I knew I'd lost my bag which had something very important in it. I kept feeling round on the carpet around my seat, crawling about desperately looking with no one helping and feet everywhere. Then someone kicked me on the side and I woke up in agony – and of course the wound was hurting and the stitches pulling, but it took a while to get rid of the feeling I'd been kicked.'

'What was in your bag?'

'No idea. Just something precious, something I couldn't afford to lose. I know I felt sick that I might have lost it.'

'I don't really need to interpret your dream, do I? We can both guess what it means.'

'I've had such a lot of dreams since the op.'

'Lots of people have rejection nightmares like yours. I think it must be all the drugs. So many, and all so powerful. No wonder your subconscious is over-active.'

'That was my father on the phone, by the way – I've spoken to him at last. He was a bit annoyed with me for not being over the moon about my transplant. Just like Mr Fellows – he did his round this morning and was so cheerful and optimistic it made me cross. And he shouted at poor Deirdre when she kept asking him why she was losing her kidney.

You said I'd have it for life. He couldn't handle it, and got really annoyed.'

Roberta gives me a little lop-sided smile at my whining imitation of Deirdre. 'He shouldn't have let her think she had the kidney for life, but just for the life of the kidney and no more, which might of course coincide with the patient's own span. Deirdre's nearly sixty, so in her case it was safe for Mr Fellows to say it, in his view.'

'And in your view?'

'False hopes help no one. You, Jane, are unusual in that you positively shun false hopes.'

'Dad says I'm being pessimistic.'

'There's a difference. Does he understand it?'

'No. But he's far away, and there's nothing he can do to help me. My sister came in for a few minutes today, and I don't think she understood either. She just thought I wasn't brimming over with Hope and Joy because I was in a post-operative trough, as she put it.'

'And that's true too, Jane. The drugs make you feel awful, I know, but at least soon you'll be on reduced dosages, and they will go down and down until you're on the minimum. Fingers crossed.'

'Fingers crossed.' We smile at each other. I'm about to tell Roberta about Georgia Hill, about her dictum of keeping your mind in hell and despairing not, but Sheena comes up at that moment to check things, and Roberta gives me another smile and leaves.

When I see Nat next day I'm feeling wonderful – the catheter is out, the drip is gone, and my surprisingly small abdominal scar is healing quickly. I've returned to the sharp, delightful sensation of peeing again. And finally I've had a strip wash and managed also to wash my hair despite the fact I've still got my neck-line, and it's still damp and sweet-smelling when Nat walks in, dressed in bright yellow.

'You look sensational in yellow, Nat. I've never seen you wear it before.'

'Freddie suggested it – he loves yellow, and had a feeling it might suit me. He's got such a good eye for colour.'

'Trained by that first wife of his. Not by you – you're useless at colours.'

'Devil. But you're right. And you look great too, Jane. All alive.'

'All clean, more to the point. My hair felt like oily string, and the nurse just helped me wash it. Clean hair's so good for the morale.'

'I brought you some toffee. I remembered how you used to love Thornton's toffee.'

'Excellent. Thanks a lot.' As I sniff the buttery caramel scent of the box, I ask how Freddie is.

'Fine. He's so thrilled with those new paintings, he talks about them all the time. He's already got the decorators in to do the drawing room, so the house is in chaos.'

'I'm longing to see the Merediths hung. They'll look so good in that room. What do you think of them?'

'I haven't seen them yet. Freddie decided he'd keep them hidden in their crates until the room was ready for them.'

'Have a toffee.' We both take one, and gossip for a while mumbling through sticky mouths.

'It's great you can eat and drink what you like again. And on the subject of food and drink, Freddie and I want to throw a party for you, to celebrate your new lease of life. Would you like that?'

'Oh Nat.' I concentrate on dealing with the toffee in my mouth while I work out how not to hurt her. (Me, worried about hurting my big sister – there's a turn of events.) 'I'm not ready for a party yet.'

'Tell us when you are.'

'It might be never.'

'What do you mean?'

'I'm frightened of counting my chickens.'

'Oh, go on – you'll be fine now. Modern medicine and all that. Have faith. Everyone's thrilled you've had a transplant and they want to celebrate it with you. Sara thought it was a brilliant idea.'

'Sara's been such a good friend—' I stop because I can see Nat is not listening.

'Oh, here's some news for you, Jane. Dave has sold his novel to a publisher, or so he says. It's coming out in the autumn, according to him. None of us have really believed in its existence, so perhaps this is a spoof too.'

'It's hard to believe anything Dave says. I asked him how his book was getting on when I saw him at Ginny's party, and he just waffled. To be honest I thought he just hadn't finished it and probably never would. So you surprise me. How exciting.'

'Well, it would be the first novel to be published by one of my contemporaries. Odd feeling. Everyone's going to read it to see if we're in it.' Nat is looking distinctly uneasy.

'What's the title?'

'I don't know.' Nat shifts abruptly, sending the contents of her bag on to the floor. When she's finished picking them up, she remains standing, a glowing yellow figure in the drab ward. 'I don't trust Dave. I'll comb the book for libel.'

'Perhaps that's why he's being so secretive. He knows he's going to annoy his friends.'

'Enough of Dave. I'd happily banish him from my life for ever. Tell me, Jane, when are they going to let you out? And please, please, when they do, come and convalesce with us. I'd hate to think of you on your own in that dismal flat.'

'It's not a dismal flat. I like living there.'

'But you'll be much more comfortable with us, and you'll have more support – Sara's never there, it seems to me.'

'I'll manage. And Sara's very supportive. Anyway, you've got the builders in, you surely don't want me as well.'

Nat opens and shuts her mouth without saying anything. Her eyes are expressionless as she finally says, 'Well, the offer of a bed remains open. As does the offer of a party.'

'I'm sorry to be so negative.'

'Jane, you always are as far as I'm concerned, so what's new?'

'Nat . . .' As I speak I see the Registrar come in, leading the Consultant's ward round, and they're heading towards me. 'You'll have to go, Nat. Sorry. The doctors are here. Let's speak later. Thanks for coming . . .' But she's waved and hurried out before I've finished, obviously annoyed and hurt. I turn towards Mr Fellows and his cohorts, my heart cold. If anyone brings back the old Jane, it will be Nat.

*   *   *

Ben Barton comes in after the ward round, and sits on my bed. 'I was just going off duty, came to see how you were.'

'Have a toffee, Ben. My sister brought this big box so that I can binge on them.'

'Thanks.' We both go into mumble-speak.

'So it's home on Monday, then?' I nod. 'We're all going to miss you, Jane. I mean on the dialysis unit. You've been such a stabilising influence there.'

'Who says?'

'Chantal. Everyone. It's obvious you've maintained a high level of self-care – I quote Chantal – and it set a good example.'

'Some people would say that's because I'm a self-centred person.'

'So what?' Ben's medical coat is a total wreck, barely hanging together. At least it's clean. 'Who else is going to look after you when the chips are down? The hospital? You must be joking. We support you when you step through the doors, but most of the time, Jane, you're out there on your own. You know that, but some don't. They expect the doctors and nurses to work miracles, to make them whole again while they sit back, doing nothing but watch.'

'Roberta's helped me as well to deal with life outside.'

'Yes. It's a pity she's such a bone of contention despite the good she does. The great Mr Fellows thinks looking after the psyche is a total waste of time. I expect you've noticed.'

'Have you had a bad day, Ben?'

'Yes. Never mind. And I'm a cynic.'

'Have another toffee.'

'I must go. I just wanted to tell you you're triffic. Don't let the bastards grind you down.' He takes a toffee. 'See you, Jane. I hope I'm on duty when you next pass through.' He lopes off, frayed gown flapping behind him. Sheena turns to watch him go with a brief warm look. He's far away the most attractive young man around, and high up on the nurses' heart-throb list. Sex is permanently in the air amongst hospital staff, I've noticed, perhaps because they take care of sick bodies and the fit, lithe ones stand out by contrast.

*   *   *

It's Monday afternoon, and I've been given the all-clear. I can go. I've arranged with Sara that she leaves work early to come and collect me. So. Now I must leave and start a new phase of my life. Right this minute I feel absolutely leaden and disinclined to move. I should get up, pack my stuff, get ready. Instead I eat toffee, drink a glass of water, shut my eyes. I finger my fistula, now unused; it will shrink, become less of an eyesore. I could have it surgically removed, but then if my kidney failed the doctors would have to make another point of access above my elbow for haemodialysis. I lie there, frozen with a fearful lassitude. I should be dancing down the corridors – everything is going well, my blood levels are as good as they can be, my new kidney is behaving itself beautifully, and I can't even get out of bed.

'Jane! Wake up.'
'Oh my God. They'll think I'm ill – relapsing.' I sit up wildly, staring at Sara.
'Time to pack and go home. They let me go early to come here, and I find you snugly tucked up and looking as if you're staying here for ever.'
'The nurses must think I'm mad. I'm surprised no one woke me and told me to get going. They would have if they'd needed this bed. Pull the curtains, Sara. Where the devil are my clean knickers?' I start to rummage in the locker, pulling everything out in a heap.
'One of the nurses said they'd decided to leave you sleeping until I arrived.'
'Sara, even though I knew it was likely to be today, when they said I could go it was a shock. I hadn't quite prepared myself – I'm so dependent on the hospital, it's difficult to imagine life in a new phase.' I pull on a light cotton jersey top in blue, over darker blue linen trousers which have got very creased despite the care with which I folded them. I put a blue and white chiffon scarf round my neck to hide the dressing over the neck-line scar, and stand there looking useless.
'I seem to have lost the tote bag I came in with. How am I going to get this stuff home?'
'Ask one of the nurses for a bin liner. I'll go.'
'No, I will.' I find a new staff nurse at the desk, completely unfamiliar. Her badge says she's called Cheryl Hignett.

'Hallo, I'm Jane Harper, on my way home today.'

'Yes, I know. Sister said not to disturb you.'

'Is anyone around? The Transplant Sister, or Vera Akram, or Sheena?'

'Sheena's gone off duty. Sister Fisher is down in theatre. I don't know where Sister Akram is.'

'Could you bleep her? I must say goodbye to Vera.'

'You could go and see if she's in the dialysis unit.' Cheryl Hignett's eyes remain cool – she clearly thinks this isn't important enough for a bleeper and she's right. I forget to ask her for the bin liner in my disappointment that there's no one familiar around, but when I get to my bed Sara's found the tote bag and has almost finished stowing my stuff. She puts Sydney the kangaroo in on top.

'What about all your flowers?'

'They've more or less had it, but that daisy thing is fine – let's take it if we can carry it.'

I look around the familiar ward. My fistula gives a little buzz to remind me of its existence. I must have knocked it packing. Deirdre has gone home, to try and enjoy what's left of the fading life of her kidney. The others are all strangers who've recently been admitted.

'Could you wait for a while by the lifts while I go and find Sister Akram to say goodbye?'

Sara sits on the seats by the lifts and I walk through various areas of the renal unit looking for Vera and other familiar faces. But everyone is busy; Vera herself is involved with a new admission, and can only give me a minute. But she hugs me and tells me the sleep did me good.

'You were sleeping like a baby, Jane. I had to laugh. We tell you to go home, and you go to sleep!'

'Thank you for everything, Vera. Your face was the first I saw all that time ago when I collapsed, and you're here now, beautiful as ever.'

'Get on with you, Jane.'

'And perhaps this new admission is another young woman like me—'

'No, he's a man in his forties. I must go. I'll see you next week no doubt, when you start coming for your check-ups.' She rushes away, and finally I face the fact I'm discharged. Sara's sitting in a heap by the left when I get back, her eyes shut, my old bag on her knees along with her briefcase.

'You look like a bag lady.'

'I feel like one. Come on, let's go and have a drink somewhere nice on the way home, and banish the smell of this place.'

8

My room is dusty and drab – Nat would have said dismal. I give the surfaces a clean and put my plant on the window-sill. There's a car siren screeching in the street, and the window-panes rattle as a tube-train passes deep beneath the building.

I put Sydney on a shelf, and all my transplant paraphernalia on my chest of drawers – my record booklet, my thermometer, and the army of drugs I will always have to take. I pin up my instructions: Neoral twice a day, which works with Prednisolone, a steroid, to control rejection. These two have charming side effects – things like increased hair growth all over, increased appetite, a 'moon face', mood swings, high blood pressure. But as my dose goes down, Vera Akram says, I'll have fewer problems with these than some people because I take good care of my body, and I'm slim, fit and young.

I have to take three more drugs: Azathioprine which reduces my white-cell count because white cells play a crucial role in causing rejection; Ranitidine to minimise the gastric irritation all the lot above cause; and Septrin, an antibiotic to prevent chest infections to which apparently one is particularly prone after a transplant. Azathioprine has the most serious side effect: it makes me super-sensitive to sunlight and dramatically increases the risk of skin cancer. This doesn't bother me too much – everyone in Australia was paranoid about skin cancer, and covered themselves in sunblock, so what's new. But I also have to wear a hat in the sun – any sun. I've never worn hats in my life.

'Let's go shopping tomorrow for hats, Sara. Can you take tomorrow morning off?'

'I can't, Jane. I have a meeting first thing and there's too much work on. Why the sudden interest in hats?'

'I wasn't really serious about you taking time off. But I have to wear hats from now on when I'm out in the sunlight. I'll go shopping on my own. I've got to get back into ordinary life.'

'Borrow my new straw hat if you like – it's on the back of my door.' It's dark blue and shaped like a bowler, but there's no brim to speak of. I put it on. 'It looks good on you, Jane. You're lucky, you've got the right jawline for hats. Lucky you. I don't look good in them – too round-chinned – but I love them so I wear them anyway.' She puts it on and she's right – her chin spoils the effect of the hat. 'See? But you should make a thing of wearing hats since you have to. Become Jane, the Girl with the Hat.'

'I'm getting very good at making necessities into virtues.'

'I know you are.'

The phone rings and it's Nat, still in chambers but offering to come over and take care of dinner for me. 'Or take you out. Sara too of course. Freddie's dining in hall, so I'm on my own. I could arrive with a take-away or whatever. Just tell me what you'd prefer.'

'What I'd really love and haven't had since goodness knows when is fish and chips.'

'Brilliant idea. I'll get the fish and chips on the way over. What do you want? Cod? Haddock? Plaice?'

'Haddock. Yes, haddock if they have it. If not, cod.'

'See you in about an hour.'

Haddock. Dad used to buy us fish and chips, and always chose haddock. The chippie he liked continued to wrap his fish and chips in newspaper long after the others stopped, and I loved the way the newsprint smelled as it grew warm and translucent with oil.

Haddock. I lie on my bed to rest and miss my father piercingly for a space. I must tell him I'm out of hospital. I'll ring him before I go to bed, catch him before he starts his day.

When I get up I find Sara has laid the kitchen table with a cloth and put candles into two ceramic holders. There's a bottle of champagne cooling in a plastic bucket, and the glasses are ready. She's chopping up a salad and won't let me help.

'Sit and talk to me, Jane. I'm doing a mix of all the odds and ends in the crisper drawer: cucumber, a ratty bit of lettuce, two nice tomatoes, and a carrot. Not very inspiring, but is that all right for you?'

'You can chuck in what you like. I can eat what I like. Whoopee! Tomorrow I'm going to buy the biggest ripe avocado I can find and fill it with prawns and mayonnaise. Wicked bliss.' I watch her big hands chopping neatly. 'How's Joe? Doesn't he need his car back tonight?'

'I'm taking it back later. Just dropping the keys in. I won't stay. Things are not great at the moment – we're going through a bit of an off phase.'

'Thank him for lending his car.'

'He'd do anything for you.'

The doorbell rings at that moment, and I go down to let Nat in. She's looking very cheerful and happy, and I'm relieved – I was afraid we'd have tension about the fact I'm back up here and not up at Primrose Hill. I'm feeling tired and thin-skinned and a cross word would finish me off. She hugs me before leading the way upstairs.

'Hi, Sara, I like the new haircut. This is lovely, just the three of us.' Nat puts the packets into the warmed oven and stretches. 'I'm in the mood for a good laugh. My life is so proper most of the time – putting on a good face in front of solicitors, clients, judges et al. I get tired of being a serious adult.'

'Me too. Let's regress.' Sara gets the wine out. 'The dreadful age of thirty looms ahead and I don't like it.'

'Freddie said hitting thirty was much the worst. Forty's a doddle, according to him.'

'Pull the other one.'

I listen to them chatter on, aware of how much my approach to my own age has changed. Getting to thirty at all will be wonderful.

'Oh, by the way, guess what Dave Rosenberg's book is called?' Nat stops pouring champagne for a moment.

'What book?'

'Sara! You must be the only one who hasn't heard – I'm surprised Ginny hadn't told you. Dear Dave has a novel actually being published in the autumn, and it's called *The List*.'

'What a terrifying prospect.' Sara gazes at Nat and they both look so apprehensive I can't help laughing.

'You both look as if he has a hold over you.'

'We don't trust Dave.' Sara looks at me with speculative eyes. 'I'm surprised he didn't try his usual gambit with you, Jane.'

'If you mean that stupid list of his, yes he did. Well, he told me I was on it and how I could cross myself off it by going to bed with him, and I told him to get lost. Don't tell me you both fell for it!' Nat is busy bent over the oven retrieving the fish and chips. Sara rolls her eyes and shrugs.

'I was young and foolish. Students do stupid things.' She makes a face towards Nat and puts a finger on her lips. 'That food smells divine, and I'm famished. Plates. Lemon. Salt, vinegar. Let's get stuck in.'

'Dave is a complete pseud. I honestly can't believe anyone's going to read a word he's written.' Nat's face is pink from the oven. She's piled our plates high; I'm never going to get through all this food but I'm loving the effort.

'Oh, they will. Being a pseud never stopped anyone being successful. In fact, I think it helps.'

'Ever our cynical Sara.'

'I'm just being observant, not cynical. Dave has always had an eye on the main chance, despite his seeming lack of contact with reality. By the way, Nat, did he ever get your wedding dress off you?'

'No, he damned well did not.'

'Good. I feel quite proprietorial about that dress – after all, it was me who rescued it, had it repaired and cleaned up.'

'Freddie was so pleased with you for doing that.'

'How is your lovely man?' Sara picks at the label on the champagne bottle.

'A bit depressed, actually. There's a lot of tension in chambers about the admissions policy, and it gets him down when all the various factions come and backbite. He'd love to give up being Head of Chambers, but unfortunately the next in line is a woman he can't stand. I don't mind her, in fact. You know exactly where you stand with her: in front of a tiger with teeth bared to win. Lots of clients prefer an attitude like that, but it's not Freddie's style.'

'Oh brash new world.' Sara pours more champagne. 'These chips are divine – did you get them from the usual chippie?'

'No, from a place I passed in Victoria that looked good so in I went. Quite near the Court Gallery. When are you going back to work, Jane, by the way?'

'Henrietta insisted I took the summer off. So I start at the beginning of September.'

'You must have a holiday first. Come and join us in Italy.'

'I can't go away for at least three months. I have to go to the clinic for a check-up three mornings a week every week for the first three months – it's almost as bad a tie as dialysis. So no proper holidays until I'm on a fortnightly check-up.'

'And Jane can't go in the sun, either, without total protection, so Italy in the summer wouldn't be much fun. More champers, anyone?'

'Not for me, Sara, I'm driving. What about walking in the Scottish mountains? Freddie tries to do that every year as well.'

'Now you're talking, Nat.' I raise my glass to her.

'We stay in the most freezing draughty house you can imagine, but so beautiful, right on the edge of a loch. We light huge fires in the rooms, but you still need serious thermal underwear to survive.'

'I've got some – I felt the cold so much one of the nurses told me about special underwear made for skiers. Not exactly unsexy, but I'm for comfort over sex-appeal these days. Hark at me, oh sister mine!'

'I hark.' She's looking at me with a frown. 'And I'm also thinking – thinking that if you've had a boyfriend since you've been in London, he's passed me by.'

'I haven't. I haven't met anyone I've gone for, and no one's gone for me.'

'Oh go on, men's heads always turn when you're around.' Nat tries to say this in a completely neutral voice and fails. 'You just haven't been interested.'

To my relief the phone rings and I answer to find it's Ginny. 'Come round, Ginny. We're having a hen party.'

'I can't. I haven't eaten yet and I'm knackered. But, Jane, when did you come out of hospital?'

'Today.'

'How are you?'

'Fine, but knackered too, to be honest. Did you want to speak to Sara?'

'Nat too. I have news for them.'

I pass the portable to Nat, who starts pacing about the kitchen, clearly not enjoying what she's hearing. 'Have you spoken to Dave, then? No, I suppose you're right, Ginny. He'll just laugh and say read the book before you start flapping.'

'Tell me what's going on,' hisses Sara. Nat hands over the phone and explains to me that Ginny's seen a blurb of Dave's book listed in some catalogue.

'It says something along the lines of: *A teasing enigmatic story of a twentieth-century Don Juan, whose serial conquests lead him down strange obsessive paths*. That sort of thing. What a rat that man is—' Nat's voice is rising.

'Calm down, Nat. It'll make no difference.' Sara turns away and disappears with the phone to her bedroom. Nat groans.

'The whole business knots me up. I've got such a lot to lose.'

'You can deny anything he says. Everyone knows how unreliable Dave is. They'll believe you.'

'I must go in a few minutes. I said I'd collect Freddie from the Temple.'

'Tell you what, I could try and find out from Dave exactly what the book's about. Dave likes me, and don't forget I'm not crossed off his list so I remain a challenge.'

'Don't worry, Jane. We're all upset because we've got guilty consciences, and over such a shit too.'

'I might give devious Dave a ring all the same, and see what I can find out. I could try and get hold of a proof copy, for instance.'

'You're good at dealing with him. You can be devious yourself, after all.'

'Thanks. Thanks a bunch.'

'I didn't mean it as an insult. It's a fact. You said so yourself more than once.'

'You always assume I haven't changed.'

'Of course you have, Jane. You've been to hell and back and that would change anyone.'

'But once devious always devious?'

'No, I didn't say that. I said you *can* be devious. Oh, don't let's quarrel. It's been such a nice evening.' Nat stands up, running her hands through her hair.

Sara comes back in and crashes the phone back into its base.

'I must go, I must go. I'm going to be late for Freddie.'

'I could chop Dave Rosenberg up and roast the pieces.'

'Don't let's panic, Sara. Jane is going to try and get hold of an advance copy.'

'It'll probably be innocuous . . .' This effort to calm the two of them fails completely.

'Dave innocuous? You have got to be joking, Jane.'

'I must go, I really must.' Nat kisses us both and I press a ten-pound note in her hand.

'That's for the food.'

'No, it was my treat, put it away. Go to bed and have a good night's sleep. I'll ring you in the morning to see how you are. 'Bye, both of you.' And she's gone.

Sara flops into a chair. 'I don't know why I'm so upset about this but I am.'

'Wait until you see the book. It's pointless to get in a state now.'

'Have you done things in your life you ought not to have done, and regretted ever since?'

'Plenty. Plenty.' I'm about to add that regret's an unfamiliar feeling, but Sara goes on too quickly.

'I wish I'd never met Dave. And there he is, in place on the London scene, a permanent thorn in our sides.'

'Perhaps he'll move to New York or Paris if fame hits him.'

'We should be so lucky. But the thing is, Jane, that Dave can give a true version of what happened over his list, and why he's ticked us off it, and there's nothing we can do because that's not libel. It would be dreadful and embarrassing but we can't stop him or sue him.'

'I'll definitely try to see him soon and ask to read the book.'

'He'll be suspicious.'

'Why? You're all assuming he's going to tell the truth about his list but you might be quite wrong. And if that's so, he'll be quite happy to show me the book. If you're right, though, he'll be shifty and he won't let me see it. Either way it's a step forward. I'll ring him soon. I'm going to need entertainment on my blank days.'

*   *   *

Blank days. That's how the days between the check-ups feel at first: I'm so worried I might be beginning to reject the kidney without knowing it, each visit is essential to put my mind at rest. So the first couple of weeks at home pass like an endurance test; I'm obsessed with filling in my record book with the results of checking my blood pressure, my temperature, and my weight twice a day. I write down my fluid intake and output; I make a note that I have started menstruating again (this further return to normal was immensely cheering). The slightest abnormality puts me in a panic and I sit with my arms wrapped round myself imagining my new kidney losing its battle with my white cells. I've been told to expect at least one episode of rejection, but when it does come in the form of a high temperature three weeks after the transplant, genuine panic fills me. The nurses are calm, I'm told to come to the clinic every day for three consecutive days for a blood test, my dose of Prednisolone is increased temporarily, and the danger passes. Down go the drug doses again, and six weeks into my transplant I wake one morning and feel that rise of hope that comes with well-being, and with hope comes the word 'future'. I lie in bed staring at the blue sky through my window and start, tentatively, to plan ahead.

My future's been my present for so long I'm nervous of the change of viewpoint. Yet if this transplant continues to work well then I do have a future again. Not the same as it was; my old careless, greedy attitude to time has gone for ever. All those roads ahead of me I assumed I was always free to follow have faded off my map. I used to feel angry when my plans didn't work: I was in control of my life, they should have worked. Now I'm not in control and know I never will be, despite a new kidney and a new lease of life, my anger has withered. I've got plenty to be angry about yet it is no longer a relevant emotion. Very strange.

One hot sunny July day I arrange to meet Dave for a drink. I cover myself as usual in factor 20 sunscreen, and put on my densest straw hat. It's dark blue with a wide brim; I wear a bright blue long-sleeved shirt and jeans. I've got used to wearing hats, and I'm tall enough to carry off wide brims.

'Jane! How svelte and well you look – what a transformation. Let's take our beer into the garden.'

I follow Dave and we sit under the shade of an inadequate tree. Dave's looking pretty svelte himself; his hair is for once well cut, he's shaved, his T-shirt is clean. His bare arms are coated with black hair, even his sandalled feet are hairy. He's quite the hairiest man I know.

'So your op's been a success?'

'So far so good.'

'You're too cautious. I'd be wildly celebrating.'

'How do you know I haven't?'

'Well, have you?'

'No.' I smile. 'And you, Dave, you must have celebrated over the news about your book coming out.'

'Who told you about it?'

'Ginny. She saw it in a catalogue of forthcoming titles. Very exciting. You must be thrilled.'

His eyes are expressionless. I have no idea what he's thinking. I decide to play down what I know as I wait for him to say something.

'I wanted my book to break upon the unsuspecting world. I told no one. I'd forgotten about the catalogue.'

'Remind me what the book is called.'

'*The List.*'

'Intriguing title.'

'Thank you.'

'Why that title?'

'You should be able to guess.' He's now looking sharply at me.

'Ah. *That* list. Don't tell me you're making it public as it stands.'

'Not quite like that. This is a work of fiction, after all.'

'I'm glad to hear it.'

Fencing with Dave is exhilarating; I know my eyes are sparkling. We both sip our beer. Patches of sweat are staining Dave's T-shirt, perhaps not wholly the result of the heat. He's now smiling his maddening smile.

'So, Dave, have you made lots of money out of it? Did you get a big advance?'

'You must be joking. A first novel, experimental to boot? They've paid me peanuts, Jane, absolute peanuts. But I'm not complaining, because they've commissioned, actually paid me to write, a second novel.'

'That's wonderful. I'm really pleased for you.'

'I think you mean that.'

'Of course I mean that.'

'Where's the Jane of the acid tongue gone?'

'Currently out of action. Maybe dead.'

'I'm rather sad. What a loss.'

'Too bad, Dave. I'll let you know if she makes a comeback.'

He laughs. 'Don't mess with me is still your message?'

'That's right.'

'So the new-style Jane is all wholesome and sincere but counteracts this impression by wearing flashy and alluring hats?'

This time I laugh. 'I'm glad you like my hat.'

'I didn't say I liked it. I mistrust women who wear hats, but I have to admit it suits you.'

'It keeps off the sun. But let's talk about your book. Tell me more about it.'

Dave taps his glass against his teeth. 'Did the Harpy put you up to this?'

'The Harpy?'

'Your dear sister. She's become a very tough cookie, has Nat. I think Harpy is a rather good soubriquet for her.'

'Have you always called her that?'

'Since she got married. But you haven't answered my question.'

'No, she didn't.'

'Liar. Do you know, I love the idea of her running round like a headless chicken at the thought of my novel.'

'I don't think she's that bothered.'

'Frankly, dear Jane, I don't believe you. I know the Harpy too well.'

'Sara's more bothered.' As soon as I had said them I wished the words unsaid.

'Well, well. Cool, collected Sara. You surprise me.'

'I think she wondered why you'd kept it so quiet. But she's very impressed.'

'And suspicious.' Dave looks smug.

'Wouldn't you be? Why did you keep it so quiet?'

'My natural reserve.'

'Your natural bloody-mindedness more likely.'

'Have another beer?'

'No, thanks. But a sandwich wouldn't go amiss. Why don't you use part of your tiny advance and treat me?'

'Why don't I, indeed? Leave it to me.'

I watch Dave saunter off, and notice that his hair is beginning to thin on the crown of his head. He's going to be bald by his mid-thirties. Bald and probably fat.

It's very hot and my clothes are sticking to me. My hat's making my head boil. I take it off and run my hand through my damp hair, then put it back again because the glare around me is intense. London feels like Sydney today. I remember that this time last year I was still with Jake, our relationship unstitching, my recent abortion an agony. How my life has changed.

'In the end I didn't ask him. I don't think he would have let me see a proof copy or a typescript anyway. He was extremely cagey.'

'Joe says a bit of notoriety never did anyone any harm, so I've given up worrying about *The List*. If Dave has spilt the beans about us, too bad.' Sara crams toast in her mouth and drains her tea. The *Today* programme is burbling quietly in the background; I'll turn it up as soon as Sara goes to work. I like these sunny summer mornings and always get up for breakfast with Sara even though there's no need.

'Dave told me the publishers have commissioned another book.'

'Wouldn't it be strange if he becomes a well-known literary figure?'

'I think he probably will, even if the book's not much good. Dave is good at self-promotion in his own way, on his own terms.'

'Have you got hospital today?'

'Yes. Then I'm going to see Henrietta, to talk about when I start work.'

Sara throws her mug and plate in the sink. 'Leave the kitchen, Jane – I'll give it a good clean this evening. It's my turn to do it. Just ignore the mess.'

I have a shower and stand naked in front of the mirror afterwards. I've put on weight – not much, but I'd lost so much during dialysis that I'm still not what I was a year ago. My face seems slightly rounder, but not the 'moon face' some people develop; I've got more body hair, but it's fine and fair and just looks like down. The slanting scar on my left side has faded to a neat line, and the one in my neck is just a pucker of healed tissue. My fistula is its usual ugly self, and I put my arm behind me. Despite your urging, Georgia, I can't love it.

'I want to have my fistula removed.'

Vera Akram hesitates before she answers. 'Think about it a little longer, Jane. Give yourself a year, then see what you feel.' Her eyes meet mine. 'We had a transplant patient recently who waited two years and then had it done. Soon after that she caught chicken pox from a neighbour's child and lost the transplant, and we had to make a new fistula above her elbow which has given a lot of trouble. So I always advise people to think very hard before they do it. And your fistula's not bad, Jane. I've seen many worse. You're far more aware of it than other people.'

'I know. I feel so self-conscious showing my arm when I'm wearing summer dresses.'

'Keep it covered then. By the way, we think you're ready to start coming once a week. Don't look so put-out!' She laughs at me.

'I've become hospital-dependent, Vera. The idea of coping without you all terrifies me!' I laugh too, but we both know I'm more than half serious.

'Most people feel the same – not that that's a comfort to you. If you get worried, you know there's always someone at the end of a phone.'

'My father has asked me again to go and join him in Sydney, and I told him I couldn't imagine being cared for in a strange hospital. Isn't that a feeble reason for not going!'

'Do you want to go back?'

'Not at the moment. Perhaps not ever. I'm enjoying London.'

'But you may well change your mind as your horizons lift and you find lots of things possible again.'

'My horizons are lifting already.'

'Good.' She sits and smiles at me, her elbows on my fat medical file. 'Sometimes I think about how you were when you were first admitted: so bitter and furious.'

'Vera, I am ashamed when I recall how rude I was to everyone.'

'Your eyes used to blaze at us when we refused you any more to drink. Four-letter words poured out, remember?'

'Don't remind me.'

'So, next check-up a week today?'

'OK. Oh, could you give me an update on Jacob? I tried ringing his home but there was no reply. I wrote him a note but got no answer and that's not like him.'

'He and his mother have moved to Lewisham, and he has haemo there.'

'That explains it. I'm sad to have lost touch with him, he's been a good friend to me in the last year.'

'Having a transplant cuts you off sometimes from those who are waiting. Maybe he couldn't cope at the moment with a friend who'd been lucky.'

I think about Jacob as I go down in the same lift that we once got stuck in. I'll send him a postcard to the Lewisham hospital, and see if it brings a response. If it does, when I'm back at the gallery I'll invite him to an opening. If it was for Devon Diamond, surely he'd come.

When I get out in the sunshine I decide to walk along the river towards Southwark Bridge and the Globe Theatre. I find a table outside a pub looking on to the river, and buy myself a juice and a sandwich. This area of London has become a part of me – the old city of Southwark, with its ghosts of past theatres and brothels. The unfinished recreated Globe along the bank is too new to fit in yet, but its pugnacious smallness compared with the cavernous Bankside Power Station beside it always touches me. I often walk past it to see how the building work is going.

Behind me is old Southwark Cathedral, hemmed in by London Bridge and a ring of commercial buildings. I'm told it's beautiful inside, but I still haven't entered the doors, though I've sat outside on the benches and admired the worn paving stones under my feet. Freddie once told me it was the oldest Gothic church in London, built in 1220. I'll go in one day. Religion has played no part in my life for years, but Georgia Hill's views have unsettled me. I stare at the Thames pouring past and think of the old Jane, of her carapace of control, of her extreme sense of self-awareness, of her rigid strength, of her ability to bend others to her will. Of her fury, her bitterness, her futile violent battering against the collapse of her body: she, I, preferring death to her/my utter loss of control.

I was full of virulence, full of poison, a monster when thwarted. And now? I'm still Jane, my life's still that river, but I'm not a water-tight little boat with a powerful engine any more. I'm that empty milk bottle, still upright and floating, but at the mercy of waves, wind and tide.

9

Henrietta hands me a cup of tea as she says how good I'm looking. So is she – her hair's been styled and given highlights, her make-up's better done, she's even painted her nails.

'So, when can you start again, Jane?'

'Soon. I'm getting bored. I don't want to wait until September, if that's all right.'

'I'd love to have you back. Start when you like.'

The phone rings, and Henrietta turns away to reply. 'No, that's fine. Half an hour later would suit me better in fact. I'll meet you in the foyer. Don't be ridiculous, Thomas, of course I don't mind.' She laughs and rings off, and goes over to the kitchen to fill the teapot with more water. I see the softness of her private smile in profile, and know then that my suspicions about Thomas were right. By the time she turns round the smile is for me, and we go downstairs with our tea to look at a folder of new work from Devon Diamond.

'He's doing well. That show gave him confidence.' Henrietta props a picture up.

'They're bigger than the last lot, aren't they?'

'Apparently he always used to paint big pictures – two or three metres in size – and suddenly got fed up and squeezed everything small. It doesn't surprise me that he's beginning to expand again. I don't feel he's a natural small-scale painter.'

'Is he having another show soon?'

'I told him he should work for another six months, then we'll see.' Henrietta closes the folder. 'He's in a hurry, is Mr Diamond. Haste doesn't go with fruitful development, I sometimes find.'

'But many great artists work quickly—'

'I didn't say *speed*, Jane. I said haste. Very different. A great artist can draw at great speed, can create a marvellous finished drawing in minutes. But his speed is to do with confidence, talent, absolute mastery of technique. He didn't acquire that in a hurry. For instance, Sam Meredith painted the *Arboreal Memory* series very quickly – some perhaps took less than an hour to paint – but Freddie Mentieth knows how good they are and the fact that he "belted them out" – Sam's own phrase – matters not one jot. They are hung now, I think?'

'I honestly don't know. They've had the decorators in for ages because they decided to do more than just the sitting room. I'm sure they'll invite you round when they're hung.'

'His brother thinks he's thrown his money away.' Henrietta sounds delighted at this judgement. 'He thinks Lol and I are on to a good thing, selling people all this rubbish!'

'Do you mind comments like that?'

'Not at all, Jane. People often get on very well partly because they hold totally opposing views. Now, what do you think of these?'

She shows me some colour photographs of delicate constructions suspended from a ceiling. They appear to be made of wire and a substance that looks like dough.

'Don't ask me to judge these, Henrietta. If I found one in the corner of my flat I'd probably put it in the bin.'

'I don't like them much from these photos. But when I actually saw them, I was impressed. The artist is called Shona Rivers. She won the odd prize and then disappeared to North America for a while. No, Mexico – that's where. A mind-expanding experience, she called it. Good track record. Lol thinks we should take her on.'

I don't say anything; I know that Henrietta's just thinking aloud. She's the one who has the eye and makes the decisions, though she pretends Lawrence helps her decide. He comes in as we're putting away all the stuff I've been shown, and to my surprise gives me a delighted hug.

'Welcome back, my dear! Not a moment too soon. I've been working far too hard while you've been away. Have you got fifty pee, Hen? I need to tip the taxi. He's waiting. I've got a pound, but that's too much.' He's holding a pound coin in his hand.

'Oh, for heaven's sake, Lol, give him the pound and be done with it. All my change is upstairs.' She turns to me as Lawrence goes out unwillingly to tip the taxi driver. 'Sometimes I despair. It isn't as if he's basically mean, either, just fussy and meticulous. If it's meant to be ten per cent, then it has to be.'

Lawrence returns and comes over to take my hand. 'Look at you, Jane. Quite transformed. What a picture of health.'

'I do feel so well now.'

He stares at me. 'It's odd, but I never considered you looked ill. In fact, I caught myself thinking that if dialysis kept you going so successfully, what was the fuss about. Oh dear, have I put my foot in it?'

'Lol, just shut up.'

'I am sorry, Jane. Didn't mean to hurt you.'

'You didn't. I'd rather people said what they thought. When you're ill people tread so carefully they aren't natural with you.'

'Champagne – let's have champagne! A drink of bubbly to celebrate your return to health and to us. Come on upstairs, both of you.'

'Not for me, Lol. I'm out tonight, going to the theatre and dining afterwards. I ought to go and change.'

'I can't either, thanks. Actually, I ought to get moving. I'm meeting Nat at six.'

'Another time, then. And do I take it you'll be back to work very soon? Next week? Wonderful. We've missed you, haven't we, Hen?'

'Yes, indeed we have.'

And so, slowly, the ties that bind me to the hospital are loosened and undone. I have one check-up only in the week before I start work again, and time hangs heavy. I go out for long walks in parks or along the river, I decide to take trips out of London to make day trips to places I've never seen. Oxford – I could go to Oxford. Sara tells me there's a convenient coach from Victoria which takes an hour and a half, and if that trip went well I could go to Bath, to Cambridge, to Norwich – all cities I've never seen.

But it's easy to lose heart; the day I ear-marked to go to Oxford is windy and wet, and my period started during the night, and getting out of bed becomes impossible. I breakfast in bed, I read a thriller all morning, I have lunch in bed and finish the thriller before tea. I look at Sara's *Time Out* when I finally get up, and as usual feel daunted by it. London has so much happening all day, all evening, all night, that my mind feels shrivelled by the choice. I drop it on the table, and watch the rain dripping down the kitchen windows. My uterus is aching. I'm bleeding hard, and for once I relish the process of menstruation. When it stopped I didn't miss it, but now it's returned it's like an old friend. Work, body, work, be normal, do the things you should do. I think of the little kidney in my groin, not far from my womb, making it fertile again. I could have children now, my Consultant said. One of his patients has just had twins a year after her transplant, and everyone is doing well.

Children. Of course I don't want children, but I'm pleased to have the choice. The doors around me have all swung open; I don't want to go through them necessarily, but it felt like a prison when they were all tight shut.

Freddie rings from chambers just after four. 'You sound a bit low, Jane.'

'I hate all this rain. That's all. I've been terribly lazy today.'

'Well, I rang to ask you to have dinner with us tonight. Come to chambers and we'll drive you back with us. I want you to come and see the new pictures. They were finally hung yesterday.'

'And how do they look?'

'Splendid. Extraordinary. Nat says they are rather overwhelming, but the whole room is so different she's reacting to the change as much as anything.'

'I can't wait to see them.'

'Can you get here by six?'

'Of course.'

Freddie and Natalie's new chambers are just outside Middle Temple, in a handsome street of eighteenth- and nineteenth-century houses. But these seem to be mainly façades now, for the inside of Freddie's building is modern and impersonal, full of corridors, fire doors, and small square rooms. Freddie's new room looks out on to the street, and is half the size of his old room. I try not to look disappointed.

'Yes, Jane, I know. Don't compare them. Everyone else in the old set was squashed three and four to a room. I was virtually the only one with a really big space – I couldn't veto the move, even if I lost out. And there are advantages: very efficient central heating, a lift, much better clerks' facilities. Everyone's much happier.'

'Except you.'

Freddie shrugs. 'I'm fine. And it made me sell some pictures which I was getting tired of, so that was a good thing. I'll give Natalie a buzz and see if she's come in yet – she's been in Snaresbrook all day, and I know she was seeing her client after court rose.' He rings her room in vain; as he does so, I feel very warm towards Freddie: so it was entirely his own idea to ask me over. 'Let's have a drink, Jane, while we wait.'

'Can I see Nat's room too?'

'We could go up now if you like.'

Freddie leads me up the staircase smelling of new paint and carpet to the top floor. Nat's own room is very small indeed, with only space for a desk, a console with her PC and fax, and a bookcase. She's hung a black and white mask on the wall, with red and white ribbons hanging down from it; the empty eyeholes are sinister.

'Nat bought that in Venice last spring. She said it reminded her of a certain judge we know. I don't see the likeness, but it's a splendid mask.' He touches one of the satin ribbons. 'Nat adored Venice.'

'She told me.' I walk over to her window, a pang of old envy going briefly through me at Nat's good life. 'Not much of a view.'

'No.' We stare at a web of downpipes clamped to streaked concrete walls. 'She's going to continue the Venetian theme by having venetian blinds painted with a suitable Canaletto-type scene to cheer her up. They're in the process of being made.'

'My blinds – I can't wait.' Nat arrives at this moment, looking hot, sticky and irritable. 'Wretched Central Line. I've spent half an hour waiting outside Leytonstone in a packed train – it was like a sauna. Hi, Jane. Surprise.' She pecks my cheek after she's kissed Freddie. 'So you even wear a hat in the evening.'

'When I set out, the sun was still strong.' I almost take my hat off, but stop myself; it's only a small hat, a cream straw trilby. I'm building up quite a collection of hats, and this one is a particular success. Freddie's already admired it.

'Poor you, always something to worry about.' She snaps open her briefcase.

'How did your cross-examination go, darling?'

'Fine. Better than yesterday. I was finished by lunchtime and I got all the information I needed from the little rat. If the jury find him innocent I'll eat my wig. Look, Freddie, why don't you take Jane off for a drink and give me ten minutes to sort myself out, listen to my voicemail, and sort my post.' She kicks off her shoes. 'These shoes were not a good buy – they're agony. Look at the hole in my tights.'

We return to Freddie's room and he pours us both small whiskies.

'So Nat is very busy.'

'She's doing well again after a trough. It's a good life for the right sort of woman. Nat has a tough-enough skin and a good objective attitude, and of course it helps to be tall and strong-voiced. And you, Jane, didn't you toy once with the idea of studying for the Bar?'

'Only when I was determined to outshine my big sister in her own field.' I can see myself in a wall mirror. I'm looking good, what with my hat and my blue linen top and trousers, and my hair tinted blonde again. I take my hat off and run my fingers through my hair, pleased with the colour and cut. I meet Freddie's eyes in the mirror and smile at him. I know he used to find me attractive and I can sense that the feeling is returning. It's one of those small moments that are quite dangerous and I dispel it by moving towards the window. 'Oh good, it's stopped raining. No, Freddie, I'm not interested in the Bar – I think I might have found my career by chance. I really like working in the gallery, and learning from Henrietta. And I enjoy selling pictures – so I think I'll stick with it for the moment.'

'There isn't much money in being Henrietta's assistant, I should imagine. Like publishing, I'm sure it's not highly paid.'

'No, it's not well paid by your standards, but these days what really matters to me is job satisfaction, not money. I can hardly believe that's me talking!'

'Why?'

'I used to be totally driven by money and ambition. It was like a disease – and how funny it is that I'm now cured of it because I acquired another. *Keep your mind in hell and despair not.*'

Freddie looks at me sharply, but just at that moment his phone rings and he has to deal with some complex inquiry. Before he's finished Nat slides in looking much less hot and harassed. I hand her my glass of whisky.

'You have it, Nat.'

'I thought you could drink anything you wanted now.'

'I'll have wine later. Sometimes the smell of spirits hits me and I'm afraid I might be sick if I drank this. Perhaps it's to do with all the drugs I have to take.' I pour a glass of mineral water, and Nat takes a big swallow of the whisky as we move to the window, our backs to Freddie and his conversation.

'Alcohol's what I need after that ghastly journey. So are you coming back with us to eat then? Did Freddie ring you?'

'Yes – he wanted me to see the new sitting room and the paintings. But if it's a bad evening for you I can easily come another time.'

'Don't be silly, Jane. He's so proud of the way the room's turned out. All that training from Anthea.'

'Maybe it's just innate talent coming out.'

'What are you talking about?' Freddie replaces the receiver and comes to the window.

'Your interior-decorating abilities.'

'Well, I admit I'm delighted with the result of my efforts. Anthea never let me anywhere near the choosing of colours because she was so good at it, so I never got any practice. Now, time to leave before someone else catches me.' On cue, his phone rings. 'Ignore it. Quick, out.'

As we reach the lobby Francis Bates erupts from the lift. 'Must have a word with you, Freddie!'

'We're just off—'

'There's been a development in the BT case.'

'Can it wait till the morning, Francis? Or if it's really urgent we could speak later tonight . . .'

'Tomorrow first thing would do.' Francis's foxy eyes are fixed on me as he speaks to Freddie. 'Haven't we met before? You're Natalie's sister Jane, aren't you?'

'That's right.'

I watch his eyes uneasily remembering the things he knows about me. I sometimes feel a bit like public property.

'Nice to see you looking so well.'

'Thanks.'

'Come on, Jane. Freddie's got a taxi waiting.'

'Let me give you a drink sometime, Jane.'

'Good idea – sometime.' I wave and follow Nat out of the door.

'You don't want to have anything to do with Francis. He's a rodent of the first order.'

'It won't happen. Don't give him my number when he asks you.'

'Do me a favour, Jane. As if I would.'

'On the other hand, if somebody totally gorgeous asks for it, well . . .'

'Different story.' She laughs, but glances at me with that shadow in the back of her eyes; I'm afraid she'll never completely trust me.

The room is now a cool off-white, with a greeny-grey carpet. The sofa and chairs have been re-covered too – all the warm apricot colours have gone, replaced by a palette of greens, greys, off-white and a few intense patches of viridian and cobalt. Sam Meredith's series fill the walls: Freddie has put all of them in the same room, and only broken the sequence with a fine black and white abstract which used to hang in the hall.

'*Arboreal Memory One to Ten*. I'm sure Meredith would love to see them hung like this.' Having said this, I doubt my own words: Meredith is not someone whose reactions can be foreseen.

'I intend to invite Henrietta Court for a drink – do you think Meredith might come too?'

'Ask her. He's a fairly unreliable man – it might not appeal to him to meet a client.'

'I'd love to hear how he came to do them. I know you've told me what he told you, but it would be fascinating to see the map he mentioned, and hear him talk about the place itself.'

'Perhaps we ought to visit the village in Essex ourselves.'

'Jane, what a good idea. I remember you saying it was

near Stansted Airport. There are several old villages round there.'

'I'll try and find out which one it was.'

Nat reappears having changed out of her black and white into jeans and a T-shirt, and Freddie now goes off to change too.

'Nat, this room is a complete success. I'm almost afraid to sit on those pristine chairs.'

'I hate it when things look so new.' She flings herself into a chair, leg over the arm. 'I find it all looks too much like an art gallery. I shall have to put my mark on it – a little bit of Nat's bad taste is needed. A few ugly touches. Anything I buy for it is bound to be wrong, therefore right.'

'You sound defensive.'

'I've lived in Anthea's house for the large part of a year, and it's all so perfectly tasteful it's become oppressive. So for that reason alone, I'm thrilled Freddie's changed this room and the staircase. I just wish it was all less successful.'

'You are funny, Nat.'

'Everyone's so obsessed with their physical surroundings. Cars, clothes, houses. Everything has to be so good, so expensive – the Bar is full of possession snobbery. Oh, look, so-and-so's got a new Porsche – personalised number plates too. Oh Natalie, don't tell me that gorgeous suit is from M&S? How unexpected, I didn't quite see you as an M&S person. All that sort of rubbish. Then I talk to someone like Colin Stimson and my faith in human nature is restored. But most of chambers regard him as a freak and a failure and are not at all surprised he's left the Bar to work for some legal advice bureau.'

'What's the matter, Nat? Something's getting at you.'

'I've just told you what's getting at me.' She opens a bottle of wine with a violent tug. 'Here's your wine, I'll pour you a glass.'

Freddie comes in, changed and carrying nibbles, and his eyes immediately feed on his new pictures. 'It was so difficult to get them level – do you think number nine is slightly lower than the others or is it an illusion?'

'Freddie dearest, I love you and I love the pictures, but we spent the whole of the weekend talking about hanging them, and then hanging them and then talking about how they looked. Can we just talk about something else for a change while we sit and enjoy them? Like dinner? There's no food in the house.'

'Oh, we'll go round the corner to the Trattoria as usual. I've just booked a table.' I notice Freddie doesn't seem to notice Nat's edginess, or maybe he's just ignoring it. He fiddles with the offending picture which is indeed slightly lower than the others but I'm certainly not going to say so. 'I gave Thomas a ring to see if he'd like to come over and join us but he's out.' Freddie sits down. 'He's out all the time these days when he's in London. It used to be difficult to prise him out of his flat and now he's never in it.'

'Are you surprised? He's probably noticed at last how ghastly it is and can't wait to get out of it.'

'Oh no, Nat, Thomas still loves that flat. He just doesn't see his surroundings. Anyway, I thought we were rather in favour of people who weren't obsessed with their surroundings . . .' Freddie's eye glints as Nat throws a cushion at him. I could tell them who Thomas is going out with, but I don't.

We eat at Freddie's usual place and it's very pleasant to be welcomed as part of the family. Sergio, the owner, joins us at our table for a few minutes and asks me how my operation went. I'm surprised he knows and remembers, and we talk for a while about it. Nat's drinking wine at a great rate, and not paying attention. Then Sergio goes off to greet new arrivals, and we are brought our starters.

'I need to eat. I'm getting drunk.' But she only finishes half of her gnocchi, and continues to knock back the wine. Her eyes have that glitter signifying heightened emotion as well as alcohol levels, and her facial muscles are taut. She's in an odd mood this evening, and I mistrust it.

'So you said you were going back full time to the Court Gallery. Don't you have any hospital check-ups any more?'

'Only every two weeks, Nat.'

'But giving Henrietta Court a hand is hardly a career, is it?'

'Jane's getting a very good eye for art, and that can only come with experience. Nothing better than looking at a lot of it with an expert.'

'What exactly do you mean by a good eye in this context? Do

you mean Jane can look at a picture and say immediately: "Oh that's worth five thousand", or "That's a promising artist with a future"?'

'Finish your gnocchi, Nat. Sergio will be upset if you don't – his home-made speciality tonight.'

'OK, but answer my question.' She forks in a couple of mouthfuls, not looking at me.

'Well, Jane's certainly got an eye already for what is good. Given the lack of guiding rules in current art, a good eye is essential.'

'And I certainly haven't got a good eye.' Nat drains her glass.

'You've got good legal judgement – I haven't.' I say this to pour oil, but instead of calming the waves it ignites.

'How the hell would you know anyway? I take it your old decision to read for the Bar has been abandoned? No longer wanting to beat me at my own game?'

'Of course it has. How can I justify a long expensive training—'

I stop. Nat stops. Freddie asks for more wine and more water from the hovering waiter.

'Don't give me any more to drink.' Nat puts her face in her hands, and then gets up quickly and disappears through the toilet door.

'What on earth was that all about?' Freddie is genuinely bemused.

'Just going over old ground.'

'You're upset, Jane.'

'Don't talk any more about my job, or anything to do with art.'

'Why ever not?'

'Because it's a passion of yours, it's becoming a passion of mine, but it's not her thing at all.'

'Nat wouldn't be so childish, surely.'

'I've probably got it all wrong, Freddie.'

'I think you have.'

When Nat returns, smile in place, he keeps off the touchy subject, however, and peace descends for the rest of the meal. I refuse to return to their house for a nightcap, and leave in a taxi from the restaurant. Nat kisses my cheek but doesn't meet my eye.

Life is a strange thing. What I've experienced in the last nine months – is it really only nine? – has changed me in ways I could never have foreseen. Nine years of ordinary living could never have brought the changes about. When you know that what life you have is on loan, that it is wholly in the end dependent on hospitals and doctors and drugs, you are left with a very simple choice. Do what your doctors tell you to do or you will quickly become very ill and die. The harshness of this choice burns away the dross in your life, and you value what you have, however limited.

And that has its own beauty. Just for the taxi ride, just for this moment, I feel more fortunate than Nat. She is the same Nat she has always been, slowly developing in her new life, but still suspicious of me, still unsure of herself despite Freddie's support, still jealous. I am sure her annoyance this evening stemmed from the fact Freddie rang me and asked me to come and admire his pictures, and she felt he'd done that because she'd let him down, fallen short in her own reactions. Which she had, not that it mattered to Freddie from what I could see.

Perhaps I'm wrong, but perhaps not. For whatever reason she was being childish and irrational. I can't help feeling pity for Nat that she hasn't been through the fire, and how she would hate me for that. I put my hand on my fistula and feel the blood buzzing. The fire has extracted its price.

'All your blood levels are good – creatinine, urea, phosphate, potassium, albumin. I doubt if you've ever had a better blood chemistry in your life, considering that you had one non-operative and one faulty kidney for all those years without knowing it.'

'I do feel well at the moment, Sheena. And I seem to have got used to the drugs and they to me. So I was really upset about having such a stupid accident . . .'

'Go down and have your ultrasound scan now; they're quiet at the moment and can do you at once. I'm sure the ache round your kidney is only from that bruise, but let's put your mind at rest. When did you fall?'

'A couple of days ago – tripped going down the stairs and tried to save myself. When the pain came I really started to panic.'

'Jane, all your levels would be up if there was a problem. And they're not, so I'm sure it's a superficial pain, nothing to do with your transplant. Take your notes, stop worrying and down you go. And I think that if the scan is clear, you could now come for check-ups on a monthly basis. Of course if anything worries you, come to a clinic or ring us at once – don't wait.'

I go down to the ultrasound scanning unit, part of the X-ray department on the second floor, and of course find that an emergency has just come in and I will have to wait after all. I sit down in the lobby and open the large folder that contains my medical notes. Every detail of my career since the first admission is catalogued here, and I've rarely looked at the folder partly because I've always been told what I wanted to know. Anyway a lot of it is illegible and medical, but I catch sight of two letters tucked in at the back, edges fresh enough to indicate they are fairly new.

I tug them out, mildly curious. I notice that one comes from an address in Epsom and is dated 15 September 1992 – just over a month ago.

Dear Melanie Sampson,

You told me to get back in touch if I ever needed to know anything more about the recipients of Alfie's organs. You were wonderful to me all through that awful time, and I was in no state to thank you properly. So thank you now. A bit late in the day, but I mean the thanks.

I'm still sad that the man who had her heart and liver died so soon after – but maybe the month he had was worth it. How are the recipients of her kidneys doing? I keep thinking about them walking about with Alfie's kidneys inside them. I wish I could meet those two people. Is it possible? I believe my grief and sense of loss would be helped if I met them. I feel so unfinished about Alfie's death – as if there are ends of grief inside me that I can't tie off. I sometimes imagine my life's like a damaged tape that gets more and more blurred and distorted so you can't hear a thing properly. I feel half alive. And also very guilty.

What I didn't tell you about before was this: I was responsible for Alfie's death. I knew my car's brakes were faulty; I knew they were dangerous. But I kept putting off having them seen to – lack of time, lack of money. No excuse really.

You'll say that this sense of guilt is the reason I feel so bad now. Yes, it is, but only partly. What I really need is to meet the people who've been given new leases of life by Alfie – I know it would help my sense of loss. Alfie was such a caring person; she'd actually put all her organs on the national donor register, which I had no idea about until her mother told me.

By the way, I've told Mrs Berwick I'm writing to you about asking to meet the recipients, and she doesn't mind. She's not sure she wants to join me if/when I do, but says to keep her informed.

I will live with the sense of guilt and 'if only' for the rest of my life, but I know the feeling would become something I could live with if I could see Alfie living in others, celebrating the way she herself lived for others when she was alive.

Yours sincerely,
Toby Sherwood

My hands are shaking as I finish this letter, and I'm breathless. I scrabble back through my notes to see if there's the name of the donor anywhere, and I find it: *Alfreda Berwick. Aged 23. Traffic accident cadaver.* Alfie. I look at Toby Sherwood's letter again, and the guilt seems to come off the page at me. *I feel half alive.* Bad luck, mate. Should have got those brakes seen to. Brusquely, surprised at my sudden anger, I shove the letter aside and read Melanie Sampson's letter to Esther Fisher, the Transplant Sister.

Dear Esther,

After some consideration, and a meeting with Toby Sherwood, we have decided that perhaps it would indeed help him to meet the recipient you have at Guy's, Jane Harper, if she's willing. I enclose Sherwood's letter to me, and would fully understand if you, or if Harper herself, chose not to proceed with a meeting. It puts quite a burden on Jane Harper. The other recipient, a fifty-year-old man in York, has rejected the new kidney, so I'm afraid there is only Harper left with a functioning organ of Alfreda Berwick's.

Sherwood is not under any delusion of finding his fiancée 'alive' in Jane Harper. He knows her age, sex, and a little of her history, but not of course her name. It is unfortunate in a way that Harper is quite near in age to Alfreda Berwick, but I believe Sherwood when he says he's not looking for a living and semi-reincarnated version of his girlfriend. He only wants to help his own grieving process to heal. I would guess him to be in his mid-twenties, and emotionally fairly immature.

This is the first time I have had to approach a recipient in quite this way, and would fully understand if you felt it should not go further and did not pass on this request to Jane Harper. Sherwood accepts this, and has taken on board the fact that the recipient herself could refuse to meet him even if you allow the request to reach her.

Do give me a ring if you need to discuss this in any more detail.

Yours sincerely,

Melanie Sampson, Transplant Co-ordinator

Scrawled on the bottom is a note: *Rang 2 Oct. Melanie reassured me about Sherwood, who sounds a bit of a nutter?? Still not sure if Jane should be told. Vera Akram and Roberta Mason equally unsure. Decided to leave it for the moment – tell Jane about it after Christmas, if Sherwood still wants meeting.*

A nurse comes out of the ultrasound unit and I hastily push the letters into their concealed position at the back of my folder. But she only tells me I'm next, and pops back through the door she came out of. Any minute the notes will be taken from me, and I won't have access to them until the next time I carry the folder round the hospital myself. Angry and confused, I quickly copy out Sherwood's address from the top of his letter, and then reread Esther Fisher's handwritten note. Why should Vera and Roberta feel I can't be told about this letter? I'm fine, I'm in good heart at the moment, why haven't I been asked to make my own decision about this?

Feeling strangely betrayed, I start to reread Toby Sherwood's letter. I get to the bit about having ends of grief he can't tie off when I'm called in for my scan. Again I shove everything back into the folder, feeling guilty. Although I know patients have a legal right to read their notes, to be honest the whole hospital regime has somehow discouraged me from freely doing so. But I'm going to tackle Vera or Roberta about this letter – not Esther, I don't know her so well. Why didn't they tell me?

I lie on the bed and stare at the monitor screen as the ultrasound waves show up the kidney in its new home. It's not easy to make out all the 'plumbing', as the consultants call it, but I can more or less see the shape of the kidney, and the ureter joining it to my bladder. I know it's also joined by its renal artery and vein to my own blood vessels, but I can't see that join. Alfreda Berwick's kidney, Alfie whom Toby Sherwood loved and grieves for. Perhaps Toby Sherwood ought to see this scan, and then perhaps he'd feel better. Actually it's most unlikely he'd feel better – he'd more likely feel squeamish and pass out.

But I realise, as I get dressed and leave having been told nothing is amiss, that my instinctive anger has faded to depression because I'm suddenly saddled with a new dimension I didn't imagine or expect. Though my very first question after I'd had the transplant was to ask who the donor was, I haven't thought about it since. I could have looked before at my notes and seen Alfreda Berwick's name if I'd really wanted to. I didn't want to – I didn't want to know the name and now I can never unknow it. Alfreda. So unusual; I haven't met anyone else called Alfreda in my whole life. Aristocratic . . . perhaps she was the typical English débutante type, all long bones and pale skin, the sort of horsy, glossy female one sees in *Tatler*. The Hon. Alfreda Berwick. Very grand.

But Toby Sherwood sounds decidedly ordinary, and lives in a faceless and suburban part of outer Greater London, 14 Chesapeake Avenue. He didn't fix his car because of lack of time, lack of money. He said Alfie was a caring person who lived for others. Despite her name, they don't sound like socialites.

I admit I am curious, but no more – I'm not sure I want to move in any closer than speculation. Knowing about Alfreda Berwick's life won't make me feel any different about mine. And the effort needed to do anything is depressing and upsetting me. Or something is.

The flat is empty when I get back. Sara's left a note to say she'll be late back, and though I want to talk to someone, I don't want to talk to Nat. Nat, who could have taken Alfreda's role, and offered to do so – perhaps I ought to ring her. She's been close enough to all this, she understands as well as anyone does. But when it comes to it, I can't dial her number.

I make myself some food, watch television, have a bath, read, watch more television, and finally ring my father in Sydney.

'I can't see anything wrong with it, if it helps this Toby guy and you don't mind.'

'I don't know if I mind or not. At first I was angry with him for wanting to use me to make himself better, and then I was angry with the nurses for making up my mind for me, and now I don't know what I feel.'

'I can see why you might be annoyed with him for proposing to burden you with his guilt so that he can lose it.'

'That wasn't what he said, Dad.'

'It might be what he meant, though. My advice would be not to do anything, just let the matter lie and see if the hospital bring it up later on. Then you can make a decision about whether to meet him, with their help and advice.'

I listen to my father's level, sensible voice but it makes me feel no clearer. 'I suppose that is the best thing to do, but it galls me to follow the nurses' line.'

'Well, it may not be the best, but it could be right for you now.'

'I did take Sherwood's address.'

'You must be interested in meeting him, then.'

'I didn't think it through, I just had the urge to copy it down while I had the chance.'

'Then it's your subconscious at work. Don't rush into anything, let it come naturally is my advice. Hey, it's a beautiful spring

morning here, I'm on the terrace having breakfast in the sun.
The kookaburras in the park are in full shout. Come out to Sydney
soon, Jane. Best time of year.'

'It's bloody cold here, feels like winter already and we're not
through October. I feel the cold so much these days. Winter's
going to be hard.'

'So leave London and come and live with me here.'

'Dad, I've taken a full-time job at the gallery, and I'm really
enjoying it. Learning a lot. I can't pass this chance up.'

'You didn't tell me you were full time now. So no more
check-ups?'

'Once a month from now on unless I have a problem.'

'Excellent.' I can hear Sydney street noises in the background.
'Well, I can understand now is not the time for you to leave
London. But the offer stands.' Yet am I imagining it, or does he
sound relieved?

'Thanks, Dad. If the winter becomes unbearable I can escape.'

'You can escape. I must go, Jane. Open the mail, get ready for
my first appointment. I can hear my receptionist letting herself
in. She's new. Greek. Her English isn't up to much, but her smile
makes up for it.'

'Hang on a minute, what shall I do about Toby Sherwood?'

'I meant it when I said leave it. Just pretend you never read the
letter. Burn the address. Let the professionals decide for you.'

'Decide how much?'

'I just mean let them tell you themselves about him. Whatever
the reason, you have to accept they didn't think you were ready
for something like this.'

'I'm fine.'

'Do you trust Sister Akram and this Roberta woman?'

'Yes.'

'Well, then.'

My father's on-going offer of a home in Sydney has had a profound
effect on me without my fully realising it. I sit now in the empty
silent flat, sipping a cup of herb tea, and think about it. Because
I know I can leave, I honestly find I don't want to. And now that
going to the hospital is not my constant activity, my perspective
on it all has changed in spite of myself. I'm not dependent on

those familiar faces in the renal unit in the way I was; I even can imagine transferring to another hospital if I had to. I see how interdependent renal patients are, how hospitals have to be a central part of their lives even if, like me, they are only touching base once a month or less. They know they are not 'cured'; they can never be in anything but a contained situation, constantly monitored. So their relationships with hospitals are unusually close, unusually constant; and therefore the staff on a renal unit begin to matter to them a great deal. I know I've been lucky, and feel that the hospital has done as much as possible for my mental and physical good, but I can also now see that no renal unit can be patient-led: despite the intensity of the average kidney patient's relationship with their unit, in the end we must see ourselves as transients in a permanent structure. Consultants, Senior Registrars, Registrars, Senior Housemen, Senior Sisters, Ward Sisters, Senior Staff Nurses, Staff Nurses, Health-Care Assistants – it's like the Indian caste system. And on this analogy, what are we, the patients? Tourists, I suppose. Long-haul, long-term tourists. Well, at least I'm beginning to feel I could be a 'tourist' anywhere.

I take out the slip of paper on which I've scribbled Toby Sherwood's address. If I burn it now, it'll be another month before I have a chance to get it again should I change my mind. I tuck it into the back of my address book. I still have no idea what I should do with it, and until I do, I might as well keep it.

It's as if the piece of paper is lodged in the corner of my mind like a speck of grit in the eye. When, a week after I heard of Toby Sherwood's existence, my first waking thought is still about his letter and its request, then I know that for good or ill, action is needed. What harm can it do if I contact him? For him to meet me now, while I'm well? If he thinks it could help him heal his grief, then who am I to deny him something which is so simple? I'm healthy again because of his girlfriend's death. I can at least tell him how grateful I am.

I sit up, and take a pad out of the drawer in the cabinet beside my bed. I'm about to write my address in the corner when I stop. There's another way of doing this. I could use the proper channels but be pro-active; I could tell Vera or Roberta I've seen

the letter and ask them to contact the transplant co-ordinator –
I've forgotten her name – and get her to set it up. Then at least
though the decision's mine, there's a safety net.

I can't get Vera, she's not in yet, but I've got Roberta's home
number and she's never bothered if one rings her there. But she
does sound very surprised it's me.

'Goodness, Jane, what's the matter? Is something wrong?'

'No, I'm fine.'

'Thank heavens, you've been doing so well.' I can hear young
children crying in the background, and realise I've caught her at
a bad moment.

'Look, I'll ring you at Guy's later on if you like—'

'I'm not in this week, Jane. I've got some leave, and I'm taking
it now while the weather's still nice and I can do things with
the twins. Hang on a minute . . .' I can hear screaming in the
background, and childish shouts of mine! mine! and tears.

'Let me sort this out and ring you straight back. Remind me of
your number.'

By the time Roberta rings me I've swung right round again to
not wanting to contact Sherwood, and wishing I hadn't phoned
her in the first place.

'Now the twins are peaceful pro tem let's talk.'

'I didn't know you had twins, Roberta.'

'They're three. Little monkeys. Toby and Tim.' Her voice is
dense with love.

'Toby and Tim. Nice names.'

'Not Tobias or Timothy, but just the shortened forms Toby and
Tim. Now, my dear, what can I do for you?'

'I shouldn't have bothered you.'

'I'm here to be bothered. What was it about?'

'I read my notes the other day.'

'Don't sound so guilty. Since November 1991 patients have had
every right to do so.'

'Roberta, I saw the letter from Mr Sherwood about meeting
the recipient of his dead girlfriend's kidney.'

'We were going to show it to you sometime.' She sounds very
relaxed. 'What are your feelings about it?'

'Mixed.'

'So were mine. But Melanie Sampson, one of the transplant

co-ordinators in this area, seems to think the man is sane and balanced, and just finding his grief extra hard to handle because of his guilt.'

'But he may not find seeing me helps him.'

'That's his problem, Jane. Not yours.'

'So you think I should see Toby Sherwood?'

'I'd forgotten he was a Toby. If you feel like it, yes. Can't do you any harm, can it? Melanie would sit with you throughout. Do you want me to ask her to set it up?'

'What does Vera think?'

'Oh, she'd agree with me. We were both being over-cautious about telling you – mainly because we haven't had to deal with something like this before.'

'So it's unusual?'

'Seems to be. What usually happens is that the recipients want to thank the family of the donor, not the other way round. In addition, here we have not a member of the family, but a fiancé, and that's a first for Melanie and for us.'

'I'm curious to meet him.'

'I've always thought curiosity a healthy emotion. Give in to it and satisfy it! I'm quite curious too.'

11

'What a strange idea – I can't think of anything more unappealing than meeting someone who was giving house room to the kidney of my dead fiancée.'

'Put like that it does sound a bit weird, Henrietta.'

'Do you know anything about this man?'

'No, except that he was a post-graduate of some sort, a bit younger than me.'

'Are you sure he's not just looking for a new girlfriend?'

'When I read his letter I didn't think he was. I was annoyed with it though, because he seemed to be hoping for an easy way out of his grief.'

'What does the hospital think?'

'They feel a meeting can't do any harm. I waver.'

She's only half listening, and in an odd mood, so I stop talking about my current worry and start filing letters that have been dealt with and leave Henrietta to finish going through the mail. Lawrence comes down with a tray of coffee.

'Have you told her yet, Hen?'

Henrietta goes pink and shuffles sheets of paper. 'No.'

'You must.'

'You do it, Lol. I am overcome with a most unnerving coyness.' She laughs as I stare in puzzlement at her.

'Henrietta is getting married to Thomas Mentieth. Quite soon.'

'Oh, Henrietta, congratulations!' I hug her. 'How wonderful – Freddie and Nat will be so thrilled.'

'Don't tell them yet. Let Thomas do it.' She's blushed even pinker, and her eyes are a bit weepy. 'I can't really believe it myself. I never wanted to marry again.'

'Thomas hasn't been married before, has he?'

'Goodness me, no. He never wanted to get married at all. We're both a bit surprised we've got this far.'

'When did you decide?'

'At the weekend, Jane. Thomas has gone back to Chile to finish whatever he's doing there, and then he's back in London for a bit so we thought that was the time to get married. In a register office, no fuss, no big party.'

'Freddie will insist on a celebration. He's a great one for doing the proper thing. I mean, he likes to mark significant events.'

'Naughty Thomas went off without telling them. He promised he would but he lost his nerve. I think he feels a bit shame-faced about the whole thing.'

'Oh come, Hen, not shame – he adores you!' Lawrence laughs at her.

'Maybe, but that doesn't count when he has to face his brother. There he is, the bachelor older brother, living only for his work, utterly monk-like in his habits, getting married suddenly – he thinks Freddie will feel he's let the side down! And I can understand it – if you hadn't been aware of the build-up, Lol, I'd have found it very hard to tell you. And think how awful it was telling Poppy and Grace – they pretended to be thrilled but I know they are rather appalled. Their mother getting married again was not on the agenda, however much they'd paid lip service to the idea.'

'So has Thomas left you to tell his brother?'

'No, he's going to write. Says it will be easier.' She doesn't sound totally convinced Thomas will do anything. 'But promise you won't let it slip out, Jane, when you're chatting to your sister.'

'We're unlikely to discuss Thomas.'

'I suppose to you he's an old man.'

My face instinctively says it all, and she laughs at me. 'Oh Jane! Believe me, love isn't confined to the young. In fact, if it didn't sound so corny, I'd say that I felt far more romantic about old Thomas than I ever did about young Jeremy. Anyway, I suppose you're wondering where we plan to live?'

It hadn't occurred to me, but she doesn't wait for an answer. 'Thomas will continue to go on missions for the UN, and he did suggest I might go with him sometimes. I've refused to live in that flat of his unless it's made fit for human habitation, so until he decides what to do with it, he's going to live here while he's in London. Lawrence has his den up in the converted loft, and I'll have the second floor with Thomas, and we'll share the kitchen and sitting room as we always have. That's the pro-tem solution. We continue to live over the shop.'

I smile at Lawrence. I wonder how in his heart he views these arrangements, but his face gives nothing away. He smiles back at me.

'So, Jane, you can see you become an even more important part of the Court Gallery. Hen and I have agreed that since you've done so well we'd like to make you a director, if you're agreeable. You can continue to develop your role as Henrietta's assistant, taking over when she's away, and I'll go on concentrating on the books.' Worried by my silent reaction of stunned surprise, he rushes on: 'Of course if you'd rather keep things as they are, fine, but we both felt you needed to be brought into the business . . .' He tails off. Henrietta stands up briskly.

'Just think about it for a few days, Jane. No hurry. We've landed rather a lot of new things on you this morning, poor thing. Oh look, Lol, there's Alvin Seaton arriving with all his stuff for the exhibition – can you go out . . .'

In the rush of dealing with the delivery of thirty paintings with a traffic warden hovering nearby, I'm left to digest the new offer. Perhaps my face showed too clearly what I feel: that I'm not sure I'd enjoy working alone with Lawrence while Henrietta was away. Though good-hearted and kind, he's a hugely irritating man. Henrietta can shut him up and send him off when necessary, but I'd have to grin and bear him. I'm not sure I can, and I'm not sure I want to.

'Kneel before me, Sara – I've been made a director. You may kiss my hand.'

'What are you talking about?'

'The Courts want me to join the board. Actually, it just means I'll earn about the same, but be much more involved, and it'll look great on my CV!'

'When did this wondrous development take place, oh mighty one?'

'Today – they offered me a directorship and I said I'd think about it.'

'For two seconds.'

'There is a serious drawback.' I explain the situation without mentioning who it is Henrietta is marrying.

'My feeling is, accept. Come on, poor Lawrence can't be that bad, can he? And if it doesn't work, then move on. But they're prepared to take a risk on you, and you should be prepared to do the same, in my humble view.' Sara is lying on the sitting-room floor, half-heartedly doing yoga exercises. 'Hell, I'm so stiff. I must loosen up, start going to yoga classes again.'

'If I didn't accept and decided to remain just an employee, it would probably spoil things anyway. They'd wonder why. Most people would leap at the chance.'

'I used to do a perfect shoulder stand. Look at me, I'm a wreck.'

'So I'll accept.'

'Good for you, Jane. Why don't you do yoga with me if I find a class near here?'

'I might. I've never done it. Goodness, my life's full of novelty at the moment.'

'Talking of novelty, Ginny says that Dave's book is in the bookshops and she'll be bringing a copy round to show us tonight. We'd better get a move on – look at the time. You make the salad, I'll do the sauce. We'll grill the tuna at the last moment.'

I make two salads, one of avocado, red beans and sliced red onions, the other green. As I slice the dense yet soft pale green avocado flesh, and drain two cans of kidney beans, I suddenly feel an extraordinary pang. I've already got so used to eating these potassium-rich foods that I'm taking them for granted. I've forgotten what it was like to avoid them, or only to eat a tiny portion and cut out something else. I stare in intense pleasure at the pretty combination of foods as I stir in olive oil, lemon juice, salt and pepper, and recognise that what can keep this pleasure sharp is the shadow of fear it could all so easily end.

'Shall I put garlic into it?' I hold up a plump clove.

'Absolutely. Crush that clove, baby, crush that clove.'

'Are you sure Ginny likes it?'

'Don't let's give her the choice – but surely she does.'

'My mother used to hate garlic. I never ate it at all until I left home and went to Australia. Australian food was a revelation.'

'My mother, on the other hand, was given a copy of Elizabeth David's *Book of Mediterranean Food* as a wedding present. Very avant-garde – it's a hardback first edition to boot. Probably worth a packet now. Mum didn't use it much, but as soon as I was old enough to cook, I did.' Sara is an excellent cook – I've learned a lot from her in the last few months. Before that she didn't often cook when I was around, because she didn't want to upset me. Sara is all gold. I'm very lucky.

Ginny is holding a book in a Waterstone's bag as if it's going to explode on her. 'Now I've got it I just haven't had the courage to look at it.'

So Sara pulls the book out. The jacket is clever and simple – a long list of women's names hand-written on ruled paper in black ink with the title in dark red: *The List*. The paper list is torn off roughly to show, plain black on a plain white ground, the name: D.N. Rosenberg.

'I feel sick.' Sara drops the book on the sofa as if it's hot. 'What if . . .'

'What if. Give me a drink, quick. Red wine, yes. Stop looking so smug, Jane, and get reading. Rip through it while we withdraw to the kitchen and get drunk. Tell us the worst. Come on, Sara, let's leave her to concentrate.'

'We're not going to get very drunk on this half-bottle. Let's go out to Oddbins and get more. We're going to need it. Get started, Jane – thank goodness it's not very long.' They rush off and I'm left laughing.

I pick up Dave's small book – it's hardly more than a novella. I riffle through the pages and see immediately that Dave only uses Christian names in the parts that look like a list of conquests. There are also long passages that seem to be nothing to do with the names. It's not going to take me long to check through. I start reading.

THE LIST
by
D. N. Rosenberg

I begin with:
Charlotte, *for no good reason except that I particularly liked her signature. Charlotte, who was five foot three, with gap teeth and grey eyes. The grey was so light I thought her pupils sat in bluey white eyeballs without an iris. Her hair was short and full of colours; it was hard to guess how it started out, but, as I later discovered her bush was blonde, then it began as fair or mouse. Nice waist.*

First sighting in Hay's Galleria. She was sitting near the big metal statue supposed to recall our great city's merchant marine past, eating white bread sandwiches from a plastic box, and dreaming. I liked the way she was dreaming, so I listed her. This takes care and concentration.

'Are you sketching me without my permission?'

'No.' *I slip the notebook away.* 'Not at all.' *Give her my best smile, eyes shining with honesty.*

'Sorry then.'

'Would you like a coffee?'

'Haven't got time.'

'Tomorrow? I work round here. I'll come and look for you.'

'So if you weren't sketching what were you doing?'

'Compiling a list. Meet me tomorrow and you will learn more.'

It never fails. She was there.

Oh, my list. My lovely list. Look at them all.
Lucy. *Brunette, tall, no chin but excellent figure, legs almost unnaturally long. Bony ankles, short toes. Black bush so thick and wiry fucking her was like doing it through heather. Didn't come. Afterwards, offered me bacon and eggs. Refused to sign.*
Jo. *Long droopy clothes, granny glasses. Long straight brown hair, same colour bush all fine and silky. Didn't like me stroking it; she rolled away and wouldn't go any further. Found I didn't mind: I'm beginning to see that a great part of my pleasure lies in the hunt, the sighting, the listing. Almost enough if I can just see their bush. Could I be performing a useful act of social anthropology?*
Emma. *I meet an anthropologist. Emma was black, lively; tried to steal my list but I caught her hand in my pocket. Then she*

offered to buy it. She asked me if I had a huge porn collection to further my researches, and I said no and was angry she'd got me so wrong. It's hard to explain, but titillation is an accidental and unimportant result of compiling my list. I don't stare at a mons veneris to get a hard-on, I told her. So why do you stare at them? Tell me, I'm interested.

If I could explain it to her, I wouldn't be writing this book.

'So tell me about this list. I don't much like the sound of it.' asks Charlotte as we sit in Hay's Galleria on fake French chairs and sip thin bitter coffee. Her pale eyes are the same colour as the sky through the arc of glass high above us.

'Don't worry, Charlotte. It's just impressionistic notes about you. Your eyes – remarkable by the way – your hair, your looks. You caught my attention, and I thought you deserved recording.'

'And that's all you do? Make a list of women you pick out of the crowd?'

'Well, not quite. We often become friends—'

She interrupts, laughing. 'So it's just a chat-up gimmick then? Go on, that's all it is really.'

I laugh too. I know that she would prefer to see it that way, and I don't mind. Unlike many, she hasn't even asked to see the list. Later, if there is a later, I will ask her to sign it – she probably will. I manage to lure about half of those on the list to bed, and a good third of them will sign; the others I cross off myself. The other half of my list remains incomplete and tantalising. Many friends are on it, girls I was at university with, girls I have worked with or met at parties. I leave every name on the list even if I don't meet them again, because one never knows, one never ever knows. For example:

Mirella. Italian, copy-book Italian. Full lips with defining edges, brown eyes in whites so startlingly white they don't look natural, long lashes. Olive skin saved from being sallow by the vividness of her colouring and the flush of her cheeks; dark thick shoulder-length hair that she kept pushing her hands through, making me long to do the same. Large firm breasts on a thin body. She looked fabulous in a bikini, but it was a firmly structured bikini that gave no hint of the way her bush grew at the base of her flat stomach, and all bikini-line hair was removed.

I didn't expect to see Mirella again, but two years later, there she was, at a New Year's Eve party. One thing led to another, and her pubic hair was – well, she had none. Completely smooth. Born *with no body hair, she said. I've seen a shaved mons veneris – hated the sight – but never a bald one like Mirella's. The top of the cleft was like a deep pimple, leading to the dark, unmasked labia and clitoris. I prefer a veil of hair. She looked like a Greek statue, I suppose, except that statues don't have deep clefts and usually no clefts at all.*

'Fancy a cinema? I love going to the cinema in the late afternoon. Then we could have pizza.' I know that if I play my girl carefully I could achieve my goal before the pizza; there's a cinema near my flat, we go back for a drink before we eat – easy.

Charlotte's pubic hair is pale and sparse. I have no desire whatever to make love to her, but she's keen. I love doing it with strangers, she says as I enter her. Ooh, that's nice. As I go through the motions I wonder whether women would mind if I just asked to photograph them. Just the bush, from the front, legs relaxed but no pornographic spread. For research purposes. The idea's exciting, and I speed up. That was very quick, says Charlotte, aggrieved. She orders the most expensive pizza on the menu.

I begin to think I was stuck for ever in a groove, having to behave like Don Juan in order to continue my research, and then one day I saw an image that changed everything. It was a photograph of a painting by Gustave Courbet. (Had I heard of him? Had I hell.) Just over a hundred years ago, he painted the most wonderful picture, which he called The Origin of the World. A woman's body is shown in section: above the knee to below the breast. No feet, no face. She's lying relaxed on her back, with the left knee up and sideways so that her pubic area is revealed. The hair is as black as coal, and thick as a pelt. It grows so thickly it completely masks her clitoris and vulva. It's a black forest, lovingly painted. It is not erotic, it is not pornographic. It is graphic. Courbet was looking at the girl with my own observing cool eyes. He painted her mons veneris with my own obsession, my own delight at its individuality. I glued the photo inside the back cover of the notebook that held my list, and there it stays, an end and an inspiration.

'Jane, we're back. Sorry we took so long, but we decided we needed some dutch courage so we popped into the pub. Tell us, tell us, what have you found? We're strong enough to bear it!' Ginny strikes a posture at the door. She's a bit drunk.

'I think it's going to sell well. Do you know a French painter called Courbet?'

'Jane! Is the book dangerous, is it dropping us in the shit? That's what we want to know! Who cares about Courbet?' Ginny's voice is a shriek.

'Does he mention any of us?' So is Sara's.

'I think the girls are all imaginary – maybe based on his experiences, but so lightly as to be unrecognisable. He only uses Christian names, and as far as I could see none of yours.'

'Oh joy. What a relief. Good old Dave. Nat's in a complete state about it, refused even to buy it. I must ring her.' Ginny picks up the phone and stabs out a number.

'I haven't read much – there may be stuff that you recognise—'

'As long as it's not attached to females called Sara or Ginny or Nat, who gives a damn.' Ginny, flushed with drink and relief, starts to talk to Nat while Sara and I go into the kitchen to cook the tuna.

'It's going to sell, Sara, it's just what catches the public's eye. Racy content, a man's sexual conquests etc. But it's not a pornographic read in any way. It's more a study of pubic hair—'

'*Pubic hair!* Dave is mad. Mad, bad and obsessive.'

'It's obsessive all right. But it's a novel – it might not be his own obsession. It feels like fiction.'

'Watch the grill. I must take a look at this book.'

Supper is spent reading bits of Dave's book out loud, interrupted by calls from the web of Dave's ex-conquests as the word gets around they are in the clear. By the end of the evening the novel has stirred up so much curiosity without doubt they will all rush out tomorrow to buy their own copy. I can't wait to buy mine; Ginny refuses to leave her copy behind and I'm fascinated to read more. I must find a book about Courbet and see the picture.

Henrietta looks pensive when I ask her whether she knows *The Origin of the World*, and goes to her extensive collection of exhibition catalogues.

'Somewhere, somewhere, I've seen that picture. Now where? I think it was in an exhibition in New York, but I'm not sure. Those catalogues are upstairs . . .'

'Don't bother now, thanks. I'll have a look in my lunch break if you tell me which ones.'

'Why the sudden interest in Courbet?'

I explain, and Henrietta to my surprise has heard of *The List*.

'Oddly enough, I looked at a copy yesterday in Sandoe's Bookshop, but it didn't look my thing at all. It just seemed to be an account of all the people the young author had bedded.'

'It is. His ex-girlfriends were in a state of panic.' Henrietta laughs with me. 'They really were.'

'Don't tell me your sister was an ex!'

'Dave had a wide experience. Let's leave it at that.'

Lawrence hurries through the gallery, stopping to ferret for an umbrella. 'The forecast is rain – where's my brolly?'

'If you put it in that umbrella stand, you're asking for someone to walk off with it.'

'Surely our clients wouldn't steal an umbrella?' He tips up the tall holder to see if anyone is lurking in its depths.

'People are without a conscience about stealing umbrellas, even our clients. Take mine, Lol. But please don't lose it.'

He rushes off down the street, and Henrietta leans back in her swivel chair, her eyes following him. 'Jane, I perfectly understand your reluctance to work alone with my brother while I'm away.'

I stare at her, unable to answer.

'Don't worry, your face didn't give anything away when he made you that offer yesterday. I could sense what you were thinking, though, and if you hadn't been worried about him, I'd have been worried about you *not* worrying, if you see what I mean.'

'It seems ungrateful.'

'No, Jane, it's just being realistic. He's a dear good man in many ways, and I hang on to that when he drives me crazy. I cope because most of the time he pulls his weight. I'm the ideas person, he's the back-up. You're like me, an ideas person, and better than me at back-up. So you might find Lawrence more irritating than I do.'

'Henrietta, I'd decided to accept your offer even before I arrived here this morning. Don't worry about Lawrence. If I can't put up with him, it's my fault as much as his.'

'You relieve me, Jane. My goodness.' She lets out a pent-up

sigh of relief. 'I'd made my mind up you were going to refuse. Lol can be so silly. You can't imagine how relieved I am. I was even thinking we'd have to postpone the wedding if you left us.'

'Henrietta, I couldn't leave. I love this job; I like the art side and I like the business side. And there's the added bonus of meeting the artists. I feel very lucky.'

'The money is not good.'

'The job is. You can't have everything.' I hear myself come out with this cliché and marvel. Jane, not wanting everything, not wanting to be the best, the richest, the most successful, the starry one. I'm sitting in a gallery that's small, not smart, and not particularly successful; the floor needs resanding and sealing, there are too many damage marks on the walls. But hung on them is a lovely exhibition of paintings by a woman who started to paint late in life, and has discovered a strong and individual talent. Henrietta saw a picture by her at a friend's house, sought her out, encouraged her. And now Elizabeth Bullock is so sought after she sells at once. She insists on low prices, however, so no one benefits much except the buyers.

Henrietta disappears upstairs after this conversation, probably to try and contact Thomas about the good news. I long to tell Nat about their engagement; she certainly didn't know about it when we talked for ages last night about Dave's book. Henrietta comes downstairs again almost at once.

'Jane! I've found it. I suddenly remembered which catalogue it was in. Only a black and white photograph, I'm afraid, but it'll give you an idea.' She lays the book in front of me, open, a gleam in her eyes. 'It's quite a picture. Full frontal stuff.'

It's just as Dave described it, neither erotic nor pornographic, though possibly if viewed in colour the effect might be different.

'I think it must have been a shocking picture in its time.' Henrietta looks over my shoulder. '*The Origin of the World*. Quite a portentous title, but true too. Everyone has to pop out the same way.'

'Dave says in his book he doesn't find this erotic.'

'No. Hypnotic would be more accurate.' She closes the catalogue as a visitor comes in to look at the pictures. 'Perhaps I'll read *The List* after all, Jane. Lend it to me sometime.' Both Henrietta and I smile encouragingly at the visitor but leave her alone. She looks round very quickly and stiffly and walks out again.

'People have no confidence, I want to say to someone like her – relax, you can spend as long as you like, I don't expect you to buy, looking's enough. But when I've said it, it's not always been well received. I'm in a hurry, they say, always keen to keep their pride intact. Anyway, dear Jane, I'm going to leave you in charge now and go off and look for a nice outfit to wear at my wedding. Whether I find it or not, I'll be back by lunchtime.'

'Good hunting.'

'Not that Thomas would notice what I wear. He's completely blind to coverings and settings and surfaces. He can't understand why I refuse to live in his flat.'

'Nat says it's a total slum.'

'Not a slum. That implies laziness and carelessness and filth. Thomas cleans the bits of his flat that he uses. It doesn't smell. But the curtains, wallpapers, flooring, kitchen fittings – everything is just as it was when he first took the flat over thirty years ago, and it's got very decrepit. Nothing's ever had any tender loving care. And he doesn't see or mind.' She's put on her coat and is winding a scarf around her neck.

'I hope he's going to show *you* some t.l.c.'

Her eyes swing to mine. 'Oh yes, Jane. He's got a huge store of it all unused and beginning to come out. I'm the lucky one.'

12

'Tolstoy speaking.'

'Dave, come off it.'

'Who's that?'

'Jane.'

'I've never been so popular. All my girlfriends ringing up in the greatest relief that I haven't landed them in the shit.'

'I wasn't a girlfriend – you never got a chance to tick me off the list, remember?'

'I'm beginning to regret publishing that novel already. All you all talk about is whether you were on the list or off the list. Tedious. I have two lists, to confuse things further.'

'Two?'

'My private notebook and this list I've dreamed up. They intersect of course, but the second is becoming more real to me than the first. What it is to have such an overwhelming imagination. I can see it's going to drive me insane.'

'Stop complaining, Dave, you're loving the attention. Any reviews yet?'

'I'm not reading the papers. Reviews are irrelevant.'

'And sales? Are they irrelevant?'

'Not at all, Jane. I'd like to make some money. What do you think – is it going to sell?'

'I've only looked at the first part, and skimmed the rest, and I can't wait to read the book properly. I'll buy a copy, and so will lots of people. It will sell – it's the kind of subject that does.'

'My catty Jane. You said you'd reformed.'

'Only partially. By the way, I'm looking at a photo of that Courbet painting right now. It's extraordinary.'

'Shall I get my copy of it so that we can stare at that beautiful cunt together?'

'It's not a cunt.'

'Are we talking about the right Courbet?'

'In my definition, a cunt would be a split-crotch, porn-mag image. This is an objective, non-manipulative study of a woman's genital area. As you yourself said, it's painted with a cool head.'

'What a good pupil you are, Jane. One reading and you've got my hero's views pat. But don't confuse them with mine, will you? *The List* is a work of fiction. I personally might feel *quite* differently about the painting.'

'I see your point. Reality and illusion getting blurred. I'm sorry.'

Dave laughs but he isn't amused. 'Most people aren't aware of the difference. On that subject, when is the Harpy going to let me have her wedding dress?'

'Never.'

'How unkind she is. She owes it to me.'

'Only in your eyes.'

'My eyes are enough. You tell your sister that I won't change my mind. I want that dress. I'll pay her whatever she asks.'

'Risky. She might take you at your word.'

'Don't underestimate what I can pay when I really want something.'

'But Dave, why? Why do you want it?'

'For my next book. It'll be called *The Dress*, and be about the unreality of modern marriage concepts.' He's laughing again, this time in great amusement at the reason he has given me. 'Actually, that's not a bad idea. Not bad at all. Why did you ring me, by the way?'

'To talk about the Courbet. The gallery's quiet, I'm on my own, I first saw the painting this morning and it impressed me. I'm sorry if I disturbed you. I must go – see you sometime, Dave.'

'Hang on, what's the sudden hurry?'

'A client is looking through the window and is about to come in.'

'Let's have a drink again soon.'

'Let's.'

'Tell the Harpy to work out a price for the dress.'

There's no one outside, but a little of Dave goes a long way. As we ring off, I remember Nat in that dress, standing at the top of the communal stairs leading up to the flat, silhouetted against the light. I'd just arrived from Sydney, and was feeling distinctly crook – jet-lagged and headachy and slightly feverish. (I'd had a hellish flight; many yelling children with streaming colds were all too near my seat.) I was feeling unreal as well as unwell, and there was Nat in a dream wedding dress of cream silk which she insisted on wearing all evening, ruining it with crazy dancing and spilt drink. It didn't make sense. And dominating the evening was a tasteless character called Dave who danced with Nat in the street, the full silk skirt swirling around them.

The reviews all ensure that *The List* is going to sell and sell. '*A strange and powerful novella*' . . . '*The sexual cynicism of Laclos's* Liaisons Dangereuses *combined with a serious anthropological inquiry – why indeed does mankind in general have so many inhibitions about female pubic hair?*' . . . And so on, and so on. I notice an unsubtle change in my friends' attitude towards Dave: now that the threat has proved to be unreal, they all feel a great desire to see him.

'He never answers the phone or picks up his messages. When did you speak to him, Jane?'

'Last week.'

'He is a wretch.'

'He's probably fed-up that everyone is suddenly trying to invite him round now he's a success, having ignored him before.'

'We ignored him because we were nervous of what he might have put in that book.'

'Feels the same to him, whatever the reason.'

'You might be right.' Nat sighs. 'I wanted him to come round and meet an American writer we've got staying who's particularly keen to get to know him . . .'

'Dave will never change, Nat. He'd disrupt your dinner party. Don't expect success to tame him.'

'I've noticed it often does.'

'I don't think it's going to make much difference to Dave. But I'm surprised he didn't return your call, because he's still after your wedding dress.'

'He hasn't mentioned it to me for some time.'

'He told me to tell you he'll buy it off you. Just name your price.'

'He can ask me himself.'

'He probably will, when he wants to.' I smile, thinking of his nickname for my sister. 'What will you say?'

'I've always said no.'

'Why not reconsider?'

'Jane, it's my wedding dress.'

'Are you going to wear it again?'

'Probably not. It's very much a nuptial gown, to quote the wonderful blue-rinse lady who originally sold it to me.'

'Put a high price on it and see if Dave bites. Buy a picture with the money.'

'Why a picture?'

'It will please Freddie. Ask his advice, he'd love that. Or mine, if you want to give him a surprise.'

'But you only know about the stock at the Court Gallery—'

'Thank you very much for that comment, Nat.' I stand up – we've met for lunch. 'I'll pay for this. I must go.'

'Jane, no, let's go dutch – I don't mean you're totally ignorant of art—'

'Dig the hole deeper. You're right in it.'

She follows me out, taking my arm to stop me hurrying off. 'Sorry, sorry, sorry.'

'It's not pleasant being patronised. I know you think I'm just a glorified sales assistant. Which I am in one sense, but I also happen to be selling objects of worth and beauty. You're hurting my fistula.'

She drops my arm, looking stricken. 'Sorry.'

'You've made such a point of not being interested in modern art that I can't help but feel you despise it. Perhaps Freddie feels the same.' I'm on dangerous ground here, particularly after her behaviour at our recent dinner together, but I'm past caring.

'Freddie has nothing to do with this argument. Please don't bring him into it. I know you'd love to get your claws into him, you'll never really accept he's mine and not yours.'

'You're wrong. You couldn't be more wrong. I don't believe this is happening.'

We stand there on the pavement, our pulses racing, all the old antagonism exploding between us despite ourselves.

'Oh my God, is that the time! I must run – I'll ring you this evening . . .' Nat tears off towards the tube station. Whether she's late or just escaping I have no idea. I want to shout after her and let my fury out, but instead I walk back to the gallery the long way round to calm myself down.

When I arrive, Henrietta is full of news: Thomas Mentieth has finally rung and told his brother about his impending marriage, causing Freddie the biggest surprise of his life. She also tells me that Sister Akram has rung from the hospital and would I ring her back urgently to discuss the date of a meeting.

Life suddenly seems appallingly complicated. I foresee phone calls this evening which will not only try to smooth over the row, but will be full of recrimination: why didn't you tell us about Henrietta and Thomas if you've known for so long? I decide there and then to be out all evening, and book myself a seat to see a film so that I can't change my mind. Then I sit back and consider my other call.

I now feel no desire to meet Toby Sherwood. It will simply bring more problems into my life; I can't think why I ever thought it was a good idea. I'm about to ring Vera when the gallery door crashes open and Sam Meredith breezes in unannounced, with Ingrid in tow. She's actually brushed her hair slightly and is wearing more clothes, but the general impression she still gives is that she's just got out of bed. She stalks over to look at Elizabeth Bullock's pictures on the walls, ignoring Henrietta and me.

'Sam!' Henrietta sounds delighted but I know she dislikes surprise visits from her artists. 'How nice to see you.'

'Hail, Henrietta. Hail, Joan.'

'Jane.' Henrietta corrects him crisply, and I notice he doesn't make the mistake again.

'Ingrid wanted to see my gallery, so here we are. Meet Henrietta, Ingrid.' No surname is ever mentioned. Ingrid moves leggily in high-heeled boots from picture to picture, tossing her hair back as she consults the price list. I dislike her intensely.

'These pictures are crap,' she says over her shoulder to Sam. 'No wonder they're so cheap.'

'Who's the painter, Henrietta?' Sam is enjoying himself.

'Elizabeth Bullock.'

'Never heard of her.' Ingrid comes up to join Sam.

'Quite a colourist.' Sam puts his arm round Ingrid, his mind more on her than our exhibition. 'Jolly stuff.'

'This show is a sell-out. We have a wide range of clients, and these pictures suit some of them. The people who buy a Bullock wouldn't dream of buying a Meredith or vice versa.' Henrietta is at her coolest and most articulate. I'm watching her closely; even her body language gives little away. She is the business woman who deals in pictures and she doesn't take on failures, says her whole attitude. I'm learning.

'They probably wouldn't be able to afford a Meredith for a start.' Ingrid is lazily scratching her thigh.

'Probably not, dear.' Oh, the deliciously patronising undertone of Henrietta's seemingly comforting remark. I could hug her, and turn away to hide my pleasure. Ingrid says no more, and the ill-assorted pair leave soon after, Ingrid demanding a lengthy kiss from Sam outside on the pavement in full view of us before moving on.

'I give that relationship two weeks.' Henrietta goes and bangs shut the door they have left open. 'Sam has no taste in women.'

'She was there when I went to collect *Arboreal Memory* from his studio. I think she's living with him.'

'More fool Sam. He's an old goat. I wish he hadn't chosen to drop in now – I knew he would dislike Elizabeth's stuff. Not his thing at all. And what particularly annoys me is the fact I happen to know Ingrid is the only daughter of Terence Bellasis. You should know that name.'

'I do. Oh dear. The Bellasis Portman Gallery.'

'Terence has always wanted his gallery to handle Sam Meredith. He must be rubbing his hands in glee that his darling girl is in there, working as an excellent sapper. Terence probably suggested this visit. Goodness, I'm angry.'

'Just pray that they break up with such a big row that the last thing Meredith will ever do is join Bellasis and Portman.'

'Cheerful thought. Don't let's talk about them any more, it's bad for my blood pressure.' Henrietta turns to go upstairs, pointing as she does so at the phone. 'Don't forget to ring that nurse. She was most insistent.'

'Sorry, Vera, I've been too busy to ring back before.'

'Melanie Sampson has fixed the meeting between you and Toby Sherwood to follow your check-up next week. Everyone's very pleased. I hope that still suits you.'

'I – yes. That's fine.'

'It doesn't sound fine. Are you all right? You sound a bit low.'

'I'm not low, Vera. Just a bit stressed. So busy. I've been promoted and my job's quite demanding.'

'Congratulations. Tell me about the promotion.'

'I've become a co-director of the Court Gallery.'

'My, that sounds very grand!'

'I'm still doing what I was always doing, just feeling more responsible about everything.'

'We're all so pleased with your progress, Jane. Keep it up.'

'I've been lucky. I know I have.'

There's a small pause before Vera goes on. 'Are you nervous about this meeting, Jane? You don't have to have it if you don't want to. I can easily tell Melanie you've changed your mind.'

'I was thinking if I said no now, it would make things worse for Toby Sherwood. I raised his hopes and then I dash them.'

'He's nothing to do with you. You owe him nothing. You might feel you owed the mother something, but though she's coming too, it isn't her that seems particularly to want the meeting.'

'The mother's coming?'

'Didn't Melanie speak to you about her?'

'No, she didn't. That settles it. I can't possibly cancel now.'

'I don't think the meeting will be difficult, Jane, but you're still free to change your mind.'

'See you next week, Vera. I won't be changing it.'

When I get in after the cinema, I find a long message from Nat on the answerphone, saying how sorry she was for her outburst, and taking the blame for our row. I promptly feel guilty and ring her, late though it is, because she's also said she's dying to talk about Thomas and Henrietta.

'I was as surprised as you, Nat.'

'I just can't believe it. Thomas getting married – Freddie's shell-shocked. He's gone to bed, grey and silent! He was quite upset his brother hadn't told him a thing until it was a *fait accompli*. I told him Thomas was probably too embarrassed to tell him and he didn't like that either. Poor Freddie – I'm sure he's pleased at heart, but it isn't showing yet. They're not going to live in that dreadful dump of his, are they?'

'Henrietta refused. He's moving in with her.'

'Sensible Henrietta. Mind you, sharing a home with a professional bachelor like Thomas is going to tax her patience.'

'What does Alice Mentieth think?'

'No one's dared tell her. She'll be horrified. She regards her oldest son as utterly impossible, a cross between a genius and a mad monk. Thomas is too chicken to tell her, so he's asked Freddie to do his dirty work. Alice will be told when she comes to Sunday lunch. Please come too, Jane, and give us moral support.'

'I can't, thanks all the same. We've got to take the Bullock show down this weekend and put up the Seaton.'

'Is Henrietta going on working after she's married? What will happen when Thomas goes abroad on his missions – will she go too?'

'She'll go sometimes. I don't really know. It's all got to be worked out.'

'The thought of the two of them in bed together boggles the mind.'

We both get the giggles and it's difficult to stop. 'Come on Sunday, Jane.'

'I really can't. Even though I would dearly love to see Alice Mentieth's face when she hears the momentous news, I can't let the Courts down.'

'Never mind. I'm sorry I was so awful to you. Heavy period, too much work.'

'It doesn't matter. I wasn't exactly blameless.'

13 ∫

Melanie Sampson comes to collect me from the clinic, and having introduced herself leads me off to the office put aside for the meeting.

'It's all right, they haven't arrived yet. Don't look so worried, Jane. I just wanted a few minutes on our own first to see how you're feeling.'

'Nervous, to be quite honest.'

'Not as nervous as they are, I should imagine.'

'Why should they be more nervous than me?'

'Because you have a part of their beloved Alfreda in your body, and they're worried you might disappoint them.'

'But that's why I'm nervous.'

Melanie Sampson looks at me with her rather protuberant eyes. She speaks in a soft Northern Irish accent which is oddly comforting. 'These meetings can be hard to predict. But one thing I can say for sure, Jane, is that you won't disappoint them. They will be thrilled that someone young like you has been given a new lease of life. Thrilled.'

As I follow her, I can feel my panic subsiding a bit. My high heels click, my hair is newly cut and tinted, I've come from a morning in the gallery so I'm in my smart suit. Too smart, perhaps, even intimidating, but never mind. I have to go back straight to the gallery, and I know that Terence Bellasis is calling on us later and Henrietta needs complete support. Hence my new dark blue suit.

When we reach the office, we find that in the interim Mrs Berwick and Toby Sherwood have arrived and are already sitting down, tensely waiting. Mrs Berwick stands up at once. Toby

Sherwood is slower. She's a large, handsome West Indian; she smiles shyly at me, teeth gleaming white. I smile back, but I can't help being utterly surprised that my donor was black. No one told me. I can't take my eyes off Mrs Berwick though I'm aware of the plain-looking young white man behind her. She takes my hand, and looks at me in silence. Then she drops my hand.

'I can see they didn't tell you my Alfreda was black.'

'No. But it doesn't matter at all. I was just surprised.'

'This is Toby, her boyfriend.' Mrs Berwick stands aside.

He shakes my hand, unable to meet my eyes, his gaze rising no further than my lapels. He's nondescript to look at, but his handshake's firm and nice despite his crippling shyness. He ducks back behind Mrs Berwick.

'They should have told you she was black. Melanie, why didn't they?'

Melanie sits us all down in a tidy ring as she answers. 'We all take the view it is irrelevant, so the policy is never to tell the recipient the nationality of the donor.'

'It would have been kind to tell her now, Melanie, before she met me.'

Melanie is going rather pink, and her eyes are popping out more than ever. My feelings are inchoate, but uppermost is Melanie's statement that it is indeed irrelevant. I decide it's up to me to change the subject.

'Mrs Berwick, I can't tell you how pleased I am to meet you. I can now be grateful to you instead of to an unknown family. My life has completely changed and it's all thanks to Alfreda.'

'She put herself on the register, you know. The doctors didn't have to ask me first.'

'How wonderful.' I can sense Toby Sherwood's gaze, but when I look at him, he drops his eyes at once. 'Tell me about her. Or perhaps you don't want to . . .'

'I love to talk about her. She was my only child, such a lively lovely girl all her short life. I miss her so much. Always up to something – but she did well at school even though she was naughty. Then she went to Oxford University to study, and I wished her dad was alive to know that. He'd have been proud. He died a long while back.'

'So you're alone now.'

'Not at all, my dear. I have a big extended family. I have my friends at my Pentecostal church, and I have God. I'm not lonely. Toby's the lonely one.'

Poor Toby blushes dark and keeps that gaze down. Mrs Berwick talks on about Alfreda, how she had started teacher training, how much she liked her pupils, how keen she was on her new life. Tea arrives and as the plastic cups are handed round and the biscuits are nibbled it seems to me Toby's disappointment in this meeting is almost palpable. He sits in complete silence though Mrs Berwick does her best.

'Toby and Alfreda met in her third year at Oxford. Tell Jane about it, Toby, how she fell off her bike on Headington Hill and you helped her.'

But Toby can't; he spreads his hands and shakes his head. Maybe he doesn't trust his voice. Mrs Berwick finishes her tea and sighs. I don't know what to say.

'More tea, Mrs Berwick? Toby?'

'No thanks, Melanie. No more. It was love at first sight, wasn't it, Toby? Such a nicely matched couple, both so tall and dark. From the back they looked like brother and sister, Toby with his black curly hair, and Alfreda when she had hers short looked the same. My husband was white, so if they'd had children goodness knows what they'd have been – lovely dark coffee mulatto like her or white like Toby, or even black black black like me!' She laughs and holds out her hands palms down.

I don't know if she's aware how consumed with embarrassment and misery she had made Toby. Poor Toby, he asked for this meeting and he is having no part in it. Melanie must be having the same thought, because she turns to Toby and pushes the biscuits at him.

'Go on, do have one. So where did you come from today, Toby? You're studying at Oxford still, aren't you?'

'No. I've come from home, from Epsom.' It's a very deep voice. 'I – I've given up doing my post-graduate degree.'

'You never told me that, Toby!'

'I was going to, Susan. I've only just made the d-decision.'

'What a pity.'

'I think my brother's probably right. He regards it as a waste of time.' Toby speaks with his gaze down, but at least he's speaking.

'You mustn't let Alfreda's death stop you fulfilling yourself, Toby dear.'

'I won't.' Toby visibly goes back into his silent shell. I feel for him; Mrs Berwick hasn't got a light touch.

Luckily Vera Akram joins us at this moment and conversation becomes a little easier. Within minutes she's got Toby chatting to her, while I'm stuck with Mrs Berwick who's telling me how Alfreda came to her in what sounds like a seance. I say yes and no and begin to long for the meeting to end. Finally, I have to end it myself because I genuinely need to get back to the gallery. I shake hands with Toby first; his dark eyes give nothing away, but at least he meets my gaze and even smiles. Mrs Berwick gives me a hug.

'Bless you, Jane. You shine like a beacon. Alfreda will come to you one day, never fear.'

'Goodbye, Mrs Berwick. Goodbye, Toby. I'm so glad we have all met.'

'Alfreda shone too. Your souls are alike.'

Melanie coughs and opens the door for me.

I rush out of Guy's and treat myself to a taxi. I sink back and shut my eyes, relief seeping through me. It's over. I met them, and all went reasonably well. I breathe deeply and think about the two of them. Alfreda's blackness is now familiar, a comfortable part of me. Mrs Berwick's large persona fades quickly from my mind, but Toby Sherwood's strained watchfulness doesn't. It's sad he has given up his post-graduate studies – it seemed to be because of Alfie's death, but maybe not. Sheer lack of money could also be the reason. He didn't look well off, though again one shouldn't assume anything from his clothing.

I'm the one that looks rich. I rub the good cloth of my suit between my fingers and wonder whether Toby Sherwood saw me simply as a rich bitch, successful and glossy; perhaps he found it hard to accept that his girlfriend's kidney had gone to a woman who seemed to have so much already. I feel a sharp twinge of frustration; I bought this suit on my credit card in a sale, and without Freddie's help I would still find it difficult to make ends meet. He's paid my rent until the end of the year. After that I'm on my own.

I wish I'd seen a photograph of Alfreda Berwick. I'd love to know what she looked like; perhaps I'll write to Toby Sherwood and ask to see one. Tall, dark, with skin like coffee. Like a sister to Toby from the back. I want to see her face – I want her to turn round.

I run through a sudden downpour into the gallery. Henrietta's talking to a tweedy tow-haired stranger. I can see from the way she's standing she's not enjoying the conversation. I slip past her and go upstairs to make a tray of tea. Henrietta loves her afternoon cup, and there's no sign she's had it yet. I carry the tray down, laid for three.

'Jane, how welcome. This is Terence Bellasis. Jane Harper, our new co-director.'

Bellasis asks for hot water instead of tea, and I have to fetch the kettle. He is looking through a folder of photographs of Sam Meredith's work and taps the set showing *Arboreal Memory*.

'So these are the new small pictures?'

'His first in that size as far as I know.'

'Very nice. Have you sold them?'

'They went as a set.'

'Pity I didn't know about them until too late. I would certainly have bought them.' He sips his water. 'How much did they go for?'

'I can't tell you that.' Henrietta pours herself a second cup. 'Sorry.'

'Meredith tells me that despite this little set, his work is getting bigger. They will hardly fit in here, I'd say.'

'There's a surprising amount of space in this building.'

'If it runs out, I could be of help. My gallery has seventeen-foot ceilings.' He puts down the folder and starts pacing down the gallery as if measuring it. Henrietta's eyes meet mine with the briefest possible eye-roll. 'We could show half the works here, half in Bellasis and Portman.'

'It's an idea.'

'I can't put this delicately, so I won't try. Sam's in your stable, and I wish he was in mine. He's absolutely loyal to you, says you gave him a show when the rest of us weren't interested, took a risk on him which took a while to pay off. He'd be better off with me and he knows it, but he won't consider letting you down. However, he did agree that to show in my gallery with your permission and involvement was a very good idea. So I leave it with you. Talk it over with Sam and see what he says.'

'I will.'

'Regards to Lawrence. Sorry I missed him. Must go. Goodbye, Miss Harper, goodbye Henrietta. Did I tell you how well you are looking?'

'Bastard.' Henrietta locks the door of the gallery after he's left. 'I'm shutting early. The rain will stop any casual visitors, and I'm not expecting anyone else.'

'I'm sorry I was late. He ignored me anyway.'

'He's the greatest male chauvinist on the art circuit. No wonder his daughter refuses to behave like an ordinary human being, with that for a father.' Henrietta clatters around, switching lights off and tidying already tidy heaps of brochures. 'Damn him for getting at Sam.'

I don't speak. I've learned that when Henrietta is very angry, nothing I say will help. I carry the tray upstairs and start to wash the cups out. She thumps up the stairs before I've finished.

'Oh, put them in the dishwasher. Don't waste time washing up.'

'I'll remember next time.' I've noticed how hard it is to please people with dishwashers. Either you load the thing wrongly, or offend if you take avoiding action.

'Lawrence is the same. Always rinsing cups inadequately and unnecessarily. Leaving scummy marks in them.' She pulls down the blinds and sighs. 'Jane, how rude I'm being. Blame Bellasis. And I didn't ask how your meeting went.'

'Not too bad.'

'Tell me about it. Come, sit down for a minute.'

'I learned that my donor was black. Her mother married a white man, she told me. The boyfriend is white.'

'Did you like the mother?'

'Yes. Overpowering, but quite a character. Impressive.'

'And the boyfriend?'

'Cagey. Shy. I think I disappointed him.'

'How so?'

'Perhaps it was inevitable. No one could live up to his Alfie, I suppose.'

'I still think it's strange that he wanted to meet you. A rite of passage maybe.' Henrietta's attention has wandered, and since I suddenly feel too tired to discuss Bellasis or anything else that is on her mind, I leave soon.

To my relief, the flat's empty even though Sara said she'd be back, possibly with Joe in tow. I have a long hot bath and pinch some of Sara's green pine crystals. I look down my body in the pale green water; my old delight in it has gone for ever. Once upon a time I used to stand in front of the mirror and purr at what I saw. So slim, so fit, so well formed. Now I've got scars, and my figure's a bit heavier, and most important, I don't care in the obsessive way I used to. Either I'm not so vain or—

The phone rings and, as the bath is getting cold, I heave myself out and answer it. It's Dave Rosenberg.

'Hi, Jane. I'm just round the corner. What are you up to tonight?'

'I was going to have an early night.'

'Do you really mean that?'

'I do. It's been one of those days.'

'Can I drop in for half an hour? Have a beer with you?'

'Not sure we've got any.'

'I'll bring a six-pack. Is Sara in?'

'Not yet. But Dave, I really don't want a long session—'

'Trust me.'

He's rung off before I can reply, so I quickly pull on a warm jumpsuit – deeply unsexy – and blow my hair dry very thoroughly. Jake always said women with wet hair gave him ideas, and I don't want Dave to have the same reaction. I shut the bedroom doors, and put all the lights on. He rings the bell as I finish.

The prospect of Dave is always more intriguing than the sight of him, with his louche manner, deep stubble and black clothes. He's as tense and laconic as ever. I lead him towards the sitting room.

'Let's sit in the kitchen. I like that kitchen.'

'It's in a mess.'

'You should see mine.'

'I'd prefer to sit in the other room, it's warmer.' I know I have to call the tune. He follows me unwillingly.

'It doesn't feel warmer.'

I ignore this and get some glasses out. He in his turn ignores them and opens a can.

'How's the famous writer?'

'Infamous would be more accurate. Everyone without exception makes the mistake of thinking *The List* is about sex.'

'Isn't it?'

'It's about mores, it's about erotic perceptions, it's about the human need for categorisation. It is not about sex.' Dave has clearly said all this many times, and indeed I've heard him myself on a late-night show. I'm beginning to regret letting him in already.

'You said you never read reviews, Dave, so how do you know what everyone is saying?'

'My publisher keeps sending me copies of them, keeps arranging press interviews.'

'I can't think why you're complaining.'

'I'm complaining about the level of intelligence of the interviewers and reviewers. For instance, as far as I know you're the only person who's bothered to find the Courbet painting, look at it, and realise what it means.'

'I've no idea what it means, Dave.'

'You corrected me when I called it a cunt. Quite right.' His eyes are bright with something, and I don't trust Dave. 'You know exactly what that picture means.'

'No I don't. I was looking at the picture as an art dealer, not a reviewer.'

He laughs and stretches back in the armchair. He hasn't touched his wretched beer after opening it. He clearly plans a long stay.

'What does Miss Art Dealer think of my pubic hair thesis, by the way? I take it you've now read the whole book?'

'Interesting. I hadn't appreciated how blank the Classical period and the Renaissance were on this crucial matter.'

'Not just them. The amount of information coming in from other people because of the publicity is astonishing. Different parts of the world, different mores, different religions – the range of attitude is is unbelievable.'

'Another book there?'

'Could be.' At last he downs a good half of the can. 'Could be.'

'Everyone's complaining you never respond to messages or letters.' Dave laughs but says nothing. 'Nat wanted you to go to dinner to meet some Americans she's got staying. You should have gone – she might have let you have the dress.'

'I'll get in touch in my own good time.' He swishes his beer gently in the can. 'That was her magnificent moment – the way she danced with complete disregard for the dog shit and the dirt in the street, the mess in the kitchen. Torn skirt, Bloody Marys all down it – she just laughed. What a sacrifice. She was wild. A maenad.'

'I think she was just drunk.'

'Not at first.'

I yawn and finish my glass. Dave pays no attention and having drained his can rips the next open.

'She should never have worn that dress again, they should never have cleaned it up. I wanted it to stay all stained and ruined—'

To my relief I hear the sound of Sara's key in the lock and the usual sound of her dropping her bag and rushing to the loo. I quickly go to the sitting-room door to warn her of Dave's presence.

'Hallo, Dave, elusive Dave.' She kisses his cheek. 'And famous Dave. Congratulations on the success of the book. Well, this is a nice surprise. I didn't know Jane was expecting you.'

'She wasn't. I like dropping in.' He finishes his second can and looks round. I've noticed often that Dave prefers a one-to-one talk – it's harder for him to dominate general conversation. And Sara is not one of Dave's admirers. She didn't like the book and tells him so when he asks.

'Well written, brilliant, clever, all that jazz. But no, I have to admit, I didn't like it.'

'Good. It would be depressing if you all did.' Dave stands up.

'Now I've upset you.'

'Of course you haven't. Dear Sara, a book like mine is bound to offend some people.'

'It didn't offend me.'

'So what didn't you like?'

'The attitude to women, I suppose.'

'I can't be answerable for my fictional characters' opinions. They think what they think. See you, Jane. I'll be in touch.' He leaves so quickly Sara looks quite taken aback.

'I really did upset him. Oh dear. Shall I write him a note?'

'Don't worry. I'm not sure you did. I was longing for him to go anyway – I'm exhausted.'

'He's had such a lot of fawning adulation I thought he'd appreciate it if I was honest.'

'Dave's strange, and completely self-obsessed to a degree undreamt of by most people.'

'You're obviously the only one he likes.'

'It's odd because I don't like him.'

'That might be why he likes you. He knows where he stands.'

'It's not that I *dis*like him exactly – he interests me, and I found his book fascinating. I actually think he's a real writer. He's got something to say and his own way of saying it. Underneath all the posing he's very serious, but that's not a part of Dave he will ever share with anyone.'

'I can see precisely why he likes you.'

14

Dear Toby Sherwood,

I keep thinking about our meeting, and remembering it was you who wanted it to happen, and I'm not sure it went very well for you. Mrs Berwick rather took it over.

I just wanted to say I'm sorry if it, or I, was a great disappointment, and to hope that even so, you were helped a little by our meeting. And also to ask if you have a photo of Alfreda to show me – I'll post it straight back, but I would love to see what she looked like. I hope you don't mind.

Yours sincerely,
    Jane Harper

Dear Jane Harper,

Here's the photograph you asked for. Please keep it if you like. I have dozens of Alfie.

Thank you for meeting me. The fact it didn't go very well for me wasn't your fault.

Yours ever,
    Toby Sherwood

Dear Toby,

What a wonderful-looking girl Alfie was. Yes, I'd love to keep the photo – her smile is one of the most cheering things I've ever seen. No wonder you are finding it so hard to live without her. Now I can see what she looked like, I find I can't help grieving for her too.

All the best,
    Jane

Dear Jane,

What's making it so hard for me is not only that Alfie was special – you can see at once she was – but that I behaved so badly on the night she died. And I also caused the crash to happen – my car's brakes were faulty and I knew it and I didn't do anything about it. So my last memories of her are smirched, as if I'm seeing her through a cloudy, dirty window, and the window is me.

If I'm honest – and it hurts me to say this, something I've never told anyone yet but writing is easier – my relationship with Alfie was changing, had changed, by the time she died. I was losing her love, I'm sure of it. She never said so, but her new life at teacher training college in London was opening a gap between us, just a small one, but a gap. And gaps between people once they appear only go one way, in my experience. They just get wider.

I was desperately trying to ignore the gap during that last weekend. We had to go to a big fancy dress party at a house outside Oxford, and getting ready for that was such fun I started to kid myself there wasn't a gap at all. But I went and got totally drunk at the party, absolutely legless, as if my body knew there was a gap and was taking a crude way out. It was a stupid, self-destructive thing to do, particularly as Alfie herself was drinking nothing mainly because she'd decided to drive. I can't imagine what she thought of me when she found me lying on the floor so drunk I had to be helped to walk to the car. I crawled on to the back seat and lay down, afraid I'd be sick again. I'd been sick at some point earlier, so I probably stank of vomit. What a turd, she must have thought as she drove us back to Oxford; how could I be engaged to such a creep. Ten minutes into that journey she was dead.

Just writing this all down for the first time has helped – please forgive me for boring you with it. I think that what I'd hoped from our meeting was that I could somehow pour all this out to you in person and absolve myself. What a stupid assumption. As soon as I saw you, I realised that I couldn't possibly burden a stranger with all my emotional guilt.

Then you wrote, and here I am, doing exactly that. But you are free to tear this letter up now and walk away from all I've told you knowing that you've helped me simply by giving me this chance. There's nothing more you or anyone else can do for me. The rest is up to me.

Yours ever,
Toby

These letters go back and forth between us with hardly a day's gap; when I receive the last, I read it many times before I do exactly what Toby tells me to do and tear it up. Alfie's photo remains propped on my chest of drawers beside all my medication as if that's her rightful place. The photo shows her leaning against a wall, a bag of books at her feet, and a wide, mischievous smile on her face. Her skin is no darker than a deep suntan on someone of dark colouring; her hair is long and plaited. Her eyes are large and slope up slightly, as do her cheekbones; her nose is short, her lips less prominent than her mother's but still well defined and full. It's a remarkably even and lovely face, and the smile causes you to smile back. Yet from the way she's standing, with shoulders slightly hunched and one foot hooked behind the other, she's lacking in confidence in herself. She comes out of the photograph as a vulnerable, loving, extrovert person who's not really aware of her beauty.

Sara comes in and picks up the photo. 'Who's that?'

'Alfreda Berwick. My donor.'

Sara stares at it in silence. 'Oh Jane. What a love she looks. I want to cry.'

'I just have.'

Tearing a letter up isn't a solution. In fact, in many ways it ensures that you remember the words – or perhaps more exactly, the emotions – with extra clarity. I can see Toby's breaking heart in his drunk body: I can imagine his misery as he lay huddled and smelly in the back of his car. These images remain in my mind though I try hard to banish them.

We are very busy at the gallery preparing for the Meredith show. There is a minor crisis when Ingrid Bellasis suddenly disappears and is found a few days later in Paris with a new lover. Sam has spent frantic days tracking her and not finishing important work, but for once this doesn't bother Henrietta.

'Best thing that could have happened.' She exults with relief about the end of this affair. She's in a highly excitable state: her wedding looms, with Thomas due back from Chile only a few days before it. He's had to stay on because of political problems, he says.

'Freddie doesn't entirely believe that. Thomas has a terrible track record for missing important family occasions.'

'Oh come on, Nat – surely he won't miss his own wedding.' Nat and I speak most days on the phone, but haven't met since our row. I think we both need time without a meeting; when we're physically together there's more risk of the temperature rising.

'Freddie wouldn't put it past him.'

'Freddie took days to believe he was actually getting married, so he's likely to take a very pessimistic view anyway.'

'True.'

'How's Henrietta taking the delay?'

'Not particularly bothered.'

'Or so she says?' Nat is clearly sceptical.

'She really isn't worried. I know her well enough now. Thomas told her he couldn't help it, and she believes him. End of story.'

'This wedding is going to be the oddest ever. What's the bride wearing?'

'A very nice Jean Muir suit. Henrietta said she'd always wanted one and just for once in her life she was going to spoil herself. Then Lawrence paid for it as a sort of wedding present.'

'What's his sexual orientation, Jane? I can't make him out. Is he gay?'

'No. He just doesn't seem to need women. He likes them, though.'

'Has he made a pass at you?'

'No.' I stare at the rain outside the kitchen window. 'No, he hasn't.'

'But you think he might. I can hear it in your voice.'

'It isn't so much that, it's just a general unease about working with him when Henrietta's away. I'm afraid I'm going to be irritated all the time and he'll clam up and be uncooperative as a result.'

'Let him make a pass, shrug him off but give him leeway, get him under your thumb that way.'

'How very manipulative. And don't say you learned it from me.'

She laughs and we ring off. If we'd been in the same room I'd have wanted to spit at her, and vice versa no doubt. Perhaps we ought to remain telephonic sisters for amity's sake.

There's nothing more you or anyone else can do for me. This phrase from the destroyed letter floats in and out of my mind. I try to remember Toby's face but I can't very well. Mrs Berwick's and

Alfie's push it out. I know he had brown eyes, very dark curly hair, was tall, pale-skinned, thin. But his face is a blur.

He's given up his research, he's lost all the structure he had. He's living with his parents, which I imagine isn't from choice but necessity. He called himself a turd and a creep in that letter. Rock-bottom self-esteem. His mind is in hell and he despairs.

He lost his love and she's given me life. I owe Toby Sherwood more than just a letter or two. His pain hurts me. I'd like to help him if I could.

The old Jane lifts up my liking and inspects it for hidden motives, but she can't find any. There aren't any. I feel no interest in Toby as a man. I'm not looking for a boyfriend, I can't even visualise him well enough to see if he could be attractive. As far as I can see my motives are 'pure'. I'm aware of his pain and could at least offer a hand of friendship. In fact, a good handshake, firm and warm, is all I can remember clearly about him.

We don't shake hands when we meet; I'm wearing gloves and by the time I've got them off the moment has passed. He's not as white-faced as he was, but it may just be that waiting in the cold outside the theatre has brought the blood to his skin.

'I'm so glad you could help me out at this short notice – such a pity to waste a seat.' My story had been flimsy, but even if he wasn't taken in by it, he didn't appear to mind.

'I haven't seen a play in the West End for ages. Thank you for thinking of me.'

'We've still got twenty minutes – let's go to the pub opposite and have a drink.'

The pub is full and very noisy which makes conversation difficult. Even so I'm talking too much to cover for his nervousness. It's a relief his face is no longer a blank: his long nose, his good teeth, his scarred chin, his bushy eyebrows and extra-long eyelashes which curl up as if he's been at them with tongs. Given the careless way he is dressed, tongs don't seem likely.

'Another drink? My turn.'

'No thanks, Toby. Save it for the interval.'

We start to cross St Martin's Lane.

'An all-male *As You Like It*. Unusual these days.' He stares at the list of names on a billboard outside the theatre.

'It's had wonderful reviews. Apparently Rosalind is played by a tall black actor, and sister Celia by a short white actor, and in no time you accept the anomaly.'

'Alfie once played Rosalind at school, she told me.'

The crowd around us saves me from replying, though I wish I hadn't known this slightly unfortunate coincidence. But he doesn't seem perturbed, and follows me happily to our seats. It is indeed an excellent production and both of us are rapt, which is exactly what I'd hoped. We have plenty to talk about in the interval discussing the finer points of the production, and after it's over Toby dashes off to catch a train and I take a tube home, pleased that the whole encounter has gone so well yet stayed on an entirely superficial friendly level. His last letter is never mentioned.

Good, I say to myself, good. The play made us laugh, made me cry, enchanted and entertained us on many levels. I couldn't have chosen a better way of drawing Toby out of his misery. And his note of thanks says precisely that, and suggests we go to something again. *I'll be in touch*. It's down to him, and he may not do anything about it. I feel completely in balance over it: if he is, fine; if he isn't, fine. Our evening together has eradicated my feeling that Toby got a poor deal at our first meeting.

Thomas arrives back from Chile looking even more unkempt than usual, and Lawrence is commanded by his sister to take him off for a haircut. The result is not a success: Thomas's weatherbeaten skin on face and neck suddenly ends in a white strip which runs all the way round his hairline.

'Oh, Lol, why did you let them cut it so short?'

'For goodness' sake, Hen, I left him to get on with it. He told them to give him a haircut to last for six months, so what do you expect?'

'It makes him look so odd.'

In my view Thomas looks no odder than usual, just differently odd. I suggest Henrietta spreads self-tanning lotion on the white line and she perks up.

'Do you think it would work? Where do I get some?'

'Anywhere – I'll get you some. But won't he feel offended if you try to use it?'

'You could be right. Oh well, his hair will grow.' She sighs. 'I remember cutting my own hair as a child. I trimmed my fringe and it ended up a miserable ragged edge right up near my hairline. I had a white forehead which showed up my efforts beautifully. I suppose that's why Thomas's white tide-mark keeps catching my eye.'

I've noticed how everyone gets stressed about the small things when it's the big things that are really preoccupying them. Shadows pass across Henrietta's face when she thinks she's unobserved; I'm sure she's regretting giving up her single life. She snaps at poor Lawrence who spends most of his time out as a result.

'That wretched brother of mine is never here when I need him. There's a mound of bills and invoices to deal with, the new bed's being delivered this morning, and I have to go to the dentist. And where is Lawrence? Out, amusing himself. I could scream.'

'Tell me where the bed has to go.'

'Let me show you. It's easier, and I don't want them to get it wrong.'

I've never been up to the second floor. Henrietta's bedroom is pretty, quite feminine, and there's a single bed, stripped and solitary, in the middle of the floor.

'They're going to take that one away and put the double one in its place. It should fit into that gap.' She stares rather desperately at the bare wall; she's pushed furniture together so that everything is rubbing shoulders to make room for the new bed.

'Oh, Jane.' She suddenly subsides on to the bare bed. 'What am I doing?'

'Making a big change in your life.'

'At the moment the whole prospect of Thomas being a permanent fixture here is scaring me silly.'

'How did you feel when you were about to marry Jeremy?'

She gives a croaking laugh. 'Much the same.'

'You'll feel better when Poppy and Grace arrive.'

'I won't. I'll feel worse. They'll look at Thomas and think I'm crazy to give up my freedom for him. But I don't mind what they think – it's what I think that matters. And since he came back I – I've got increasingly panicky.'

'Do you still love him?'

'Yes.'

'So no doubts there.' I find this conversation with a friend old enough to be my mother rather disconcerting. I feel older than Henrietta at the moment.

'He's a fascinating, interesting man and I love him and want him permanently in my life, but I'm not sure I want him permanently in my bedroom.'

'Perhaps Thomas is wandering round his flat at this moment wishing he wasn't leaving it.'

'I'm sure he is. He's decided to keep it on as it is – he had such a horrendous estimate for putting it to rights he's planning now just to use it as a study and office.'

'Maybe you should get married but live separately – you know, spend time together, nights together, but not actually live together under the same roof.'

'I can't see Thomas in this bedroom, can you?'

'Not easily.'

We start to laugh, and Henrietta throws herself backwards on to the striped mattress as her laughter builds.

'Why don't you ask him whether he's feeling just the same? He might be quite relieved.' The phone starts ringing downstairs and I run off to answer it. By the time Henrietta appears, ready to go off to the dentist, she's looking very much happier.

As the Peter Jones delivery lorry stops outside the gallery, a young man wanders past the window carrying a bunch of vivid blue irises. It's only when he's out of sight that I realise it was either Toby Sherwood or someone very like him. And Toby it turns out to be: he and the delivery men come through the door closely behind each other.

'Bed delivery for Mrs Court?'

'Yes, I'm expecting it, Toby! What a surprise.'

'We have to collect a bed first, I believe.'

'Upstairs. Toby, sorry about this, but enjoy the exhibition for a minute while I sort out this delivery.'

Toby smiles, makes a no hurry, no worry gesture, and drifts towards the walls. I do indeed feel total surprise about his sudden appearance – how did he know where I worked? Perhaps I mentioned the gallery at some point, I don't remember. I rush up and down behind the men, who start proceedings by bringing in the double bed and leaving it in its wrappings in the middle of the gallery while they go up to fetch the old single bed.

'It looks like an installation, doesn't it? Sort of thing that wins the Turner Prize in a bad year.' Toby walks around the large package.

'I see what you mean – puckers of thick plastic and all that brown tape look carefully meant.'

'What do you think of that sort of art?'

'Now's not the best moment to discuss it, Toby.' The men are easing the single bed down the last flight and now there are two beds in the gallery. A woman is peering with interest through the window. The double bed, swathed in its protective plastic, is carried upstairs. I follow as the woman walks in, and leave her with Toby. When I return she's sitting on the single bed.

'It's Mrs Frazer. I came to collect the Elizabeth Bullock I bought.'

'Of course. It's all ready for you downstairs. One minute while I fetch it.'

'Should I get off this bed? The young man assured me it wasn't an installation.'

'No, it's not, so be comfortable, Mrs Frazer.' It takes me a few minutes to find the right picture, and as I return to the main gallery I see the morning has one more surprise to offer. Dave Rosenberg is outside looking in, obviously checking to see if I'm there. I could duck back to the lower room again but Mrs Frazier has seen me.

'Ah, there it is. What a lovely Bullock. I'm so looking forward to hanging it with the others.'

Dave is walking in, his eyes flicking from bed to Toby to me to Mrs Frazier and her Bullock. The men come rumbling down the stairs at this moment and ask me to sign the delivery note. Dave stands back, clearly enjoying himself, as the bed is carried past him.

'Let me wrap your picture for you, Mrs Frazer.'

'No, please don't bother, I'm parked nearby. Apologise to Mrs Court for taking so long to collect my picture.'

'Of course.'

'Well, I'll leave you to your busy morning.' She clutches her painting against herself as she passes sardonic Dave. Toby holds his bunch of flowers equally close to his body, and glances in Dave's direction, obviously thinking he's a casual visitor.

As my heart sinks, Dave disillusions him. 'My beautiful Jane, you look as if you are running a happening that is barely controllable.'

'Hallo, Dave. Let me introduce Toby Sherwood.' I move quickly towards Toby to forestall Dave giving me a welcoming embrace. 'Whom I have shamefully neglected because he arrived with the beds.'

'You're in the bed business, then, Toby?'

Toby goes scarlet and I could cheerfully strangle Dave.

'At the same time as the beds, I should have said.'

'Don't disappoint me. A bed dealer who delivers a bunch of flowers with the bed – what a nice idea, I was just thinking.'

Dave is enjoying my frustration and Toby's complete discomfiture. In a minute I will throw Dave out.

'Take no notice of my friend, Toby. He specialises in playing games.'

But how could poor Toby take no notice of Dave? Dave is now giving a fluent running commentary on the pictures on the walls as he looks round, and has offered me no inkling of why he's come here in the first place. Toby's lost his confidence completely, and can hardly meet my eyes – he's the Toby of our first meeting. Whatever plans he had in mind have crumbled; he's edging towards the door still holding the flowers.

Lawrence suddenly hurries in, and I've never been so pleased to see him. He smiles vaguely in the direction of the two men while ignoring them.

'Where's Henrietta, Jane?'

'She had a dentist's appointment.'

'That would account for her peevish mood this morning. My goodness, did she bite my head off!' He heads for the stairs. Oh no you don't, Mr Court.

'Lawrence, it's just about my lunch break, and I'd arranged to have lunch with Toby Sherwood here, so do you mind if we slip off now? Henrietta should be back herself soon.'

'You go, my dear. Of course. Just give me five minutes.'

Toby is standing stock still, a small smile growing. Dave prowls towards me.

'I was just passing, Jane. Wanted to see where you worked, what sort of gallery it was.'

'Sorry to disappoint you.'

'Disappoint me? What makes you say that? I arrived without preconceptions so how could I be disappointed? I must say, when I saw you in the middle of a happening, my hopes rose, but it was just real life after all.' He takes my hand and kisses it. 'Mr Sherwood's flowers, which I suppose he intends to give you before he batters them to pieces, don't quite match your eyes. *Bon appétit.*' And he's gone.

Toby holds out the flowers. 'He's quite right, they don't. Your eyes are more cobalt than the indigo of these. I got them cheap because they're all open.'

The pizzeria is busy and full; Toby and I squash on to a small corner table which luckily became vacant as we arrived. Large menus keep us occupied choosing, though I don't need to – I always have a marinara. Toby dithers, changing choices until the last minute. We give our order and as the waitress hurries off he smiles wryly.

'I always drove Alfie mad because I took so long to decide what to eat. It's not so much indecision as greed – I love food so when I'm reading a menu I'm mentally tasting the dishes. Alfie was like you – she always knew exactly what she wanted to eat.'

'Don't tell me she always had a marinara too.'

'No, she usually had the four cheeses pizza.' He is biting his way through a packet of *grissini* at speed, in between sips of Coke. He suddenly puts the packet down and meets my gaze. 'This is the first meal I've had out since she died. Pathetic, isn't it? I've been a complete recluse most of the time, and my parents never eat out.'

'Why did you give up your research, Toby? And what was your subject?'

'I lost too much time.' He fiddles with the *grissini*. 'And my subject seemed increasingly irrelevant. Who cares about the Greek diaspora in late antiquity? I expect if I got down to it again, I'd find it as fascinating as I did at the beginning, but I'm not sure I want the academic life any more, and where else does post-graduate lead you? Teaching and publishing articles etc. I saw myself as writing a definitive book one day, but I've lost all impetus.' He is staring blankly at the wall behind me. 'I can't tell you how useless I feel. I've been applying for jobs but it's not easy. I haven't even been offered an interview yet.'

'You mustn't lose heart, Toby.' The words drop between us. Lose heart. It's an apt description of a certain kind of atrophy. The losing is a letting slip of all that demands emotional input.

'I've been feeling so empty I feared Alfie had taken my heart with her.' He's snapping *grissini* into short lengths and stacking them. I take a few pieces as if he's done them for me. He stops at once and puts his hands on his lap.

'Give yourself a holiday, Toby. Go travelling.'

'No money. I must get a job, pay my parents back. Then I'll go abroad, backpack mindlessly for months.'

'Here come the pizzas. Don't they smell good? I love a thin pizza like this.'

'It's very kind of you to treat me to lunch.'

'Tuck in.'

As I cut a wedge of pizza I feel the usual sheer delight at eating what I like. I pay such close attention to the flavours of tomato and anchovy and garlic and olive oil I miss what Toby has just said.

'Sorry?'

'Another reason why I gave up my research was that I was getting bored with it. I hadn't really even admitted it to myself, but after my life changed so suddenly, I had time to reflect. I don't think anyone should do post-graduate research unless they're really serious.' Toby copies me and eats a slice of pizza with his fingers.

'Weren't you?'

'Of course I was, or thought I was at the beginning. But I didn't get a first, though I'd been tipped for one, and that was a blow. However it was a good enough degree to allow me to continue so no one questioned my decision. Least of all me.'

'And Alfie?'

'Perhaps she did. She never said.'

'How old are you, Toby?'

'Twenty-five.'

'And Alfie?'

'She was twenty-three. And you?'

'I'll be twenty-nine in January.'

'I'll be twenty-six in January. When's your birthday?'

'The fifteenth.'

'Mine's the sixteenth.'

We beam as we share this; it's always such an oddly happy thing to discover another person born on or nearly on your own birthday.

'I arrived a day early – my mother was out shopping when my birth began, and she told me I was very quick about it. She just made it to the hospital. So I should really share your day.' Toby laughs as I say this, the first laugh I've heard him give.

'I've never met anyone else who shared my date.'

'One of my friends in Sydney was born on the fifteenth.'

'Sydney, Australia?'

'I lived there for a few years. My father emigrated after he divorced my mother.'

Toby's pizza is disappearing fast, and I offer him half mine.

'I'm really not going to eat it all. I usually just pick round it and mess it up – I'm going to cut it in half now and if you feel like it you can finish it for me.'

'I'll happily eat it.' And it's true, the coincidence of our birthdays has made him happy, briefly.

'Don't hurry, Toby. I've got to leave in five minutes to go back to the gallery, but you stay and finish in peace.' The bill comes and I add a coffee on for Toby before I pay. 'It's a pity to rush. Thank you for those beautiful blue flowers, and let's speak soon.' I touch his shoulder and hurry out. He's already looking less cheerful and his shoulders are hunching over his plate. When I glance from the door he's got a paperback out and is trying to prop it against his Coke glass.

'Who's the new boyfriend? Lawrence told me you'd gone out to lunch with a strange young man.' Henrietta imitates her brother's voice.

'Oh, Henrietta, what a morning.' I'm good at telling a story, and she laughs at my vicissitudes. But she wants an answer to her question.

'So who took you out to lunch – the famous novelist or the poor student?'

'I took the poor student out for a pizza.'

'Very noble of you. But I'm sorry to miss meeting D. N. Rosenberg – we must ask him to the Meredith opening. If he makes lots of money out of *The List* he might start collecting.'

'He's not a collecting type. He's been a squatter for ages – though he has a flat or base of sorts now. He lives a deeply irregular life.'

'He'll change if he's seriously successful.'

'And were you? Successful?'

'With what?'

'Thomas and your living arrangements.'

Henrietta smiles and stretches luxuriously. 'Oh Jane, you were so right. He was dreading moving permanently here, so we've got a much more flexible arrangement lined up, and he's happy and I'm happy. Or I would be if he hadn't had his hair cut so brutally short. He's going to make a very strange first impression on Poppy and Grace.'

Not nearly as strange as she foresees, but I say nothing.

Poppy and Grace themselves are rather strange: they are non-identical twins with identical voices. Poppy is like Henrietta, dark-eyed and heavy-browed; Grace must resemble her father because she's sandy and freckled and blue-eyed. With their bright eyes, clear skins and unstressed air, they ooze the West of Ireland. Their hair is left long and tied back, their hands are rough from their weaving. I listen to them chatter to their mother as they bounce about the gallery and feel a deep envy; not of their happy and rewarding country existence but of their obvious closeness to one another and their support and trust of each other. I'm so used to my stop–start relationship with Nat and its past of dislike and dislocation, that it is a revelation sisters can be genuinely so close.

They're so pleased to see Henrietta and Lawrence they pay no attention to me beyond the first polite acknowledgments. Thomas is due to arrive soon for a family dinner party upstairs, and I make a point of leaving on time. I look back as I pass the window of the brightly lit gallery and see Poppy and Grace go up to their mother and put their arms round her, so that the three of them stand swaying rhythmically together in what is clearly an old family habit. I hurry briskly on but can't help a tear of self-pity forming. I may not have been lovable, and my family was certainly dysfunctional, but I never experienced family love like that. I walk on towards Victoria Station, desolation building up inside me. The chances of me one day being hugged by grown-up children are unlikely to say the least. Kidney patients don't have long life expectancy, however well their transplants go.

Christmas decorations are now up everywhere; there are carols being sung outside the station to hurrying commuters. I stop to watch a large choir of children do their best with 'Silent Night, Holy Night' while the cacophony of London traffic continues blindly on. In front of the choir is a donkey, its panniers collecting boxes; the animal looks resigned, its minder cold and tired. I put a pound in a pannier and, more lonely than I can ever remember feeling, join the press of people underground.

The moment I reach the empty flat, I fetch Georgia Hill's book from its accustomed place and open it. Tucked into the front is her letter to me. I unfold it with care; because of a certain nervousness I haven't reread it since I first opened it in hospital. I remembered how its stringency affected me, how I was drawn to it yet found it painful at the time. I start to read her comments on my remark to her that my future had become my present.

> . . . A new kidney would give you some of your future back, but I know that you are not stupid enough to expect the restrictions will lift or your life open out again just as before. So my advice is this: don't conceive of your life as a linear progression through time. A little poem by e. e. cummings has ever pleased me.

> seeker of truth

> follow no path
> all paths lead where

> truth is here

I put the letter down on my bed and stand perfectly still with my eyes shut. Georgia Hill, I need you. I've got my new kidney now, and yes, I'm beginning to think there's a road ahead of me and I'm going along it. No, there isn't a glow at the end, and it's a short road, and contemplating its shortness made me cry this evening, I am ashamed to say.

follow no path – but my life stretches ahead and I'm in the thick of it whether I like it or not. A road or path is a good image for this. Maybe the important word is not *path* but *follow*. To follow is after all to make a choice and then get going and move in the chosen direction. Don't we all have to do that? Or do we? If we live in the moment and let the future arrive, then the path comes to us. Is that what you mean, Georgia Hill? Damn you for dying so soon after I met you. If, when, the truth is here, I'm not sure I'm going to be able to know it when I see it.

15

The only people to witness the marriage of Henrietta Court to Thomas Mentieth are Freddie and Nat, Alice Mentieth, and me from that side of the family, and Lawrence, Poppy and Grace from the other. Freddie is best man; Poppy and Grace stand behind their mother, tears running down their faces throughout the short register office ceremony. It is over before we all take it in, and we find ourselves out on the King's Road in the cold, posing on the steps for Jason, Henrietta's freelance gallery photographer who says he's better at things that don't move than things that do but he'll have a go. We freeze as he fiddles about, and the next wedding party arrives before he's finished so none of us expect much from his efforts. He looks so put out when Henrietta suggests he comes to the wedding party lunch to take a few more shorts that she lets him off with a thank-you kiss.

'You can always take Thomas and me again in the gallery.'

'Natch, Hen. 'Bye and luck!' Jason is a man of few words, and those monosyllabic if he can make them so.

Three taxis take us up to Freddie's house for champagne and food. Henrietta and Thomas travel alone. Freddie goes with Nat and Alice, and I'm deputed to go with Lawrence and the girls since I know the house. Poppy and Grace are not over-friendly, but Lawrence takes my arm and insists I sit on the main seat with him while the girls go on the jump seats.

'Another beautiful hat, Jane.'

'Thank you.'

'Jane always wears hats. The most hatty person I know.'

'We never do. They don't suit us.'

I'm about to explain why I started to wear hats, but suddenly

I can't be bothered. I don't know how much Henrietta has told them about me, and right now I don't care. Lawrence is sitting rather too close to me, and they've noticed. I recross my legs which gives me a chance to shift slightly away. We talk about weddings. I feel a bit hot and sweaty despite the cold outside.

I nip down to the kitchen as soon as we arrive so that I can offer Nat some help. Nat is standing in the middle of the kitchen gazing in despair at a dour-looking old woman in a baggy purple cardigan.

'But how did you know, Elsie?'

'Mrs Mentieth told me, bless her. When she said Mr Thomas was getting married at last, you could of blowed me down with a feather duster.'

I wave at Nat as I disappear to the loo. When I come out, the woman has put on a white frilly apron covered in pink kittens. Nat's despair is turning to stress.

'Now, dear, tell me what needs doing, and let me give you a hand with Mr Thomas's wedding breakfast. I never thought I'd live to see the day. I had to come even though I can feel the flu is brewing. Nothing would stop me.'

'Please don't touch anything, Elsie.' Nat tries to hide the sharpness in her voice by smiling widely and introducing me.

'Hallo, Jane. I'm the boys' old nanny, Elsie. Pleased to meet you. Now, shall I chop these?' She turns away at that point to give a juicy sneeze.

'Jane, could you possibly ask Freddie to come down?' Nat is about to scream in frustration.

'You should put those funny nuts on a nice doily. They look a bit naked in that basket.'

'I'll take them up anyway and offer them round.' I grab the pistachio nuts and run upstairs to join the noisy throng in the sitting room. Freddie is holding forth about *Arboreal Memory* to Grace. I take his hand and say in his ear:

'Nat is desperate. Your old nanny is going to get murdered unless someone goes down pronto.'

'I'll go down, dear.' Alice Mentieth starts to dodder off.

'No, you don't, Alice. Stay put and talk to your new family.' Freddie puts the champagne bottle into my hand. 'Bugger Elsie.' He disappears. Henrietta picks up a strange package.

'I think it's very sweet of her to travel across London to wish us good luck, Thomas. You're being very ungracious about her. Don't you think we should open her present?'

'It's difficult to be gracious about Elsie, as you will no doubt discover. Let's see what this sausage-like object really is.' They take the Christmas paper off with difficulty because of the heavy Sellotaping. Henrietta holds up a long bright green corduroy snake with a red felt tongue and baleful black button eyes.

Grace giggles. 'What on earth is it?'

'A draught excluder, for putting along the bottoms of ill-fitting doors.' Alice touches the felt tongue. 'Elsie makes a lot of these. The one she gave me was orange with a purple tongue.'

'If you put it in the gallery, people might think it was a work of art.' Poppy takes it from her mother and swings it about. 'It would knock a burglar stone cold in an emergency – it's very heavy.'

Thomas fortifies himself with more champagne. 'I'll go down to the kitchen and thank Elsie. And make her leave.'

'If only you can – Freddie's failing dismally,' Nat hisses as she comes in, grabs a glass of champagne and immediately goes out again. I follow her to the dining room.

'This looks lovely, Nat. Gorgeous flowers.'

'I have sweated blood over this party and now that old bat is doing her best to mess the food up and make sure we all get her flu.'

'Poor old thing . . .'

'Jane, she's an evil witch. What's that fairy godmother story? You know, twelve good fairies are followed by the wicked one who casts a spell?' Nat bangs her glass down, spilling champagne. 'She's like that.'

'Calm down, Nat.'

'Why the hell did Alice tell her about this party? She's another old witch.'

'Shsh. She's standing in the other doorway.'

'She's a bit deaf, she won't hear. Oh Jane. This sort of do is a strain without any extra problem. I could wring Elsie's neck.'

'Drink your champagne, take a deep breath, and let Freddie and Thomas get rid of her before you think of going back into the kitchen.'

'You go down, then. Give me a progress report.' Nat joins the others, I go down and find Thomas sitting at the kitchen table with Elsie, encouraging her to finish her sweet sherry.

'I can't abide that champagne.'

'I don't blame you, Elsie. Dry, nasty stuff.' Thomas pretends to inspect his glass.

Freddie snorts as he heaps canapés on to a wooden board.

'You should be careful, Mr Freddie, you don't know what's been on that board.'

'I do, and it will only improve the taste of these.'

'There are some lovely floral dishes in that cupboard.'

'Your health, Elsie!'

'And yours, Mr Thomas.'

'It was very good of you to bring us the splendid useful present, and I believe you made it yourself.'

'Mr Snake will keep you snug.'

Freddie snorts again before carrying the canapés to the door. 'Bring that other load up, would you, Jane.' He disappears upstairs.

'Guests shouldn't hand round food. Let me do it.' Elsie gets up, meaning business.

Thomas suddenly leaps to his feet, full of resolve. 'Jane is family, of course she can help. You must go home now, Elsie. Go home and nurse your flu. We're very touched you came, but this is a small family party and none of us can spare the time to run you home. I'm going to order a taxi and of course pay for it, and you will be a dear and leave when it arrives.'

'You're angry that I came.'

'Not at all, Elsie. I mean it when I say I'm touched.'

'I'll get the cab organised.'

'Thank you, Jane. Now drink up your sherry, Elsie. I'll stay with you until the taxi is here.'

I run upstairs and tell Nat to summon her nearest minicab which she does with alacrity. Five minutes later Elsie is shown out with great ceremony and some warm hugs to mollify her, and then Thomas makes everyone laugh by parading round the room with the snake round his neck.

Nat and I go to the kitchen to bring up the soup. She reaches for Elsie's glass to move it to the dishwasher and it slips and smashes.

'Never mind.' She kicks the pieces under the table. 'I'll clear it up later. Thank God Elsie's gone.'

'I can't help feeling a bit sorry for her.'

'You wouldn't if you knew her as I know her,' Nat snaps at me so I just keep quiet and help. Freddie has made a beautiful fish soup and the whole party goes into contented silence to consume it. It's followed by a cold main course, and at last Nat begins to relax and look as if she's enjoying herself.

Freddie stands up to toast Henrietta. 'To a most wonderfully easy-going bride! Tom doesn't know how lucky he is – no morning suits, no big do, no hassle . . .'

'I do, actually.' That's all Thomas says as he raises his glass, but the tone is enough to make Henrietta go pink.

'I think it's a pity you didn't have a church wedding, though I suppose you're both a bit old.'

'It has nothing to do with age, Mother.' Thomas is crisp. 'We didn't want one. Henrietta is a Roman Catholic, and I'm an agnostic heavily tinged with atheism, so this solution is far the best.'

'A white wedding is so lovely. I well remember your beautiful dress, Natalie. So becoming.' Alice smiles in a half-hearted way at her disappointing daughter-in-law. No grandchildren and no sign of them.

Henrietta stands up. 'Thank you for my toast, Freddie. And for laying on such a good do. It's all very different from my first time round. When I married Jeremy I wore a white dress with a train and had to carry a bouquet that was far too heavy. And I had a circlet of flowers round my head which kept the veil in place but was hellishly tight. I was in agonies. The photographs afterwards went on and on, and I wanted to rip the bloody thing off my head by the end, it was so excruciating!' Henrietta joins in our laughter. 'I was only twenty, a lamb to the slaughter.'

'What an odd thing to say, Mum.' Grace is in purple which doesn't suit her; Poppy is in purple too, but on her it sings. 'Dad was a lovely kind man. Slaughter. Really!'

'I mean I was a young innocent bride who was so wet behind the ears you young things wouldn't credit it.'

There's a little awkward silence, then Thomas lifts his glass again. 'To Jeremy.'

The silence becomes more pointed until Grace says, 'To Dad and all our happy memories.'

'To Dad.' Poppy's identical voice meshes with her sister's.

'To Jeremy.' Henrietta looks as if she's going to add something, but instead puts her hand briefly over Thomas's and we all drink together.

'Who is this Jeremy? Should I know him?'

Freddie stands up again, ignoring his mother. 'As best man I ought to make a speech. Relax, I'm not going to, beyond saying this. My brother is famous – infamous – for never turning up to any family occasions. The weddings and funerals he's missed run into dozens. Yet, here he is, in London in time for a wedding! Even with days to spare! Unheard of. Let's drink to Thomas, and may he be more present in the future than he's been in the past!'

Everyone cheers but Thomas looks rather annoyed. 'Hold on, Freddie, there's always been a very good reason for me not turning up to things.' He is shouted down and Henrietta gives him a hug. I still can't see what she sees in him but there's no accounting for tastes. Whereas Freddie . . . I won't forget my initial feeling of pure envy when I first saw what my big sister had netted. Nets . . . I look down the table at Natalie.

She's at the far end, talking to Poppy. They've found a friend in common and are announcing this with cries of surprise to Grace. I remember that story about a fishing net on the beach – Nat swears I pinned her down with it, making her really panic, but all I remember is chucking it at her to wake her up, because I wanted her to come and play. Yet from what she said, this incident became a milestone in her life – millstone might be a better word – which haunted her and gave her nightmares. She'd wake up feeling the wet tarry rope on her face, the seaweed, the weight of it all, and want to scream.

She's screaming with Poppy at the moment, but with laughter. Nat's looking at her best today, in creams and browns and exquisite amber jewellery I've never seen before. I'm in my usual blues, and the long viridian chiffon scarf that gives such a lift to blue clothes.

'You're very quiet today, Jane.'

Freddie is sitting beside me, with Henrietta on his other side. He'd been talking to her so I wasn't aware he'd stopped and was watching me.

'A lot's happened in the last year.'

'It certainly has. And this wedding is a particularly nice way to end it.'

'More could happen – we've got three weeks of December left.'

'I hope not. How are you, by the way? Everything as it should be?'

'Yes, fine. I've got my next check-up in a few days. Haven't had one for a month.'

'You look fine, better and better. What a noise your sister is making – it must be the Irish influence.' Nat and Poppy have drawn Grace into a stream of vivid reminiscences about the person they all know. Freddie turns back to me.

'You missed our wedding. I was thinking about that on the way back here. It's nice to have you with us for this one.'

'I'm so happy for Henrietta.'

'I'm so happy for my brother. Never in a million years did I think he'd marry.'

'Nor did he, I imagine.'

'And you, Jane? Is marriage for you one day?'

'It depends. Living with someone is more my line – I wouldn't want to make the promises they made today.'

There's a pause as Freddie frowns over what I've said. 'Because of your illness?'

'Because of the way life is.'

'Nat and I made those promises.'

'I would expect you to, Freddie. I can't commit myself in the same way.'

'You might feel differently if you met the right person.'

'You are in a sentimental mood today, Freddie. Weddings do that to us, I suppose. If I met the right person as you put it, well, given my cussed nature I might not recognise their rightness, and if I did, I'd be even more wary of total commitment. They might consume me!'

'You've done very well, you know. I honestly admire the way you've got on top of what has happened to you.'

'It took a while. And I've still got some way to go – is that what you were thinking?'

'Not at all.'

'Because you're right. People say: "Oh Jane, you're back to normal," whatever that is, but I'll never get back to normal. And I don't regret it, so don't feel sorry for me.'

'I can't help feeling sorry for you.'

'Freddie, DON'T.' I'm fierce; he flinches, but holds my gaze. 'I can't bear it if anyone feels sorry for me, least of all you. There are hidden things in my life, good things, which would never have happened to me had I not collapsed. So don't feel sorry for me ever again!'

'What are you two talking about so intensely?' Henrietta's face is flushed and her eyes are sparkling.

'The art of living.' I laugh with her.

'Time for another speech.' Lawrence is also flushed, and fairly drunk. 'It's my turn to make one.'

'But no one's made a speech, Lol.'

'Well, say a few words then. I call it a speech.' He pulls a card out of his top pocket and puts on his reading glasses as he stands up. 'No one had a better sister than I've had. I didn't lose her when she married Jeremy, and I'm hoping for the same—'

'Of course, dear fellow, of course.' Thomas interrupts. 'Goes without saying.'

'Nothing goes without saying. It all should be said on an occasion like this.' Lawrence tries to focus on his card. 'Yes. Whoever marries Henrietta is a lucky man—'

Henrietta stands behind her brother, putting one hand over his mouth while removing the card with the other. 'Lol, my dearest darling brother, shut up. You're too drunk to make sense, and we don't need any speeches anyway.'

'I wanted to thank all these good people—'

'Let's thank them together then. Let's drink a toast to our hosts.' Henrietta puts her arm round her brother as she lifts her glass. 'To Natalie and Freddie!'

'And to the absence of Elsie!' Thomas raises his glass again. 'Who always had the knack of ruining one's fun.'

'You're being very mean about her,' says Alice. 'I regarded her as an excellent nanny. She kept you both tidy and clean and punctual. Very efficient was Elsie. I think all this criticism is very unfair.'

'She cast a miasma over my childhood.' Thomas is staring

blankly into space. 'I used to think when I was a boy that if wives were like her, I didn't want one.'

'Thomas, what a thing to say!' But Alice's protests are drowned by everyone's laughter and then Henrietta takes Thomas by the hand and pulls him away from the table.

'It's time we went back to the gallery to collect our things or we'll miss our train to Scotland. Poppy, Grace, would you like to come back with us or will you stay on?'

'Stay for a bit if we may. Uncle Lol needs a good strong coffee.'

'I'm perfectly all right.'

Henrietta goes round the table kissing everyone goodbye. 'Keep the party going, won't you? I'm sorry we've got to leave.'

But it's hard to keep a party going when the reason for the celebration departs. Poppy and Grace throw themselves into helping Nat and me to clear up, Freddie sits having coffee with Lawrence downstairs out of duty. I put the dining room straight while the others work downstairs, but it's an effort. I feel utterly exhausted and drained, and still have the slightly over-heated feeling that's been with me all day. Too much food and drink and excitement, says Nat, and she's right.

16

Sunday is one of those cold dark days when there is a mile of thick cloud between you and the sun. I'm feeling so tired and generally off-colour I decide to spend the day in bed; Sara is away seeing her parents and I've got nothing planned. I was going to try and see a few exhibitions but I know I'm just not up to it today. I make myself a mug of tea and some toast, and draw the curtains again to shut out the gloomy outside world. I put the radio on near my bed. Maybe I'll go out later for a paper, maybe I won't.

As I lie back I realise I've forgotten my usual routine, not for the first time recently. I haven't weighed myself for a couple of days, or taken my blood pressure, or my temperature. The habitual checking is becoming rather less ingrained as time has passed. I take my medication, but decide to skip the rest for this morning. I'll do it all this evening. I'm sure it's the weather and the pressures of life recently that are making me feel so low today – I know I've been overdoing it. I sneeze a couple of times and wonder whether I've caught that old woman's flu. It would account for my shaky feeling.

I fall asleep after drinking my tea and don't wake until midday. Not that it looks like midday: the sky is now black, and heavy with a looming thunderstorm. Lightning divides the clouds as I look out, followed within ten seconds by a good clap of thunder. I open a carton of soup and heat it, and then take it through to the sitting room and switch on the television. I never normally watch television in daytime, but I really feel I might be getting flu, and want to take my mind off the unwelcome possibility.

By chance, there's a programme about the Great Barrier Reef where I once spent an enchanted time with Jake, and I vicariously descend again with the camera through intensely blue sea to coral reefs thick with darting fish in mad shapes and colours. I leave the sound down so that it's like an underwater silence. Jake. What a good diver he was; he taught me well. Our week together on Lady Ellis Island was in early September. Low slanting spring sunlight, peculiarly golden, lit the bleached, sea-smoothed shells on the shoreline. I lay with my nose inches from honeycombed white shapes like fossilised sponges, watching Jake as he headed out across the reef that rimmed the little island. Crazy Jake – he was covered with cuts from the razor-sharp coral and any sharks around were bound to scent his blood.

Jake. I switch off the programme and shut my eyes. Jake. Large, blond, physically the archetypal Australian. Great in and on water, insensitive as a lover and friend. A hunk with a small heart and no imagination. He had a good brain though, got a decent degree, seemed very bright. I was (still am?) an intellectual snob and he fooled me.

I've got an envelope of photos somewhere; I know I brought them with me when I left Sydney. I just couldn't throw away the recorded evidence of my years with Jake, so I packed them even though looking at his image gives me no pleasure now.

The lightning and thunder continue while I search through my chest of drawers until I find the packet at the very bottom of the last drawer. I take it out and get back into bed. It's like looking into someone else's life. I can barely remember the names of all those friends we had at uni. And as for Jake – the pain I felt over him has really gone. His square smile, his pale blue eyes, his habit of sticking his chin in the air and sliding a look down at you: none of those evoke love or anger any more. There he is, astride his bike, riding into the future, looking a complete moron. How could I have been so besotted with him? Even the photo I used to particularly love, taken from above as he lay on the beach, doing nothing. I'm cured. I knew I was, but hadn't dared look at these snaps and put it to the test.

Dad looks miserable in the few photos I've got of him. He so hates being photographed and it always shows. Some-how though, his uneasy smile and his tenseness pull hard at my heart. I ought to ring him. I hope he's not still hurt that I haven't taken up his offer to share a house in

Sydney. I drop back on to my pillows, the photos lying all round me.

When I came to England I left behind an emotional mess of my own making – not that I'd have admitted it then. Breaking up with Jake after my abortion seemed his fault more than mine; my difficulties with my father I also blamed on Dad, on his selfishness, his absorption in his new work, his neglect of me. I was betrayed, I was let down, life had gone sour. I'd go back to England, make a new life. So I pushed all my broken toys into a cupboard, forgot them, and tried to find new toys in a new room. How pathetic I was.

I realise now my kidneys would have failed there as they did here, sooner or later. I try to imagine a rerun of what it could have been like in Sydney. No Jake to support me, only Dad, in a life similar to the one I've had here, tied to the renal department of a hospital so closely that it becomes a second home. With no Nat, no Freddie, no Sara, no Joe, no Dave, no Jacob, no Henrietta, and no Georgia Hill. I can see *Last Count* on the shelf—

The phone rings and photographs cascade off the bed as I go to collect it from its base and answer it. It's Toby Sherwood, his slight stammer suddenly evident.

'Hallo, Toby.'

'How d-did you know it was me?'

'I'm good at voices. Isn't it a dreadful day?'

'That's why I've rung. I hate all this d-darkness and rain. End of the world stuff.'

'I'm in bed with the curtains drawn so I can't see it.'

'Are you ill?'

'Just exhausted. Might be getting flu, but I hope not. I'm in charge of the gallery for the next two weeks while Henrietta's on honeymoon.'

'Big responsibility.'

'It is. So how's life, Toby?' There's another rumble of thunder, and my windows shake in the wind.

'Bad. I had a terrible nightmare last night. I'm glad my parents are away, because I woke up yelling and banging the wall.'

'Tell me about the nightmare.'

'Oh, it's the usual thing. A version of the crash, only this time with me in front, somehow driving, but everything breaks in my hands.'

'Poor Toby. Are your parents on holiday?'

'Just for a week. Would – would you like to come down today? I just had the idea – but I suppose the weather is too bad.'

'I'm not feeling well enough anyway.'

'It's not serious, Jane, is it?'

'No, no, I'm just tired. Look, Toby, if it helps, you could come here instead, just for a cup of tea and a chat. You're welcome. If being on your own gets you down . . .'

'I can't. I've no money for fares until my next dole payout. My mother left me well stocked with food, but my travelling is down to me. I had to go to two job interviews this week. My budget's run out.'

'How did the interviews go?'

'One badly, one quite well. It was for a job I didn't much want, so I suppose I was relaxed about it. I'll have to take it if I get it.'

'Perhaps you did better than you think in the other one.'

'No. They told me then and there they didn't need me.'

'Let me know if you get the other and we'll celebrate, Toby.'

'You're the only one who c-cares what I do.'

'I'm sure I'm not.'

'Since Alfie died, I've felt like a pariah.'

'Everyone finds it difficult to deal long term with other people's disasters. Lots of sympathy at first, and then the backing off. People feel inadequate because they don't know what to do or say.'

'And you change and they don't.'

'Maybe.'

'I feel a hundred years older than my older brother. He used to despise me for trying to be an academic. Now he's just nervous of me. I've got an incurable disease called grief which he can't handle.'

'I'll get very angry if you go on talking like that. Grief is not a disease, and it's not incurable.'

There's a longish silence before Toby mumbles, 'Sorry, Jane. That was . . . Sorry. I . . . Goodbye.'

'Let me know how the job goes. 'Bye, Toby.' But I don't think he hears me, because the phone's gone dead.

I lie on in bed and allow my annoyance to fade. I can see why

Toby's friends are giving him a wide berth, but at the same time, I like him. I like him because he's so vulnerable and open with me. He's broke, lonely, and at the bottom of his heap with only upwards to go. He makes me feel strong and wise, which is dangerous, for I know I'm neither. Neither. Just a little wiser than I was.

I fall asleep again surrounded by bright images of Australia.

The doorbell wakes me. I fumble my way to the entryphone and pause before I pick it up. Can I cope with a visitor? It might be Dave, and I certainly couldn't handle him today. The bell gives another sad little ring, as if the caller is about to give up. It's not Dave – he'd give the bell hell. I pick up the entryphone.

'It's Toby.'

'Toby!'

'I hitch-hiked. I felt so awful about what I'd said.'

'Toby, I've been asleep since I spoke to you. I'm not dressed. I can't really see anyone.'

'I just . . . Don't worry. I'll go again, it doesn't matter.' A police car is passing noisily behind him and I can hardly hear him.

'No, of course you mustn't turn round and go. I'll give you some tea, but I need half an hour to get sorted. Go for a walk and come back.'

'I'm such an idiot . . . why did I come?'

'Toby, shut up. See you in half an hour.'

And so I have to rouse my sluggish body and get up. A brisk, very hot shower and some jazz on high volume help, and by the time Toby returns the flat is smelling of hot buttered toast and the tea is made and on a tray in the sitting room, with lights brightly lit and the deep litter of newspapers dropped behind the sofa to make the place look less bleak. The flat needs a thorough clean – neither Sara nor I have done much to it for weeks.

Toby is as wet as an otter. 'It just started to bucket down again.'

'Hang your anorak here so that it drips on to the kitchen floor. I'll put the oven on to dry it. Have a towel for your hair.'

He smells of musty damp clothes, wet dog smells, and I don't want to encourage him to take his soaked trainers off. They'll dry quicker on him than off, anyway. He combs his wet hair back, and reveals his well-proportioned forehead and strong eyebrows which normally lurk unseen under his mess of hair.

'It's a nice flat. Have you got good flatmates?'

'Perfect. Sara is a sweetie, and Mark is working abroad for the moment but has paid his rent so he's ideal in a different way. They're college friends of my sister's, and in fact she lived here until she got married. I'm in her old room. Help yourself to lots of toast – half of them have honey on, half marmite. I didn't know which you'd prefer.'

'You must think I'm mad, coming to see you like this.'

'Well . . .'

'I think I'm mad but I couldn't stop myself. I thought, I'll hitch-hike to central London, and before I could reflect on my lack of wisdom, I was in a van that smelt of oily tools, on my way with a very nice chap, a plumber, who dropped me off in Balham. Then I walked. I've eaten all the marmite toast – sorry.'

'Don't worry, I like honey. I'll make more in a minute. I love hot buttered toast. And it's got to be good white bread, thickly cut. Just like this.'

Toby leans back in his chair and closes his eyes. He's so thin and tense and unrelaxed that up to now I haven't really seen what his face looks like. I suddenly imagine him a stone heavier, with a good haircut and wearing decent clothes, and see a new and different person. His face is actually rather forceful in repose yet when he talks one is only aware of his shyness and insecurity, his 'grotty student' aura.

I leave him there and go to make more toast. Sara should be back soon. She usually tries to avoid the traffic jams by coming back from the country early. She hasn't met Toby before. He's standing up in front of the gas fire almost steaming when I go back with the toast.

'Did you dialyse here in the flat?'

'No. It wasn't possible.'

'How hard it must have been for you.'

'They say one of the worst moments of all is if you have to go back on dialysis after a period off it.'

Toby's eyes flick to my face, away, and back. 'It won't happen to you. You'll be all right.'

'I may well not be. You have to understand, Toby, that I may lose Alfie's kidney. It's working very well, and I'm beginning to count on it, so I'm really talking to myself as much as you, warning myself not to take anything for granted.'

'You're telling me something is going wrong, aren't you?'

'Of course not – I just don't want you to get too much comfort from the fact that a part of Alfie is still alive inside me.'

'It's tempting.'

'I know.'

'I'm really sorry about what I said. Grief can't be anything like as hard to bear as your condition was. The trouble about grief is that you think it's unbearable for so long that you don't realise you're beginning to bear it, and when you do realise it you get upset because you are.' He laughs, a natural infectious laugh that makes me join in. When he laughs his long face becomes squarer immediately and the whites of his eyes are less noticeable as his eyes crinkle up. Does grief change the way you look? It must do – all the body's muscles must be affected by day-long sadness, tears, depression.

'Sorry, say that again, Toby – didn't hear the last bit.'

'I said, I'm sure people hang on to grief because they're afraid of forgetting the person who died.'

'You'll never forget Alfie.'

'No. But I think about her much less than I did, and it feels like a betrayal.'

'That's perfectly natural, I'd say.'

'Meeting you has helped me.' He's gone tense again, and his drying hair is flopping down over his eyes. 'I had to come and tell you how much.' His hands are clamped on his knees, he's hunched and flushed, possibly from the warmth as well as his feelings.

'It isn't me particularly, you know. Anyone in my position, given a new lease of life by Alfie, would have helped you just the same.'

'Come off it, Jane. Her other kidney went into a crabby old bugger who would have said fuck off if I'd asked to meet him. He lost the kidney anyway.'

I think of Eric and others like him and grin at Toby. 'You have a point. I just don't want you to pin too much on me.'

'It's inevitable. You are the first light at the end of my tunnel. Cliché but true.'

'How many new people have you got to know since Alfie died?' He stares at me and I stare back. 'I'm the first woman, I'll bet. Yes? I thought so. You must separate me, Jane Harper, from the natural sense of rebirth you'd be feeling now anyway. Your body's mended, your heart is mending. Eat up the toast, Toby. I've had all I want.'

Toby takes a piece and looks at his feet while he chews it. He takes another piece and another. I sip my tea, happy to be silent, waiting for him to speak.

'You're telling me not to fall in love with you.'

'If there's the slightest danger of that, yes, I am.'

'I don't know my own mind any more. I feel one thing, then I feel another. I suddenly hitch-hike to London. I am a bit mad at the moment.'

'I certainly was when my kidneys first failed on me. I was so angry at the unfairness of it I felt as if I would shrivel up.'

'You're not angry any more.'

'Is that a question?'

'Yes – no – you don't seem angry.'

'I think my anger was a bit like your grief.'

Toby finishes the toast while we both think about this.

'What made your anger go, Jane?'

'Time. Circumstances. Lack of choice. You can't keep railing at the present if your future becomes your present. There's no point – it's a dead-end.' Toby waits for me to go on. He's a good listener, I'm discovering. 'And various people helped me. A fellow patient, Jacob, was very good to me, gave me courage.' The thought of how Jacob had gone from my life pierces me again. 'My flatmate Sara has been a great support recently, though at first she couldn't cope. She was like my sister, neither of them were much help to start with. Nat still isn't. She's too wrapped up in her own world: older husband, big house, challenging job.'

Toby shifts in his chair uneasily. 'You sound jealous.'

'I wouldn't want Nat's life.'

'Your voice changed when you mentioned her, that's all.'

'There's a vast bog of past unpleasantness between us with a few bridges over it.'

'The one you were on went wobbly.' We smile. 'I haven't got a single bridge that I can use between my brother Anthony and me.'

'You said he despised you. That makes it hard. I don't think Nat has ever despised me – hated me, feared me, but not despised me. Nor me her.'

'Anthony worships money, cars and the fast lane. He's a total materialist, and it doesn't look as if he'll ever change. I embarrass him with my charity shop clothes and total lack of style. To be honest, he embarrasses me just as much. When we're together we both burn and squirm.'

'Did he like Alfie?'

'He's a racist. Not quite National Front but not far off.' Toby picks at a hole in his jeans. 'He said it disgusted him to think of Alfie and me together.'

'What about your parents?'

'They liked Alfie. Mum's open-minded, Dad less so, but he follows her lead.'

I'm just letting him talk. I suspect he's been living in a silent world of misery and talking about his everyday life with Alfie and without her has been a desperate but unsatisfied need. So he chatters on and I make little kick-start comments when he stops. He slides a look at me after one of them.

'I ought to go now. You're tired.'

'I think it's actually stopped raining.'

'And you're bored. I've become so boring.' He stands up, tipping his mug over with his foot as he does so. 'Relax, it's empty. Thank you for tea and toast and everything.'

I can hear Sara coming in, shouting hi Jane as she carries an armload of branches into the sitting room.

'Sorry, I didn't know you had a visitor.'

'Meet Toby Sherwood, Sara.'

'I'm just going actually . . .'

'Don't let me drive you out because I've come in with the forest of Dunsinane. I thought these would look good in that corner, Jane, they'd cover up the stain Dave made when he threw a samosa at Ginny. Mum gave me this old vase to put them in. What do you think?'

Toby has gone all angular and long-faced again; he leaves

promptly, firmly refusing my offer of some money for a train fare.

'Who on earth was Toby Sherwood, Jane? And he smelt of wet dog.'

'I know – he got absolutely drenched coming here.' I quickly explain who Toby is while Sara puts her branches in an ugly brass vase.

'So he just arrived out of the blue?'

'More or less.'

'Shades of Dave. Oh, and how was the wedding?'

'Great. That's why I'm so knackered – it was a long day.'

'How did Nat cope? She was in quite a state about hosting the reception, as she put it. Is Nat getting a bit pompous or am I imagining it?'

'She was fine, considering.'

'Tell me all. Let's make more tea first. And toast. I can smell toast.'

'I'll make you some.'

'Is Toby Sherwood in love with you?'

'He couldn't really love anyone in his present state.'

'Don't be too sure. He had that look in his eye. Nice eyes, pity about the rest of him. Now, tell me all about this wedding.'

17

When I reach the gallery on Monday morning, it's locked and unlit. Normally I would let myself in but I had to lend my keys to Poppy and Grace over the weekend, and Lawrence said he'd be there to open up. I ring the upper bell and wait. Perhaps Lawrence is in the shower or still asleep. I ring again, hard.

The sky above me is blue-black again with unshed rain, and the air is heavy. The storm of yesterday seems to be about to return. After a third try on the bell, I pop over to the travel agents opposite. Polly, the manager, is staring out into the street and waves at me as I cross it.

'Have you seen Mr Court at all this morning?'

'I saw him go off in a taxi with two young ladies about half an hour ago.'

'He didn't leave a key with you by any lucky chance? Oh well. Could I have a sheet of paper? I need to leave him a message. He's forgotten I gave my keys to his guests.'

'Mr Court's been locked out himself lots of times. Not good with keys, is he?'

'No, Polly. Not good with keys. I'll call back at one – that's what I've said in the note. Tell him if you see him, just to reinforce it.'

It's ten o'clock. The gallery should be open. I go and search near the door to see if there's any hiding place for keys, but find nothing. I hear the phone ring inside, and it goes on and on. He's even forgotten to switch on the answerphone.

So, deeply frustrated, I find myself unexpectedly free though I don't want to be, with three hours to kill in bad weather. I wander aimlessly along Victoria Street towards the Army & Navy Stores, cursing Lawrence almost audibly in my frustration. My first morning in charge of the gallery and I can't even get in. Say Henrietta takes it into her head to ring and see how I'm getting on? I boil.

A large stripy brick building catches my eye in a sort of piazza on my right. It's Westminster Cathedral, I realise; I'd never noticed it before, tucked away off Victoria Street as it is, though I'd seen its Byzantine roofline from a distance. Rain starts to fall so I hurry towards the Roman Catholic heart of London. Perhaps if I sit down for a while and calm myself I will think of something constructive to do with my morning. I certainly don't want to be cooped up in the flat again, even though I'm still feeling slight flu symptoms.

When a large building is hemmed in by smaller ones, there's a strong tension in the spaces between. Westminster Cathedral climbs into the sky as if stretching itself free of all the stripy offspring clinging to its skirts. Westminster Abbey down the way is calm and weighty; this cathedral is impatient and exuberant. I enter eagerly, and then stand in disappointment.

They have never finished the inside. I gaze at the blackened brick, dark like the outside sky, which arches above out of the marble-lined walls. The marble ends brusquely and the ceiling cries out for mosaic, the upper walls for more marble or fresco. The High Altar area is fully completed and while I sit and admire its gaudy splendour crashing, curdling organ music suddenly fills the building. Someone is practising. I sit and listen, conscious of the dark brick above me and the glitter ahead and around. Perhaps the unfinished building makes a point: it reminds one of the inherent conflict between Christ's poverty and these lavish surroundings of ecclesiastical life.

I haven't sat in a church for years, and would stay longer but for the painfully invasive music – one noisy discord barely resolves itself before another starts. As I leave I ask a passing priest if he could tell me what the music is.

'Messiaen. Isn't it splendid? Utterly splendid.'

He doesn't wait for an answer, and I find myself in the wet and windy piazza outside feeling I've missed something.

At one o'clock, back at the gallery nothing has changed. No sign of life, and Polly tells me she's seen nobody return.

'But there was one of your clients – I went over when I saw

him ringing away at the bell. He had an appointment but he said he'd give you a ring tomorrow.'

'Thank you, Polly. I'd better leave a note on the door. This is driving me mad.'

As I stick up a notice, the phone rings inside, on and on. Long enough to turn on the answerphone, and I can just hear Henrietta's voice leaving a message, though can't make out what. I can guess. I push another note for Lawrence through the door to say I'll try once more hoping to find him there at four o'clock, and go off to get myself some lunch. I ring Nat on her mobile just in case she's free and we can meet, but it's switched off. I think of Dave, then drop the idea. Dave can be so complicated.

I buy a copy of *Private Eye* and read it over lunch. Cheered by it, I decide not to let my annoyance with Lawrence spoil a free day. I must go and look at something in London I haven't yet seen. As my mood changes, so does the weather. Pale blue sky is pushing the clouds away; a sharp wind blows paper in wild eddies round the station. I take the tube to Tottenham Court Road, intending to visit an unfamiliar department of the British Museum, but then I notice an advertisement for Sir John Soane's Museum and my heart lifts. Yes, that's where I'll go. I check my *A–Z* and walk the short distance to Lincoln's Inn Fields. Its size is a surprise after the roar of traffic in Holborn; huge plane trees creak in the wind, round seedheads dancing. It must be one of the biggest squares in London; it's certainly one of the most beautiful. I notice where the museum is as I pass, but I'm so attracted by the open space I decide to walk through it first. As I reach the central area containing benches under the plane trees, a bundled tramp ahead of me buckles at the knee and falls heavily to one side. There are several other people about but they melt away, eyes down, with furtive speed.

I kneel beside the tramp; he's muffled in many smelly layers, and has a green bobble hat pulled low over his brow and ears. He's gasping and groaning with pain.

'What happened?'

'Ankle bloody gave way.' There's a pothole into which he must have stepped.

'Try and sit up, and I'll help you to a bench.'

'Fuck. Bloody fuck.' He heaves himself on to his knees. 'I'm lost.'

'We're in Lincoln's Inn Fields—'

'I bloody know that, lady. Lost without my feet is what I bloody mean. Fuck.' He stays on hands and knees, cursing and groaning. I'm half tempted to melt away like the others, but I find myself propping him up as he hobbles to a bench. His smell is rich, and his nose is running. He sneezes, and I manage to get well away from the spray. TB goes through my mind.

'I'm fucked if I can't walk. I walk all day.' He meets my eyes for the first time, and I see two sharp hazel eyes at odds with the mess of broken veins, scabs, stubble and grime. He looks away quickly, down at his feet in worn trainers with string for laces. He's wearing a thick assortment of socks which makes the trainers bulge open.

'What can I do to help?'

He wags his head in pain and despair, rubbing at his twisted ankle.

'Is there somewhere you could go so that you could rest your foot and have it seen to?'

'I'm lost if I can't walk.'

'I'll pay for a taxi. Just tell me where it can take you.' I realise it's probably pointless asking him this, but a hospital casualty department doesn't seem appropriate for a sprain. 'A hostel somewhere?'

'I walk ten miles a day when the weather's good. Wasn't good yesterday, had to hole up down Waterloo.'

'Do you want to go there?'

He doesn't answer. A tear trickles from each eye as he gazes at his feet.

'Look, I'm going to fetch you a cup of sweet tea and something to eat while you decide what to do.'

'Bloody hurts, it does.'

'I'll be five minutes.' From a snack bar in Holborn, I buy him a sealed polystyrene cup of tea with three sugars, a cheese and ham roll, and a Danish pastry, and hurry back to the Fields. I can't see the green bobble hat – the idiot has gone, dragged himself off – no, he's there, he's moved to another bench.

'Better bench. Out of the wind.'

I wonder if this is all an act to get food and money, and hand him the small paper carrier bag.

'I nearly fell over again, hopping to it. Ta.' He opens the tea and sips it. 'Ta. You not having any?'

'Not now.'

'Never thought you'd come back. Most people don't.' His voice and accent is unplaceable, and roughened by life on the streets, but the odd vowel gives away a middle-class background. Curious about him, I sit on the other end of the bench. London is full of tramps and beggars, but I've never talked to one before. Brisk gusts of wind shake the trees above as he coughs his terrible racking cough.

'You fell so heavily, I couldn't leave you.'

'Most would.'

'Tell me where you'd like to go to rest that foot. What about that place in Vauxhall? Bondway I think it's called?' I've passed this place often enough in bus and car.

'Is this ham and cheese?'

'Yes.'

'Can't eat cheese.' He picks the slices out and drops them under the bench. 'Never could. Allergic to it.' He rolls the word round his mouth. 'Allergic.'

'It must be difficult having an allergy when you live like – like this.'

He ignores my remark and eats his roll with a combination of dainty bites and noisy open-mouthed chewing. He stops between each bite to check for cheese. This food could take him a while to eat.

'When did you start to live like this?' The blue sky arches overhead without a cloud now, but the wind is biting. I am getting cold.

'When I lost my job.'

'What work did you do?'

There's a pause. He chews, swallows. 'Everything unbegan when I lost my driving licence.'

Unbegan. His eyes lift briefly, then go back to his roll. I say nothing, I don't want him to stop.

'Lost my bloody licence. Lost my bloody job. Lost my wife. No home. Here I am.' He belches loudly, and takes out the Danish pastry.

'How long ago?'

'Don't remember.' He starts on the pastry which clearly appeals to him more than the roll, though he still picks out the glacé cherries. I wonder how old he is; it's impossible to tell from his dirty skin and his matted hair. His eyes don't look that old.

'Did you go to college or university?'

'Too many questions.'

'Sorry. I'm – just interested. Didn't mean to pry.'

'My past is gone and my future is gone with it. And if this foot doesn't get better my present is fucking gone too.' His voice thickens, he rubs his ankle and then stands up. He puts weight on the damaged foot and sits down smartly. 'I've bloody broken it.'

'I don't think you could have. But if you like I'll get a taxi to drop you at a casualty department for an X-ray—'

'No hospital.'

'Make another suggestion then.'

'What taxi?'

'I'm offering you a taxi to take you somewhere to get that foot seen to.' If he hears the annoyance creeping into my voice he gives no sign.

'Why are you doing this?'

'I've got no idea. Kindness maybe?' I feel like adding it's about to run out.

'No taxi driver would let me through the door.'

'I'm prepared to try. There's a rank over there.' The walk over damps down my rising irritation, and I find the tramp is right.

'Sorry, love, don't need no more problem passengers.'

'I'll pay extra . . .'

'No go. He's probably having you on anyway, lay you a bet his ankle's fine.'

There are three cabs on the rank, and they all refuse. As I stand wondering what to do next, the first leans out of his cab and calls me over.

'Miss! How bad's his pong then?'

'Doesn't seem too bad, to be honest. He really fell, he can't walk. It's not a con.'

'Where do you want to take him?'

'Bondway in Vauxhall?' I hadn't planned on going too, but I see that's the only way out. The driver wouldn't do it on his own.

'Get him over, then. But if he's wet, you know, dirty and wet behind, it's no go.'

'Give us five minutes.'

I hear the other cabbies ribbing the driver with comments about Father Teresa as I head back to the tramp. He's started fumbling through his knapsack, which appears to be full of dog-eared photographs and cards. He closes it up again as I arrive.

'Ready for take-off?'

'Go on.'

'The front cabbie's agreed to take us to Bondway.'

'You don't give in easy, do you? How am I bloody going to get across there?'

'Put your hand on my shoulder and hop.'

It's not easy, and fortunately a smartly suited man passing us stops and helps by taking over the propping.

'Well done.' I'm not sure whether he's talking to the tramp or to me. 'Well done.'

Together we push the tramp into the taxi, and my helper says well done again before disappearing.

The taxi journey is surreal. It begins with the tramp refusing to wear a seat-belt and the driver refusing to go any further unless he does.

'It's called the Law, mate. The Law. Heard of the Law?'

'Put the belt on, please. You have to.'

'I know my rights.'

'This isn't one of them.' I pull the belt out as far as I can and bring it over him. Being so close makes me want to gag at the smell, but I get the belt done up. He tries to undo it but fails to find the catch, and the driver starts off again.

'What's your name?'

'Jane. What's yours?'

'AB. ABCDEFG.' He laughs.

'OK. I'll call you Alph.'

'What's this Alf?'

'Your name is Alphabet, from what you said.'

'Alph. That's a good one. I could use it in future.' He cackles again.

'What's your real name?'

'I've forgotten. Haven't used it in years.'

'How could anyone forget their own name?'

'This life makes you forget everything. That's good, on the whole. Better to forget.'

'You haven't forgotten about losing your licence.'

'I need to go to the toilet.'

'Don't even think about it, mate.' The driver's voice cuts across our conversation. 'Or out you get.'

'We're nearly there, Alph. Look, there's Waterloo Station. Just another few minutes.' I've had enough of this encounter and I'm afraid the tramp might pee or crap just to make a point. Luckily he doesn't and in silence we finish the journey. His expression is of someone whose insides are troubling him, but when we reach our destination he's in no hurry to get out of the taxi. Our driver nips off to fetch someone from the hostel, and comes back to urge his unwelcome passenger to vacate his precious vehicle.

'Out you get now.'

'Got a fag you could give me?'

'Don't smoke, mate. And with that cough you shouldn't either. Come on, out you get.'

'Never said I wanted to come to this place.'

'Slide along the seat, will you?' The cabbie's getting irritated.

'Never liked this place.'

'There's the warden coming out to help you.'

'That's not the warden, that's Ginger.'

'Hallo, hallo, if it isn't our Reg. I'm told you've done your ankle in.'

'Tell the cabbie I want to go back to the Fields.'

Eventually Alph/Reg is eased out of the cab, and his ankle is clearly very painful. The swelling is now obvious through the layers of filthy sock. He starts to hobble away leaning heavily on Ginger, then turns back to me.

'Got a fag then, Jane?'

'Sorry.' Our eyes meet for a fraction of a second. 'Hope your ankle heals quickly.'

'It bloody better, can't stand this place for long.' As he goes through a door I jump back into the taxi. I'd meant to get the tube from here and go the two stops to Victoria, but the roaring traffic is unappealing, I'm tired and my flat's a short ride away. The smell of the tramp is heavy in the cab and I open a window. My clothes smell of him and I can't wait to change. I hang my heavy winter coat to air in Mark's room, and give the gallery a ring. No one there; I leave a message, beginning to worry a little about Lawrence's absence. He's probably doing things with his nieces before taking them to the airport, but even so he should have thought of me. Sod him. He can ring me when he finally gets in. It's now down to him.

I'm feeling restless and reckless. The entirely unexpected day has shaken me loose, and I can see the old Jane peering round the door and saying it's all getting a bit dull and worthy round here and what about some fun for a change?

Clubbing. I haven't been clubbing since my renal failure. I haven't danced all night, got high, got drunk, got laid. I've done nothing that I've regretted doing next day. I've obeyed the rules, looked after myself, tried to get on better with Nat, taken a job with a lot of responsibility, behaved, in other words, like an adult. Time I went wild. Time I really went wild.

'Dave? It's Jane.'

'I know it's Jane. This is an unexpected surprise. How are you?'

'Raring for some action. Are you free tonight?'

'Well, well, an unexpected proposition from the reformed Jane. What sort of action had you in mind?'

'Take me clubbing, Dave. I've had a very odd day, utterly maddening and strange, and I need to forget it. I long to dance till I'm brain-dead.'

'This is all very sudden. I thought you'd given up such pastimes.'

'Please don't mock me, Dave. There's no one else I feel free to ask.'

'Is that a compliment?'

'Yes.'

'You'll have to convince me.'

I hear a murmur behind him, a woman's quiet voice.

'Are you in the middle of some pubic research?'

'Not at all. My mother's here for tea.'

I can sense his smile as clearly as if I can see it. 'How nice for you.'

'It is.'

'I'll buy you dinner tonight if you'll take me clubbing.'

'What about tomorrow?'

'By tomorrow I'll have come to my senses.'

'OK. Let's meet at the Sea Breeze in Soho.' He explains where it is. 'Eightish?'

'Not too ish. See you there, Dave. Thanks, and be kind to your mother.'

'I always am.'

I put music on loud, I have a bath, and then dig out suitable clothes: skinny black top, black short skirt, black tights, long black boots, a loose transparent silver shirt over the black outfit. I put on effective make-up and some bold silver earrings and a neckpiece I haven't worn since Sydney which neatly covers the scar there. I gel my hair and slick it back, spraying on some discreet silver glitter. I look at myself in a full-length mirror and laugh. Hallo, bad Jane. Calamity Jane. I dance a bit to the music. The phone rings.

'Hi, Jane, it's Toby. I was wondering if—'

'Sorry, can't talk now. Just heading out of the door. I'll ring you. 'Bye.' I cut him off, and go on dancing. People like Toby make me care and I'm tired of caring.

The Sea Breeze is a smart new bar sited in a former bank. It is packed with people under thirty, all in the latest fashions, all, from the conversations going on round me, media people or journalists. I deliberately arrive late, but of course Dave is even later. I suspect him of lurking outside, watching for me, making sure he's not first.

'Jane, so sorry I'm late. You look terrific. Let me get you a Sea Breeze. They make the best in London here.'

'What's a Sea Breeze? I know I'm out of touch so what's the use of pretending.'

'Grapefruit juice, cranberry juice, and vodka.'

'Sounds good. I'd love one.'

'Hi, Jake! Long time no see. Fill me in – are you still with Channel Four? Meet Jane, by the way.'

I tend to shy away from men called Jake so my smile is lukewarm. Jake ignores me after he's greeted me anyway, and takes his time filling Dave in. I drift away and am about to go and buy my own drink when Dave leaves Jake, takes my arm and finally gets the cocktails.

'You look different. Black suits you. I like the silver streak.'

'Thanks. How's the book going – sales good?'

'Not bad at all. Everyone's pleased, even my bank manager. It's a treat to be able to give two fingers to a smooth bastard like him.' Dave smirks. 'It's hard to believe, but *The List* has crept to the edge of the bestseller list.'

'Film rights?'

'No. Give it time.' Dave leads me to a booth and we slide in. He lights up a cigarette.

'By the way, Dave, I saw a lovely example of pubic hair in a picture the other day. I was looking through a catalogue of French nineteenth-century drawings and there it was: a very nice study of a standing nude by Pierre-Paul Prud'hon, with very naturalistic pubic hair, and it was done as early as 1815.'

'That's earlier than the Courbet. Interesting. You must jot down the reference for me.'

'I have. I'll send it.'

'My little research assistant.'

'Hands off, Dave. It's dinner and clubbing I had in mind, and that's all.'

'Shame.'

'Have you decided which club we're going to?'

'Semtex has something on tonight.'

'Fine. Shall we eat here?'

'Too many people I know.'

'Where, then?'

'You know I don't care what I eat. Any place will do. Let's have another drink.'

'This one's on me.'

As I go for the drinks Jake oozes up to Dave again and they immediately start an intense conversation. I stand trying to catch the frantic bartender's eye and think of my own Jake. I remember a wonderful night soon after we first met when we drank and danced at a beach club all night, danced and danced under a hot moon. We took a line of coke that night, the first time I'd ever tried it, though I knew Jake sometimes used it. It didn't do a lot for me, to be honest, but I've used it occasionally since though never in England. I know Dave is a pothead, and is doubtless into cocaine as well. I'm sure he'll use something tonight at some point. And me? I feel reckless. What the hell. I'm tired of being careful and sensible. I get the bartender to put double vodkas in our Sea Breezes.

We go on to a Pizza Express and eat to a background of live jazz, and I find the music and the atmosphere so good that I'm suddenly less interested in clubbing. People are dancing here and anyway I'm beginning to feel weary. The words are collecting on my tongue to suggest we stay on when Dave says firmly: 'Time to leave. We've got to drop in on my old friend Barry on the way.'

'I don't think I want another drink.'

'Who said we were going there to drink?'

So I pay and follow Dave into the street. He's in charge of events now, and he leads me to a small flat at the top of a narrow flight of stairs somewhere nearby. The warm rooms reek of cannabis, and everyone there seems to be either smoking or scoring. I spend the first ten minutes in the loo repairing my make-up, hoping that everyone else thinks I'm shooting up in there. I touch my fistula as if to reassure it and stare into my eyes. It's a strange experience, almost schizoid, as if the new Jane is looking at the old Jane. Then I look down at my fistula, having stared myself out.

I know that my recklessness has suddenly reached its limit. My body's full of powerful anti-rejection drugs and I have no idea how they would react to other equally powerful substances. I go to find Dave, resolved. He is sitting very relaxed in a corner. He pats the settee he's commandeered. He waves his joint at me and asks if I'd like one.

'No thanks. I'm fine. I'm sorted.'

'And what's that supposed to mean?'

'Whatever you want it to mean.'

'Is my Jane shocked at Barry's little set-up?'

'No.'

'Have a drag at least.' He hands me his joint and I draw on it gently, determined not to inhale. I'm not feeling too good suddenly, and the sweaty feeling is back. It must be all the alcohol. I drink a glass of water, and pretend to take another puff.

'Let's go and dance, Dave. How much does it cost to get in? I might need a cashpoint.'

'Relax, we'll get in free. I know the management.'

'Let's go then. I need exercise or I'll fall asleep.'

'In a minute. Let me finish this.' He draws on the stub, his eyes narrow. 'Tell me about that picture you mentioned. By – I've forgotten his name already.'

'Prud'hon.'

'Never heard of him. How big is it?'

'Oh, just a drawing, about A5 size.'

'Erotica?'

'No, not at all. It's a calm little study. None of the boldness of Courbet.'

Dave's looking at my naturally dark eyebrows when suddenly he says: 'So you've got a dark bush despite the blonde hair?'

'Piss off, Dave. None of your business.'

'Not even later on? Grant me my dearest wish?'

'Absolutely not.'

'What a tease you are.'

'I am not teasing, I assure you. In my experience people tease when they intend at some point to deliver.'

'But I got the impression when you rang you were in the mood for a night of excitement and delicious debauchery.'

I can't help laughing at the way Dave pronounces debauchery, so full of – well, debauchery.

'You're a devil, Dave.'

'I know. But sometimes you can't help liking me.'

'True. Not enough to grant you your dearest wish, however. If it is your dearest wish?'

'It always is, with every woman still on my list but not ticked off it. Like you.'

'Has the success of your book increased the size of your list?'

'So many women are fascinated by my obsession.' He stubs out his joint. 'So gratifying.'

'I would have expected them to be put off.'

'Not at all.'

'And what does your mother think of your success?'

He frowns for a minute, disconcerted.

'You said you had your mother with you when I rang.'

'So I did. I have a mother, you know. Carla Rosenberg, housewife and mother. House widow. She's lonely so she comes to tea on Mondays. I get in crumpets and we toast them.'

Dave is impossible to trust or believe. I follow him out into the dark, cold street and wonder at his life, at the blurring of fact into fiction. Does he himself know where one shades into the other? It's hard to take him seriously, yet we all under-estimated his talk of a book and I can't forget that. It could be true he has tea with his mother every Monday but it sounds wholly unlikely.

I won't ask him further questions, because he will simply put up smokescreens. He sounded simple and open when he spoke about his mother, but nothing is simple and open with Dave.

I sneak a look at him as he strides beside me. He's brooding about something and is hardly aware I am with him. A taxi passes and I almost hail it. I'm beginning to regret we didn't part after dinner; if I think at all about how tired I feel, I'll crumple. Dancing is the only thing that will keep me going – the rhythms of the music and the constant movement will re-energise me.

'Here we are. Let's hope it's a good night – sometimes Semtex is full of children dressed to deceive.'

We descend past the bouncers and a dodgy-looking manager who greets Dave with a warm smile and dead steely eyes.

'What's it like tonight, Tony?'

'Good. There's a good crowd down there.' Flick go his eyes, missing nothing. 'Enjoy.'

Dave pushes me through to the main room where there's a big dance floor crammed with people. We start to dance once he's drawn me well into the thick of the crowd. I'm a good dancer, and I notice within minutes Dave isn't. Cool, relaxed, but not rhythmical. I half close my eyes and lose myself in the dance, and find as I expected my energy returning. Time passes, and when I open my eyes properly to say to Dave that perhaps I've had enough, he's not there. I struggle through the crowd. He's nowhere.

The music is now very heavy, the lights flicker so fast they are disorientating, people bang into me because I've stopped moving with the beat. Getting out of the dancing crowd is harder than getting in, and a giddy panic begins to rise in me. I don't feel well, I really don't feel well. I need a familiar face, but Dave has disappeared.

It takes me ages to retrieve my coat and the girl on coat-check can't tell me whether Dave has taken his. My hands are shaking. I'm feeling worse and worse. Tony the manager passes and I put my hand on his arm to stop him.

'Has Dave gone?'

'Dave who?' His cold eyes stare at my shaking hands. 'No idea.'

I stagger to the staircase. Tony probably thinks I'm drunk or coming down from a high. I grab the stair-rail and pull myself up the stairs, but the staircase gets steeper and the treads shimmer and stretch and then give way as I faint into a carpet-lined abyss.

18

Old carpet. Dusty, dirt-ingrained, undercleaned carpet could be the covering of hell. I lie face down on this unpleasant surface, trying to anchor my returning consciousness. I'm in Tony's office; I can hear his voice and his feet in pointed leather shoes are pacing past me as he talks. He stops when I roll over and says hang on into his receiver.

'I'm trying to get hold of a doctor for you.'

I sit up with difficulty. 'I don't need a doctor. I'll be fine.'

'It's OK, she says she's fine. Yeah, don't bother.' He puts the phone down and drinks from a can of Diet Coke. His small office is crammed with messy papers and empty drink cans. In one corner is an inflated pvc gorilla.

'Please could you call me a taxi?'

Tony pulls open the door and shouts at a bouncer. 'Paul, get the lady a cab pronto would you?'

I can see the staircase I collapsed on through the office door. Tony helps me to my feet, his face expressionless, and hands me over to Paul. He waves his hand and shuts the door on me as I thank him for his help. Paul leads me to a taxi and disappears. I feel giddy again as I climb in.

'Where to?'

I stare at the driver as I shiver in the cold. Where to? Straight to Guy's Hospital? To my flat? The cab driver is beginning to look uneasy and in a minute he's going to throw me out. His digital clock moves to 3.07. A car behind him hoots and he drives slowly off.

'North? South? Make your mind up, lady.'

I can't face the empty flat – Sara's away at a conference this week – and I can't go to the hospital looking like this.

'North, please.' Nat is north, and in that moment I know it's my sister I want. She will rightly curse and complain at being disturbed at this late hour, but she'll let me in just the same and give me a bed, and love me and hate me for what I am. As I love and hate her. I give the driver the Elsworthy Avenue address to his obvious relief: an upmarket area so she must be good for the fare, is doubtless his thought.

Money. Do I still have that tenner, and my credit card? Fear chills me as I search through my bag, to find nothing has been taken. The credit card and the phone card with the ten pound note wrapped round them are still in the inner zipped pocket. Tony must have pulled me very quickly into his office before anyone had time to examine my possessions.

'Could you stop at a phone box somewhere? I need to ring my sister to say I'm on the way.'

'Do you realise how late it is?' He pulls over unwillingly.

'I do.'

'Just thought I'd mention it.'

Nat answers almost at once – she's always been a light sleeper, and the phone's her side of the bed. She whispers hallo.

'It's Jane.'

'Are you mad? It's after three.'

'I know, I'm sorry, but I collapsed in a club, I'm feeling terrible, please give me a bed.'

'Jane, are you drunk?'

'Not now. I'm on my way. I'll be with you in ten minutes.'

'You know you can always have a bed here, but what a time to pick.'

'See you very soon.'

I sit poker-stiff and still as the taxi rumbles through empty streets towards Primrose Hill. My eyes are shut and I keep my brain empty. When thoughts try and creep in I push them away. I do not want to face the unthinkable: I'm rejecting my new kidney.

The downstairs light is on and Nat is lurking near the front door because as soon she hears the cab stop she opens it. She stares at me in distaste as I come up the steps.

'God, Jane. What do you think you look like?'

My reflection in the hall mirror is so awful – white face, smudged black eye make-up in streaks down my face, hair like rats' tails, clothes sweaty, dusty and dishevelled – that I start to laugh and she drags me downstairs to the kitchen.

'Shshsh. Don't wake Freddie whatever you do.'

'I look a complete wreck.'

'What have you been up to?' Nat is in a green velvet dressing gown, hair loose, skin clear and clean and juicy with moisturiser. 'You said you collapsed.'

'I went clubbing with Dave.'

'Most unwise.'

'I asked him to take me. I needed to do something wild. I'd been so bloody sensible for too long.' I sink into a chair at the kitchen table and put my head in my hands. 'I'm so tired I can hardly think.'

'Drink this water. You're probably dehydrated.'

She's right, but I don't answer. I do drink the water, and she pours more.

'Where's Dave?'

'The bastard disappeared. We were dancing. I was loving the feeling of dancing again, I had my eyes nearly shut, and when I looked up he'd gone.'

'That man is trouble, Jane. I can't think why you go out with him.'

'I wanted to dance. I longed to dance, to go clubbing and dance and dance. Who else could I ask? Dave lusts after me, so I knew he'd agree.'

She's staring at me with a look I can't read. Then she turns away quickly. 'I'll make you up a bed in the flat.' She goes to the connecting door in the kitchen and I try to get up to follow her, but I'm so shaky I have to sit down again. She frowns and comes back to my side.

'Are you sure you're not drunk? You look it.'

'I suppose I had more than I should have, but that was hours ago. Dave took me to a nasty little drug den but I didn't join him in anything.'

'Drink this water.'

'I feel sick. I think I've got a temperature.'

'I'll make the bed up.' I put my head back in my hands, and listen to her banging about in the adjoining room.

'Come on, Jane. Bed.'

'Don't be angry.'

'It's late, I'm exhausted too, and I probably won't get back to sleep. That's why I'm a bit annoyed, plus the fact I can't honestly see why you've come at this ungodly hour.'

'Because I need you.' My voice breaks and I let the tears which have been building up for some time pour out. I sob and sob over the table; Nat sits beside me, her arm round my shoulders, doing her best to comfort me.

'Jane, Jane. Skippety Jane. Don't cry.'

'Skippety Jane. Mum used to call me that.'

'You used to skip in the back yard for hours. Here's a box of tissues – dry your eyes and wipe your nose.'

'I had to skip better than you. It took a lot of practice.' I mop my wet face again. The tissues are black with eye make-up. 'Can I borrow some cleanser?'

'You left some in the flat last year. I'll get it.'

She watches me cleanse my skin. 'Your face is quite puffy, Jane. Are you sure you're all right?'

I say nothing for a moment because what I have to tell her is so painful it's almost unsayable.

'I've been very stupid, Nat.'

'I quite agree. Anyone going clubbing with Dave needs their head examining.'

'I haven't been taking all my drugs when I should, or doing my routines.'

'Drugs?'

'My anti-rejection drugs.'

'What are you actually telling me?'

'It's the Prednisolone that's particularly awful – it makes your face round, you get spots, you put on weight. It's a steroid.'

'And you haven't been taking it at all?'

'I've been taking one a day instead of two. It didn't seem to make much difference, but if I took two, I could see it was affecting me and I couldn't bear it.'

'No one noticed. You look fine.'

'You just said my face was puffy.'

'You've been crying – is it surprising?'

But I can tell she's trying to cheer me up. She's lying. I do look different.

'I can't bear to be fat and moon-faced. Oh God.'

'Jane, you'll make me angry in a minute. You're being ridiculous. You are not fat and moon-faced in any way.'

'It's started to happen. I've got eyes.'

'You're being paranoid. You look wonderful. Fuller in the face and body, but you used to be too thin. Watch my lips, you foolish foolish woman. You-look-wonderful.'

'I've been a fool, I know I've been a fool. But the drugs are such a ghastly trio, each of them with horrid long-term side-effects, that as time passes you begin to hope you'll magically be able to do without them.'

'What do they say at Guy's?'

'I haven't had a check-up for nearly a month. They don't know I've been cheating on the Prednisolone. They'll soon find out I'm not the model patient they all thought I was.'

'When's your next check-up then?'

I meet her eyes. 'I shouldn't wait for it, Nat. I should go in now. I think I'm rejecting the kidney.'

Her face is a blank of horror. 'Oh no, Jane. No.'

'If I lose this kidney it'll be my fault. I've ignored the signs. It'll be entirely my fault.'

'But I don't understand – you can't be losing it – surely there'd be no doubt . . . ?'

'The body doesn't go into convulsions of pain when it says out, out, out to the transplant. Rejection's horribly quiet and low key – you pee less, you feel a bit off, you develop a slight temperature, your weight goes up. When this happens you tell yourself there's nothing the matter, it's a normal fluctuation, just a bad few days. You kid yourself it isn't happening, you tell yourself again and again that of course your immune system isn't winning and rejecting the kidney. You stop weighing yourself and taking your temperature because you're afraid of what you'll discover.'

'Oh Jane.' To my surprise, Nat has tears in her eyes. 'Oh Jane.' She is slumped opposite me at the table. 'No wonder you wanted a wild night with Dave.'

'It didn't do me much good. Nor was it particularly wild.' I start to laugh, but I'm crying too. Nat puts her hand out and we grasp each other's hands across the kitchen table. 'Bloody Dave.'

'He's a bastard, but what's new about that?' We smile at each other, tears ending. 'I think I should take you now to Guy's.'

'Now?'

'Now.'

'I can't go looking like this.'

'I was going to suggest we pass by the flat to collect your stuff because I imagine they'll keep you in. Give me five minutes to get dressed and we'll go.'

'And Freddie?'

'If he doesn't wake up I'll leave him a note. My clothes aren't in the bedroom so he should hear nothing.' She stands up. 'Why don't you ring the hospital and tell them you're coming in?'

'I've been so stupid.'

'You won't be the first idiot they've come across. Go on, Jane. Ring.' She puts the phone beside me and goes upstairs. I ring that familiar number and get a familiar voice.

'Clarkson Ward.'

'Chantal? I didn't know you'd transferred to Clarkson. Yes, it's Jane.'

'What's the problem, Jane?'

'I'm feeling awful. I think I'm rejecting. No, I'm sure I'm rejecting.'

'Tell me your symptoms.'

'All the classic ones. I know them too well, Chantal.'

'Come straight in. Take a cab.'

'My sister's offered to bring me.'

'Remember your medication, your record book and your night things, and see you soon. Be prepared for a few days in.' Her cool efficient voice is a tonic. I rest my head on the table and my whole body is shaken by an involuntary, post-weeping fit of shudders. The wooden surface smells faintly of good things, of the countless different foods that have been prepared on it. Wholesome good things. I think of the smell of that club carpet under my nose: dirt, dust, cigarette ends, chewing gum, food, and unimaginable other bits ground into the fibres. The most hellish of smells and textures. How Cleopatra could have had herself delivered to Caesar rolled up in a carpet – a clean, sweet-smelling carpet no doubt, but still a carpet – I cannot think.

'Are you asleep?'

'No. I was thinking of Cleopatra.'

'You are quite mad, Jane.'

'Not all the time.'

'Come on. Freddie didn't wake. I'm glad because he would have insisted on taking you himself. Go very quietly.'

We creep back through the hall and out through the heavy front door which Nat closes with extreme care. Freddie's car is parked off the pavement on the front carport area. Nat's is luckily parked some distance away.

'I cursed when I couldn't get nearer the house, but it's become an advantage. Freddie knows the sound of my engine – it's got a special rattle, he says.'

It's now getting on for four o'clock, and the dark streets are so empty we hardly see a car. Nat comes up to the flat with me, to wait while I shower off the sweat of dancing. She stretches herself out on my bed, her old bed, and is leafing through *Vogue* when I come out of the shower. She prods at a page.

'Dave's even got a mention in here – that man is everywhere.' She shuts the magazine and drops it on the floor with a plop.

'And nowhere.' I put on jeans and a jersey, and start collecting the necessary things together.

'It's sick-making how well he's doing with that book, which I honestly don't think is very good. Just a smart idea, and a good quick read.' Nat turns her head and watches me. 'It's funny lying here again. I never thought I would. I've been married a whole year – it's hard to believe. The year has gone in a flash.'

'My year has mostly felt long. Each month two months long.'

'Even recently? You've been looking so much happier.'

'Less so recently, I suppose. But the consistency of my time has altered – it passes slowly, yet I feel I haven't got enough of it.'

'Your fistula has shrunk, you know. It really has.' She's looking at it as I hold my arm out.

'It will be back to its old size in no time if I have to start dialysis again.'

'Don't say that. They'll save this kidney, surely they will.'

'If things haven't gone too far. They can't always halt rejection.

Come on, Nat, I'm ready.' Our eyes meet as she lies there, but she doesn't move.

'Now listen to me, Jane. I've decided that I am going to give you a kidney if you need another, and don't say no this time. The only thing to consider is the timing. I'll do it after I've had a child.'

There's a silence. 'Are you pregnant again?'

'Yes, but it's early days so don't let's count on anything.'

I sit down beside her. 'Forget about the kidney. Freddie would be too upset. Let him enjoy a baby in the family without worrying about you becoming a donor.'

'He's changed – he's become a lot less squeamish about things like that. He'd better be, if he's planning to be at the birth.'

'So he knows about it?'

'I told him on Sunday. He's ridiculously pleased – over the corny old moon. And Jane, never, never, never, tell him about that miscarriage.'

'As if I would. Nat, I'll be an aunt!'

'If all goes well. If. Now, back to my kidney.' She sits up and swings her legs off the bed so that we're side by side. 'You've changed your mind too, haven't you? Remember how you said you never ever wanted a little bit of me inside you?'

'I still don't, but not for the same reasons.'

'So what are the new reasons?'

There's another silence. I can just see the photo of Alfie with her heart-stopping smile. I turn my head to blot it out. 'I've risked the new kidney for vanity. Say I do the same to yours? I'd never forgive myself.'

'You won't.'

'How do you know I won't?'

'Because I'll wring your neck if there's the slightest risk of it!'

'Oh Nat.'

She puts her hand on my shoulder, and we lean our heads together for a moment. In this position she murmurs, 'Our tissues are a perfect match, by the way.'

I swing away. 'How do you know?'

'I had my tissue-typing done ages ago.'

'You never told me.'

'I was waiting.'

'What for?'

'I don't know.' She lies back on the bed again and twiddles a hank of hair just as she did when she was a child. 'Ignoble reasons. I hoped never to be called on to go further. When I first heard our tissues matched so well, I felt sick.'

I look at her profile, that beautiful profile I've always envied, and I don't know what to say. After a longish silence, she goes on:

'Freddie doesn't know about the tissue-typing. I never even told him I was having the test. I didn't want to worry him.'

'I don't think you should ever give me a kidney, perfect match or not.'

She sits up immediately. 'You haven't given me a single good reason why not except for Freddie.'

'I think that's a good enough reason. I respect Freddie a lot. I wouldn't want to give him pain.'

'And me?'

'You know you'd feel much more pain than I would if you did this for me. The op's much worse for you than for me.'

'I know all that, but I don't mind any more. Having a baby is going to be painful, but it's worth it. Perhaps the same applies to giving you a kidney. Have you thought of that?'

The phone starts ringing, making us jump. 'Freddie?' whispers Nat. But it's Chantal, worried I'm taking so long.

'Got delayed, sorry, Chantal. No, nothing's happened. We're leaving now. Thank you for ringing. I – I appreciate it.'

As I open the door, overnight bag in hand, Nat says, 'We've all changed a lot in a year, but you've changed the most.'

'It could be said that I've had the most powerful reason to.'

'It could indeed. Off we go.'

'I haven't left a note for Sara—'

'I'll tell her, and everyone else.' We walk into the street to the car, and there's a definite feeling of dawn in the air. Nat opens the passenger door for me, and I can smell the gentle scent of her night cream as she bends forward to stow her bag at my feet.

'Nat. How can our tissues match so well when we are of different blood groups? Me B and you O?'

'O kidneys can go into both A and B blood groups.'

'I thought the doctors didn't like doing that.'

'Only because if an A or B blood group kidney becomes available,' it can only be matched with itself. No flexibility. They told me it would be against their normal practice to use an O kidney for a B group recipient. I told them my kidney was for you and no one else.'

'So our DNA is identical?'

'Identical. It only happens between siblings, and not often then, apparently. But it's happened with us.'

'Sisters under the skin.'

'Exactly.'

'No one would guess, looking at us. Do identical twins always have the same DNA?'

'No idea.'

We drive for a few minutes in an easy silence, then I ask Nat if she's in court in a few hours' time.

'No, luckily. Freddie will insist I have a quiet morning after this little escapade, so I think I'll spend the morning in bed when I get home.'

'If you lost this baby because of me he'd never forgive me. He'd be devastated.'

'That's why I'm glad I didn't tell him about the miscarriage, Jane.'

'You shouldn't have taken this risk. He's going to be frantic if he wakes up and finds you gone. I shouldn't have come so late. Oh God, I'm so selfish.'

'Shut up, Jane. Yes, it was selfish but I'm glad you did it. Let's both have a sweet – there are some in there with the tapes.'

The ersatz smell of the fruit-flavoured boiled sweets is temporarily stronger than the gentle scents of dawn or moisturiser. I suddenly remember an occasion when we were small children, and my mother gave me two boiled sweets wrapped in cellophane, one for each of us, and I unwrapped them both and licked them to see which I preferred. Then I rewrapped the reject and gave it to Nat after drying it out on a radiator. She never knew.

'Look how high the tide is.' We're going along the empty Embankment, with the Houses of Parliament across the river slowly becoming clear in the growing dawn light. 'Nat, can we stop for a moment? I need some fresh air.'

Nat stops the car at once, eager for air too. We walk to the edge of the Embankment and stare down the Thames towards the east.

With no traffic fumes in the air, the smell of the river is strong and has undertones of the sea. There's a long line of freighter barges slipping downstream in the faint light of dawn. I can see a ghostly seagull sitting on one of the freighters, but otherwise no sign of life.

'What a benign form of transport.' Nat's eyes turn down to the strong race of brown water below us. 'Last year, I lost a shoe in the Thames. I was getting off the now defunct Riverbus, and in it fell. I remember I was coming back from court, and there was I, in my black and white, hopping along with only one shoe!'

I laugh at the image as I watch the line of barges slip under Westminster Bridge. In seconds the row of boats has disappeared, gull in place.

I could not have written this book without the help and advice of Lisa Burnapp, Senior Sister, and Ferga Robinson, Renal Counsellor, both of the renal unit at Guy's Hospital, London. I was also given invaluable help by renal patients, particularly Sophie Brown, Teresa Minter, Sarah Agboula and Peter Watson.

Grateful acknowledgements are also due to W. W. Norton & Co., New York/London, for permission to quote from e. e. cummings's poem 'seeker of truth', first published in *73 poems* (Faber & Faber, 1964).

Finally, I need to acknowledge my debt to Gillian Rose's remarkable book, *Love's Work* (Chatto & Windus, 1995). I have re-imagined Professor Rose as Georgia Hill, and semi-quoted from an invented book, *Last Count*, which is modelled on *Love's Work* as any reader of Rose's own book would instantly recognise. My 'open-borrowing' is a homage to a great mind and an extraordinary person, whose early death from cancer in December 1995 made her book's depiction of her illness all the more poignant. I thank her literary executors and her publishers for allowing me this freedom.